7

"Men are like melons, hard on the outside, often spoiled on the inside."

> —the opposite sex, according to
> TV chef Cathy Mallory

"The world is full of beautiful women—most of them looking for a man who can cook."

> —the opposite sex, according to
> TV chef Devlin Kilpatrick

Cathy and Devlin know each other by reputation only, but that's about to change—big time. Their rivalry—and their passion—comes to a rolling boil when the two are forced to vie for a major shot at nationwide stardom.

Dear Reader,

Our summer gift to you is a unique, dual-perspective love story, written cooperatively by two of your favorite authors, Jasmine Cresswell and Margaret St. George.

The author of more than forty novels, world traveler **Jasmine Cresswell** has received numerous awards that honor her writing achievements, including the Romance Writers of America's Golden Rose Award, and the Author's League Award for best original paperback novel. Though she now calls both Florida and Colorado home, and continues her frequent travels across America to visit her four grown children, she manages an incredibly prolific output of fascinating stories for MIRA Books, as well as contributing to various innovative Harlequin projects.

Jasmine Cresswell's friend and colleague, the talented and award-winning **Margaret St. George,** is the author of over thirty novels, in categories ranging from historical to mystery to romantic romp. A native of Colorado, she brings a wealth of life experience to her writing, having served as a flight attendant for United Airlines, as well as the national president of the Romance Writers of America.

Together they have created Cathy and Devlin, rival chefs of very different stripes! And for authenticity, Ms. Cresswell consulted her son-in-law, a professional chef in food-loving New Orleans. The challenge of writing this creatively told story has led both authors to sign on as contributors to the upcoming DELTA JUSTICE series. Watch for its debut in the fall of 1997!

Marsha Zinberg,
Senior Editor and Editorial Coordinator, Special Projects

HE SAID, SHE SAID

Jasmine Cresswell
Margaret St. George

Harlequin Books

TORONTO • NEW YORK • LONDON
AMSTERDAM • PARIS • SYDNEY • HAMBURG
STOCKHOLM • ATHENS • TOKYO • MILAN
MADRID • WARSAW • BUDAPEST • AUCKLAND

If you purchased this book without a cover you should be aware
that this book is stolen property. It was reported as "unsold and
destroyed" to the publisher, and neither the author nor the
publisher has received any payment for this "stripped book."

HARLEQUIN BOOKS
225 Duncan Mill Road, Don Mills,
Ontario, Canada M3B 3K9

ISBN 0-373-83330-X

HE SAID, SHE SAID

Copyright © 1997 by Jasmine Cresswell and Maggie Osborne

All rights reserved. Except for use in any review, the reproduction or
utilization of this work in whole or in part in any form by any electronic,
mechanical or other means, now known or hereafter invented, including
xerography, photocopying and recording, or in any information storage
or retrieval system, is forbidden without the written permission of the
publisher, Harlequin Enterprises Limited, 225 Duncan Mill Road,
Don Mills, Ontario, Canada M3B 3K9.

All characters in this book have no existence outside the imagination of
the author and have no relation whatsoever to anyone bearing the same
name or names. They are not even distantly inspired by any individual
known or unknown to the author, and all incidents are pure invention.

This edition published by arrangement with Harlequin Books S.A.

® and ™ are trademarks of the publisher. Trademarks indicated with
® are registered in the United States Patent and Trademark Office, the
Canadian Trade Marks Office and in other countries.

Printed in U.S.A.

CATHY'S CHICKEN STRUDEL

1 package frozen puff pastry sheets
Sprinkle of flour (to roll out pastry)
1 10-oz package frozen spinach, thawed
1 8-oz boneless chicken breast, split in half
Salt and pepper to taste
1 8-oz package garden vegetable cream cheese
1 egg mixed with 1/4 cup milk (to make egg wash)

Thaw one puff pastry sheet approximately 5 to 10 minutes.
Unfold sheet and lightly flour.
Roll twice in each direction, just enough to stretch 2 inches
on each side. Place on a cookie sheet.
Squeeze off as much excess liquid as possible from
spinach.
Season chicken breast with salt and pepper to taste.
Lay chicken in the middle of the pastry.
Place spinach on top of chicken and cover with spoonfuls
of the cream cheese.
Brush all edges of puff pastry with egg wash (to make it
stick better).
Fold pastry over filling. Seal by crimping with a fork.
Brush entire pastry with egg wash.
Bake at 350° for 30 to 40 minutes or until golden brown.
Serve immediately.
Serves 4.

DEVLIN'S SEAFOOD DIVINE
(Feuilleté with shrimp, lobster and scallop ragout)

Ragout Base:

Ingredients—Seafood

3 x 1 lb to 1-1/2 lb cooked lobsters.
Remove meat from tail and claws, and set aside. Rinse
inside bodies—save all lobster shells.
1 lb large rock shrimp. Peel and save all shells. Devein
shrimp, rinse and refrigerate.
1-1/2 lb sea scallops. Rinse and refrigerate.
Meat of seafood is for use in ragout.

Ingredients—Mirepoix (all cut into 1-inch pieces)

1 large leek	*1 medium fennel bulb*
2 carrots	*3 ribs celery*
2 shallots	*5 large mushrooms*
1 head garlic	

Other Ingredients

1 cup extra virgin olive oil	*Bouquet garni of 2 large*
1 oz Pernod	*ribs celery, thyme, parsley,*
1 oz white vermouth	*bay leaf*
3 oz cognac	*Pinch of saffron and*
3 oz white wine	*cayenne pepper*
Sufficient fish or chicken	*1-inch piece of minced ginger*
stock to cover shells to a	*1 cup arborio rice*
depth of 2 inches	*1 cup heavy cream*
	Salt and pepper to taste

Method:

Heat olive oil in a thick-bottomed stock pot over high heat.
Add lobster and shrimp shells (no meat). Sear until shells
turn bright red (approx. 2 minutes).
Add mirepoix and sweat (cook until translucent).
Deglaze with Pernod. **Caution:** Always remove pan from
heat when adding alcohol.
Reduce until au sec (almost dry).
Deglaze with vermouth, reduce until au sec.
Deglaze with cognac, reduce until au sec.
Cover shells and mirepoix with white wine. Reduce by half.

Cover with fish stock. (Chicken stock if no fish stock available.)

Add bouquet garni, saffron, cayenne and ginger. Simmer approximately one hour over low heat.

Strain out all shells and mirepoix. Save all remaining liquid, about 1-1/2 quarts.

Bring liquid to a boil and add arborio rice. (This is used as a thickening agent and will be strained later.)

Reduce to a simmer. Add heavy cream slowly.

Stir and simmer gently until mixture begins to thicken.

Strain out rice and season to taste with salt and pepper.

Ragout:

<u>Ingredients per person</u>

Prepared ragout base
(6 oz per portion)
5 oz shrimp
2 oz lobster meat
3 oz scallops

Thyme and parsley,
chopped fine, to taste
Lemon juice
Salt and pepper
Cream

<u>Method:</u>

Heat ragout base over medium heat—simmer, do not boil. Add shrimp, lobster and scallops and cook. Season with herbs, lemon juice, salt and pepper. Add additional cream to taste, or to thin, if required.

Feuilleté:

<u>Ingredients</u>

2 sheets puff pastry
Egg wash (1 large egg beaten with 1/4 cup milk)

Method:

Cut pastry into 8 strips 6 inches by 4 inches.

Score the top in a crisscross pattern with a sharp knife, brush with egg wash.

Bake at 350° until golden brown.

These will rise very high. Cut out the centers of each rectangle and fill the resulting pastry cup with ragout.

Replace top of pastry.

Garnish and serve.

Serves 8.

Chapter One

*She said: Men are like melons—hard on the
    outside, often spoiled on the inside.*

"WILL YOU LOOK at what he's preparing today?" Cathy
Mallory said indignantly. Lowering a tube of lipstick, she
stared at the television mounted on the wall of her
makeup cubicle.

She wouldn't have admitted it to anyone but Jean,
her best friend at Denver's station KBAB, but she never
missed Devlin Gilpatrick's show, "Dining with Devlin."
Dining! How pretentious could you get? He had a cooking show, for heaven's sake, the same as she did. But
the name of her show, "Cooking With Cathy," was
more accurate and to the point. *Dining. Jeez, what a
phoney jerk.*

"Look at that. He's cooking Fowl Stuffed with Bulgur
Wheat Dressing, and Fried Cucumbers with Sumac!
Fowl, my aunt Fannie! Why can't he just say Cornish
hens?" Scowling and irritated, she turned back to the
lighted mirror and ran the lipstick around her mouth.
"I'm sure every woman just happens to have bulgur in
her pantry and sumac to sprinkle on her fried cucumbers." She rolled her eyes. "Right!"

Jean Sadler grinned and glanced at her wristwatch.

"Better get a move on. The crew wants to start taping in ten minutes."

"I don't know how that pompous goof stays on the air!" Frowning, Cathy studied her lips in the mirror. She'd made a mess of the lipstick. Damn. Hurrying, she wiped it off and began again.

"He stays on the air for the same reasons you do, sex appeal and market share."

"Sex appeal? Me? I wish!" Leaning away from the mirror, Cathy sighed and studied her reflection.

Every woman in the Denver viewing area agreed that Devlin Gilpatrick was the sexiest man on television. Jean was right about that. Against her will, Cathy's gaze flicked to his TV image, reflected in her makeup mirror. Today His Highness wore a béarnaise-colored turtleneck that complemented his hair and eyes. His apron was brown-and-white striped. Though it pained her to admit it, Devlin was the only man alive who could make an apron as elegant as white tie and tails.

Glaring at him in the mirror, she envied the easy way he seduced the TV cameras. He chatted about a five-star restaurant in glamorous Monte Carlo, his voice as rich and smooth as caramel sauce. And you only had to look at Devlin Gilpatrick to believe that he'd actually been to places like Monte Carlo. The guy oozed savoir faire and sex appeal.

She, on the other hand, was about as sexy as a white picket fence. And she doubted that anyone had ever used the words sophistication and Cathy Mallory in the same sentence. If she had appeal, it lay in her whole-some, every woman quality, which she had stopped fighting shortly after graduating from college. She just wasn't an X-rated type. Men looked at her and instantly thought about mortgages, children and their favorite sister. Immediately following these thoughts, they performed a brisk about-face and hurried away in search of someone who brought to mind silk sheets and black negligees.

"A person has to capitalize on what assets she has," she murmured to the mirror, frowning at the blue blouse that matched her eyes. A homey gingham apron covered all but its perky collar and sleeves. She looked like the pretty young housewife next door. A woman who might be described as "cute." She shuddered. Or "nice." Almost as bad.

A deep sigh issued from her lips.

Her fantasy was to be a vamp who could bring men to their knees with a single glance. With all her secret heart she wished she could knock 'em dead in power suits with padded shoulders or slinky silk dresses and shimmery gold lamé cut up to here and down to there. She wished she could glibly drop the name of a five-star restaurant in Monte Carlo, wished she looked like someone who might possibly have been to Monte Carlo.

Jean pointed at her watch. "How about moving your assets to the set?"

Cathy glanced at the television. "That man makes me crazy."

"You and every other woman in Denver," Jean responded with a smirk.

Cathy gave her a look. "I mean, he annoys me."

"Then why do you watch his show?" Jean opened the door and shouted into the corridor, "She's coming, guys."

"I want to know what the competition's doing."

"Methinks she doth protest too much."

"What's that supposed to mean?"

Jean laughed. "It means I think you're fascinated by

Devlin Gilpatrick. I wish the two of you would get together in person."

"We've met in person, and believe me, he's as
phoney as he is on TV." Leaning toward the mirror,
she pressed her lips together and gave her blond curls
a final, irritated pat. "Fowl with Bulgur Wheat Dressing!
Yeah, that's what I'd want to go home and cook after
a long day at the office. And when was the last time *you*
fried a cucumber!"

Jean ushered her out the door and down the hallway
to the cooking set. "Give the guy a break. Hey, he
makes gourmet cooking look easy. And Bill says he's a
peach to work with."

Jean Sadler was the sound technician on Cathy's set
at KBAB while her husband Bill was the chief cameraman on Devlin's set at rival station KDID. It was a stan-
dard joke at both stations that the Sadlers' pillow talk
prevented "Cooking With Cathy" and "Dining With
Devlin" from presenting the same weekly recipes.

Nothing could have been further from the truth.
Cathy's show was as different from Devlin's as apple pie
from crêpe suzette. The possibility of their presenting
the same recipe carried the same odds as winning the
state lottery. About forty gazillion to one. It would never
happen.

The instant Cathy stepped onto the set, her insecurities evaporated like the fragrant steam leaking from the
pots on the stove. She didn't know diddly about la-di-da
restaurants in swanky places, but she could whip up a
wholesome meal for a real family blindfolded, with one
hand tied behind her back. The kitchen had always been
her favorite room, the place where she felt most comfortable.

Which, she supposed, went a long way toward explaining why she was thirty years old and had never been married. Ninety-nine out of a hundred men would have said they preferred a woman whose favorite room was the bedroom.

Surveying the countertop, she checked her supplies, making certain that everything was where it was supposed to be. Then she lifted the lids and peeked into the pots simmering on the burners.

"Is the lighting too bright?" Mike Millican, her producer, ran a hand over the hair plugs dotting his scalp in tiny tufts. "The lighting's too bright. Is it too bright?"

Cathy glanced at Jack, the head cameraman. Jack rolled his eyes, grinned, and nodded. "The lighting's fine, Mike."

Mike helped her thread the wire to the mike beneath her apron and around her waist. "Did you see Devlin's show today? They've got new wallpaper. They must have a budget that's twice the size of ours." His fingers moved like a rake between the hair plugs while he studied the wallpaper on the set.

"I like our wallpaper. Where's my favorite knife?" It wasn't in the drawer where Cathy always kept it. "I had it yesterday."

Yesterday they had taped a show to be aired after the annual Chefs' Culinary Contest. Cathy had prepared what she hoped would be the winning entry in the contest. There was always great interest in the winning recipes and all the competing chefs taped their entries to be aired later. The problem was that the crew wasn't accustomed to taping two of Cathy's shows in a week, and they obviously hadn't had time to put the set back fully in order.

"I left my favorite knife right here," she said, frustrated. She would have wagered her next paycheck that no one messed with Devlin Gilpatrick's utensils. His Highness didn't impress her as a person infected with terminal niceness. If someone misplaced *his* favorite chopping knife, heads would roll, she felt sure of it.

Irritated, she continued opening drawers until she found her knife, then sighed heavily.

"Are we ready, people?" Mike squinted at the lighting, considered angles. "Let's do it." Standing beside the center camera, he counted it down. "In five, in four, in three, in two…" He pointed at Cathy.

"Hi," she said brightly, smiling into the camera. "Welcome to 'Cooking With Cathy.' As many of you know, I'm originally from western Kansas, not far from Dodge City, where today's recipe originated. Dodge was founded in 1872 and, for a time, was the cattle capital of the world. Even so, beef was too expensive for most old-time residents to buy more frequently than a couple of times a week."

She spoke to the camera as she might have talked to a neighbor who had dropped by her kitchen to share a cup of coffee and a little conversation.

"We're making White Bean, Parsnip, Potato and Turnip Soup today. Soup sounds good on a cold snowy day like this, doesn't it? This would also make a perfect recipe for the weekend, when you have all those chores you've put off during the week. Cover a soupbone—ham, pork, beef, or lamb, it doesn't matter which—with two quarts of water and simmer for about two hours while you run some errands or catch up on the laundry."

Lifting a pot lid, she inhaled the aroma before she stepped back so Jack could move in for a close-up of a simmering ham bone. "Don't forget to soak a cup of dried navy or pea beans in boiling water while the soup bone is simmering. Easy so far, isn't it? And it doesn't get harder."

The soup was light-years easier than whipping up a batch of Bulgur Wheat Dressing.

"In today's economy we're always looking for ways to stretch meat. Well, they did that in the old days by adding beans to most dishes. And this recipe uses that stale bread we all seem to accumulate." She smiled at the camera. "Best of all, today's presentation is an utterly unpretentious soup that only costs about fifty cents a serving. But don't let the cost deceive you. This soup has a rich, robust flavor that your family will love."

While she sliced potatoes, turnips and the parsnip, she chatted about the rowdy cattle and gunfighter days in old Dodge City, blending history and cooking as naturally as eggs and cheese. Having delivered a particularly amusing anecdote, she grinned at the camera.

"Through the magic of television, our soup is almost ready. What shall we serve with it? A nice accompaniment to any hearty soup is hot, golden corn bread, that staple of the pioneer plains. And wait until you discover how buttermilk improves the flavor! The only item you need to add to your grocery list is a box of cornmeal. If you don't have buttermilk on hand, you can substitute by combining two tablespoons of vinegar or lemon juice with one cup of skim or one-percent milk and let the mixture stand for five minutes. Low-fat plain yogurt also works nicely."

It was so easy to do this, Cathy thought, stirring the corn bread, and fun, too. Sometimes she felt guilty taking a paycheck for cooking and talking about history, her two favorite subjects. The half hour flew past.

"Good show," Mike said after the camera lights winked off. "Wasn't it a good show, everyone?"

"Great." Jack paused, his spoon hovering over a bowl of Cathy's soup. "That was terrific stuff about old Boot Hill and the days of Wyatt Earp."

Jean bit into a square of hot corn bread and groaned with pleasure. "This is so good. I haven't had corn bread in years."

Mike sampled it and agreed. "I sure hope your replacement doesn't cook that fancy gourmet crap, or that nouvelle stuff. The portions are always so small. I like the everyday meals that you fix."

"Excuse me?" Cathy's voice emerged huskier than usual. "What do you mean...my replacement?"

Heavy silence descended on the set. They all stared at Mike.

He frowned at the wedge of corn bread he was turning between his fingers. "It's a surprise to me too," he said in a hurt tone. "I wish you'd told me that you were interviewing with American Universal Syndication."

Feeling the heat rise in her cheeks, Cathy lowered her soup bowl to the counter. "There's about one chance in a million that AUS will choose me. I'm sorry I didn't mention it, Mike. I didn't think there was any point in worrying or upsetting anyone when it's such a slim chance that AUS will pick me." Suddenly it hit her. "How did you find out that I talked to them?"

"AUS sent a fax to the station."

"Oh, jeez. I was so nervous...I must have given them the station fax number instead of my number at home." She stared at him. "Mike? Where's the fax? What did they say?"

"Your chances aren't as slim as you supposed. You're a finalist."

"Oh my God!" Cathy's knees collapsed and she sat hard on the stool Jean hastily placed behind her.

"Congratulations!" Jean and Jack cheered in unison.

"It's a hell of an opportunity," Mike added, smiling reluctantly. "I'll hate to lose you—you've been a ratings bonanza—but if anyone deserves a shot at syndication, it's you."

"Syndication," Cathy whispered, trying to catch her breath. She couldn't believe the news. From the moment she'd first set foot on the KBAB cooking set, she'd dreamed of syndication. She supposed every local TV celebrity hoped for national exposure, but it happened only to a lucky handful. "I've got a chance."

"Damned straight you do!" Jean beamed at her.

"May I see the fax?" Her heart was pounding.

"I have it right here. I meant to give it to you earlier but it slipped my mind." Mike patted his pockets, starting outside his jacket, then inside, then checking his pants pockets. When he found an envelope stuck in his waistband, he handed it to her with a flourish.

"I'll read it later," Cathy decided, folding the envelope into her apron pocket. A document this important was best read alone where she wouldn't be self-conscious about the crew watching her reaction. "I probably won't be chosen, but it's nice to be a finalist."

"We're all pulling for you," Jack said.

Her cheeks felt hot and her hands shook as she moved about the set, cleaning up and putting everything away.

American Universal Syndication was an up-and-coming corporation headquartered in Atlanta. Already they had built a solid reputation for producing and packaging half-hour shows for national distribution. They were willing to spend big dollars to insure a high-quality product, and the chef they chose to anchor their new cooking show would have a major shot at nationwide stardom. Cathy could envision future cookbook deals, endorsements, fame and fortune. Her mind spun with fabulous possibilities.

And, she'd survived the first two cuts. Now all she had to do was emerge the winner in the final selection.

Was that possible? As confidence was not her long suit, thinking about the final selection sent her heart diving toward her toes.

"I'M NOT A LUCKY PERSON," she insisted to Jean before she left for home. As they stood in the station lobby facing the windows, the lights winked on in the parking lot. A thin dusting of snow capped the rows of cars.

"How is the competition decided?" Jean asked, shoving back a mop of short, dark hair. "Boy, it looks cold out there. I'll bet we get more snow tonight. Our weather forecaster can't predict his own shirt size."

"I don't know how the final decision will be made."

"Doesn't it say in the fax?"

Cathy juggled a sack of fan mail to search her coat pockets for her gloves. "I haven't read it yet. I'll wait until I get home."

Jean touched her arm. "Listen, you wouldn't have gotten this far in the competition if you weren't damned good. Nobody does what you do, mixing history and food. It's a great gimmick."

"I don't want to win because of a gimmick."

"Yeah, but it doesn't hurt to have one. The thing is, Cathy, most cooking shows focus on the fancy stuff. You don't. You give women recipes they can actually make. You use ingredients most of us have on hand, and you try to hold the cost per meal to something less than the price of a new sofa."

Cathy stared out the window at the damp halos shimmering around the street lamps. "Soup and corn bread," she muttered, suddenly feeling depressed. "I must have been crazy. Who makes soup and corn bread from scratch? You can buy a can of soup and a corn bread mix right off the grocery shelf. Who's going to spend three hours making homemade soup?"

"I might," Jean said promptly. "If the recipe was easy enough, and that one was. I can see myself putting that recipe on to simmer while I do the weekend chores, and then let Bill praise me to the skies for making homemade soup. Besides, the last time I looked, Campbell's doesn't make white bean, parsnip, potato and turnip soup."

Cathy laughed. "Thanks, Jean. You're a good friend." She pushed open the door and waved. "See you next week."

The instant she slid inside her minivan, Cathy opened her purse and touched the envelope just to make sure she hadn't dreamed that she was a finalist.

Why it would be bad luck to read the fax now, she didn't know, but that was how it felt. She'd go home, pour a glass of wine, put Neil Diamond on the stereo, *then* she'd read the letter.

TWO YEARS AGO, shortly after Cathy went to work for KBAB, she'd used a small inheritance as a down payment on a modest house in an older section of Wheatridge. Some of the houses were still occupied by the original owners, but gradually the neighborhood was being taken over by young families. Cathy was the only single on her block.

She preferred a house to a newer condo with noisy singles packed around her. Privacy was important, as was having a yard with room for a garden. There were few things as satisfying as growing your own vegetables, nothing quite as delicious as biting into a ripe tomato minutes after picking it off the vine. Winter hadn't officially arrived yet, but already she was planning next spring's garden.

Another thing she liked about owning a house was the sense of living in a real neighborhood. She liked children ringing her doorbell on Halloween night or coming by to sell her a box of Girl Scout cookies. Right now she could see a paper turkey and a pair of Pilgrims pasted on the picture window fronting the ranch house across the street. In a few weeks Christmas lights would twinkle in the evergreens, and wreaths would appear on the doors along the street. From her front porch, she spotted the Wilson kid's tricycle, and noticed a snow shovel leaning against old Mr. Ludlow's porch. This was community in the finest sense.

Stepping inside, she paused a moment and braced for Romeo's enthusiastic greeting. "Down, boy," she said, grinning. "How many times do I have to tell you—don't jump on people."

Removing his paws from her waist, she bent and scratched behind his ears, laughing at his frenzied tail-wagging. "Miss me, did you?"

That was another thing. She couldn't have had a dog in most condos, particularly not a dog as large as Romeo. And she'd grown to love him.

The day she moved in, Romeo had been sitting on her front porch like a one-dog welcoming committee. Large, a bit mangy, with the face of a Boxer and the body of a Labrador, he was no beauty. But he seemed to be smiling and was happy to see her. Inquiries in the neighborhood had not produced his owner, and he wore no collar. Cathy had taken him to the dog pound but when she learned that a dog of Romeo's undistinguished lineage and age was unlikely to be adopted, she had gazed into his soulful brown eyes, sighed, and taken him home again. She hadn't regretted her decision.

After hanging her coat in the closet, she paused a moment to appreciate being home. She had decorated the interior of her house in cheerful blues and yellows, enlivened by splashes of red that were repeated in the folk art lovingly chosen for the walls. Her favorite piece of furniture was an antique wheelbarrow, complete with iron wheels, that she'd converted into a coffee table by placing a sheet of glass across the top. If she ever found a spare minute to shop, she planned to buy a brass bed, and a claw-foot table for the dining room.

With Romeo on her heels, she took the envelope of fan mail to her office, listened to her phone messages, then headed toward the kitchen, the room that had persuaded her to buy this house instead of any other.

The cabinets were plentiful, maple with Shaker-style fronts, some with glass doors. Long expanses of counter were finished in gleaming white tile that always looked clean and fresh. A flowered backsplash added interest and color, and she had repeated the blue and yellow flowers on her canisters and accessories. She never felt she was really home until she entered the kitchen and inhaled the scent of spiced potpourri and the faint tang of the herbs growing on the windowsill.

For a moment she stood beside the oversize double oven and gazed fondly at her collection of antique cooking utensils that hung on the back wall of a cozy breakfast area. She remembered Grandmother Mallory using the potato ricer and old grater, the long tongs for a woodstove and the ice pick. Cathy had added to her collection cast-iron trivets, a nutcracker, a spatula that had seen hard duty and a toasting fork.

Standing in her kitchen, surrounded by shiny surfaces and quietly humming appliances, all the things she loved best, Cathy felt the tensions of the day start to drain out of her.

A glass of California Chablis would complete the process. For some reason Devlin Gilpatrick popped into her mind as she poured the wine. Mr. Superiority probably drank nothing but imported wines. He probably had a wine cellar in his house. It would be like him to employ a butler to serve and clear at chichi little dinner parties where women in gowns and men in dinner jackets drank amusing French wines and discussed the quality of this year's truffle crop.

Cathy flattened her palms on the countertop and dropped her head. Why did she waste so much time thinking about Devlin Gilpatrick? She didn't like him, she didn't like his cooking show, she didn't like the menus he selected, and she didn't like his superior attitude.

The rivalry between their two shows brought out the worst in her. She only had to hear his name to feel a rush of competitiveness. If anyone else had hosted the cooking show at Station KDID, she wouldn't have cared about the ratings sheet. But because it was Devlin Gilpatrick, ratings were crucial. When she beat him, she felt ten feet tall, felt as if she'd been crowned master chef of the world. When Devlin beat her by a few points, the news arrived like a blow to the midsection, and she felt about as talented as a pot washer in a military chow line.

She hardly knew the man, yet he had a tremendous impact on her emotional well-being. Well, she thought, lifting her head, that was going to change. She was moving upward and onward. With a little bit of luck, she'd leave Devlin Gilpatrick in the dust.

"To success," she said, toasting her reflection in the window above the sink. "To safety and security."

Syndication. It could happen.

Her gaze settled on the envelope containing the fax that she had removed from her purse and placed on the countertop. "Not yet," she said to Romeo. "First, we'll give you some supper." Some serious tail-thumping applauded her decision.

Next, she changed into a pair of faded jeans and slippers, then pulled a yellow sweater over her head. Because this was an occasion, she built a fire in the living room fireplace and turned on the stereo.

Singing along with Neil Diamond, dancing toward her reading chair, she let the music pump up her confidence. Romeo followed her and stretched contentedly before the fire.

Finally, she was ready. She sank into the chair, the glass of Chablis beside her, and crossed her ankles on an upholstered ottoman, turning the envelope in her hands. This was the stuff of dreams. A collection of magic words on a page. She wished her parents were alive. They would have been so proud that she, Cathy Mallory from Oakley, Kansas, had a chance at nationwide syndication. Her mother would have phoned the news to the *Graphic,* and her dad would have shown the article all around town.

Resting her head on the back of the chair, she drew out the moment, making it last.

How many finalists were there? Who would make the final selection, and how would the choice be decided? What would happen next? If she won, would she have to move to another city? Would she become famous? Just thinking about it made goose bumps rise on her arms. Her life could change in so many wonderful ways.

She would probably have to sell her catering business. After thinking about it, she decided maybe it was time. Since hiring a manager last year, she was no longer involved on a day-to-day basis, no longer doing all the cooking herself as she had in the early days. She still handled the finances and coordinated large events...but Maureen, the new manager, had hinted she'd like to buy the business.

A chance like national syndication happened but once in a lifetime, and Cathy wanted it so much that her stomach ached. Everything else seemed secondary.

When she had heightened the suspense to the extent that her pulse raced, her fingers trembled, and she couldn't stand it another minute, she drew a deep breath, then eased the fax out of the envelope and smoothed it open on her lap.

American Universal Syndication's President, Eugene Montford, opened by congratulating her as one of two finalists. He wished to share his excitement about the plans for a syndicated half-hour cooking show and assured her that AUS was prepared to invest heavily in production, packaging and promotion. Their Vice President of Planning, Annette Dunning, would arrive in Denver next week to interview both finalists and make the selection. Cathy could expect a call from Ms. Dunning to set up an appointment.

Mr. Montford wished Cathy good luck and signed his letter with warm regards.

Shock numbed her senses. She stared at Annette Dunning's name, praying that she had misread it. After a moment, the fax slipped out of her fingers and fluttered to the floor.

Please. It had to be a different Annette Dunning. It couldn't be the same Annette Dunning that Cathy had known in college. Fate surely wouldn't be so cruel as to dangle success and security before her, then snatch the possibility away by handing the final decision to Annette Dunning.

To Cathy's knowledge, there was only one person in the universe who hated her.

And that person was Annette Dunning.

Two

He said: The world is full of beautiful women—most of them looking for a man who can cook.

DEVLIN GILPATRICK had had enough. "No more!" he growled, jumping out of the chair and ripping off the towel tucked around his neck. "We're done, Bernie!"

Waving a powder puff, Bernadette danced anxiously in front of him. "But, Dev, your forehead's shining."

"It's not *shining*," he said. "It's *sweating*. I'm a chef, and that's what chefs do. They cook in hot kitchens, then they sweat. Plain, honest-to-God sweat." He swatted her hand away. "No more makeup, Bernie, and that's the end of the discussion."

Ignoring her squeaks of protest, he strode out of the cubicle, marched along the brightly lit corridors of the KDID building, and slammed into the greenroom.

Bill Sadler greeted him with a friendly thump on the shoulder. "Yo, man, you look as if you just ate rancid liver."

Dev took a deep breath. "Close."

"Let me guess," Bill said. "The ditzy new kid in makeup suggested you'd look sexier on camera if you wore eye shadow."

"Pink face powder." Dev spat out the words and directed a glare at his friend that would have shriveled a lesser man. "If she'd dared to suggest eye shadow, I'd have been arrested for murder by now."

Bill shifted his two-hundred-pound frame into a more comfortable position and grinned. "Should be a good show this week. You always cook better when you're angry, Dev. Gives you a real edge."

For a moment, Dev's fists clenched. Then he laughed, his temper cooling as rapidly as it had flared. "You're a major pain in the ass, you know. I can't think of a single reason why I put up with you."

"Must be because I'm the best cameraman in Denver. Either that, or it's my great personality." Bill lumbered to his feet and gestured toward the television monitor mounted on the wall. "Want to take a look at this week's effort by the competition? Just to whet your competitive spirit?"

"No," Dev said.

Bill clicked on the monitor as if Dev hadn't spoken. The opening credits for "Cooking with Cathy" filled the screen, followed by a riff of introductory music. Smiling into the camera, Cathy Mallory delivered her opening spiel with a warmth and confidence that Dev could only envy. She made you feel you were in the company of a good friend, welcoming you into her own kitchen; Devlin stared at the screen, trying to fathom how she managed to create such a captivating illusion of intimacy.

Bill seemed to be under her spell. Forgetting his normal cynicism, he watched the screen, eyes narrowed, mouth slightly open, stroking his beard appreciatively when Cathy bent over to lift a pan from the lower oven. "Great shot," he murmured. "Terrific angle."

Dev snorted. "In case you've forgotten, the camera's

supposed to be focussed on the food, not Cathy Mallory's fanny."

"Why not both?" Bill said. "Because it sure is a nice fanny. She's real cute, isn't she?"

"Mmm."

"Hey, what do you know? She's making bean soup and corn bread, my favorites." Bill patted his ample stomach. "Damn, I can almost smell that ham broth right from here. She always makes it look so easy."

"That's because the meals she prepares are easy."

Bill ignored him. "I haven't eaten homemade bean soup since I was a kid." He gave a nostalgic sigh. "Let's hope Jean gets inspired over the weekend and decides to make it for us. I love corn bread."

"You love food, period." Dev stared at the screen, unwillingly fascinated. He wouldn't have admitted as much to anyone, not even Bill, but he never missed watching Cathy Mallory's show. "Cooking With Cathy." Hah! In Dev's opinion, the word *cooking* was a serious stretching of the truth. As far as he could tell, "How to Mix and Match Packages" would have been a more accurate title.

"What are you cooking this week?" Bill asked, lowering the sound on Cathy's show, but keeping an admiring eye on her trim figure.

"I'm going to make Wiener schnitzel according to an authentic Viennese recipe, served with potatoes Anna and a side salad of pear and watercress with a raspberry dressing."

"Sounds great. Less exotic than the last couple of weeks."

"Yeah, well, I got to thinking that last week's menu was a bit over the top. Sumac and fried cucumbers are definitely an acquired taste. Sometimes I like to remind people that gourmet cooking doesn't always involve standing over a pot, braising duck flippers."

"Praise the Lord." Bill glanced at his wristwatch. "Are you ready, Dev? Scott told the guys we'd be taping in ten minutes."

"I'm ready." Dev cast a final irritated glance at the television screen, just in time to see Cathy shake her blond curls out of her eyes and smilingly inform everyone that the addition of buttermilk made corn bread more moist and flavorful.

"Now there's a huge surprise," Dev said, unable to control his sarcasm. "That's really an insiders' tip. Explain her success to me, Bill. I don't understand how that fluff-ball stays on the air."

"For the same reasons you do, I guess. Sex appeal and market share."

"Sex appeal?" Dev said acidly. "Funny, I thought the show was about cooking."

"Only incidentally," Bill said. "Face it, Dev. Most women watch your show because they're fantasizing about how great it would be to have you take them to bed, not because they want to learn your secret recipe for Amaretto *biscotti*."

"Maybe next week I should take my shirt off and see if we can get a jump in the ratings."

"Gee, that's a great idea," Bill said. "I'll mention it to Scott."

Dev eyed his friend with deep suspicion. "You're kidding, right?"

Bill grinned. "Yeah." He paused. "I guess I am."

He should really be used to this sort of comment by now, Dev thought, turning away and pretending to give a final check to his notes. The truth was, he hated to think people watched his show for the wrong reasons.

After fifteen years of backbreaking apprenticeship in the toughest kitchens of Europe, he wanted to believe that people watched "Dining With Devlin" because they liked his cooking, not because they thought he had a sexy voice or a handsome profile. If they wanted cute, they could watch Cathy Mallory. If they wanted a guide to the great cuisines of the world, he hoped they would watch him.

Bill tapped his watch. "Time to take that smoldering Heathcliff gaze onto the set, Dev." He stuck his head into the studio. "Dev's back from makeup, folks. We'll be with you in two."

Dev gave a final glance at the monitor. "That woman makes me crazy."

"Then why are you watching her?"

"You said it yourself. I need to know what the competition's doing."

Bill laughed. "Right."

"What's that supposed to mean?"

"It means you're obsessed with the woman. Personally, I can't understand why you don't put yourself out of your misery and invite her out on a date. Turn on some of that famous Devlin Gilpatrick charm. You'd probably find you have a lot in common."

"We've met already. Trust me, we don't like each other."

Bill held open the door to the studio and waved Dev in with his clipboard. "Give the gal a break, Dev. She isn't claiming to be a Cordon Bleu chef. She just wants to show busy men and women how they can enjoy a good meal every now and then, without spending hours shopping for shiitake mushrooms and coated rice paper."

"Don't tell me you need shiitake mushrooms!" Scott

Mortimer, the show's producer and resident panicmonger, started a frantic search of his supply list. "Did I hear you say you need them for today? No one told me. Where the hell am I supposed to find shiitake mushrooms five minutes before we start taping?"

"Calm down, Scott." Dev gave the producer a reassuring pat on the arm. "I don't need shiitake mushrooms. I don't need any sort of mushrooms."

"Then why were you talking about them?"

Bill and Dev exchanged amused glances. "It's a long story," Dev said. "Let's leave it for later, okay?"

"Okay, but I need you on set, Dev. Penny, get his mike fixed up. Bill, how's the lighting? That new wallpaper is too bright. I said last week that we should have gone with the beige. I knew that yellow would be distracting."

Bill rolled his eyes. "The lighting's fine, Scott. So's the wallpaper."

Dev let the chaos ebb and flow around him, as he checked his supplies. His crew was one of the best in the business, and normally the setup for the show went more smoothly than this. But yesterday they'd taped an extra segment, ready to air Christmas week, and it looked as if the cleanup crew had done a pretty rushed job. His favorite knife was nowhere to be found.

"Scott," he called. "Where's my paring knife? I left it on the counter."

"Are you sure it isn't there? Under the cheesecloth, maybe?"

"No." Dev gritted his teeth. "I need my paring knife. I can't prepare potatoes Anna without it."

"Here," called one of the sound techs as he pulled open a drawer. "Is this the knife you're looking for?"

"Yeah. Thanks." Dev glared into the dark studio.

"The next person who moves one of my knives is going to get sliced and filleted with it. Do we all understand each other?"

"Yeah, Dev. Sure. Sorry." The sound tech hurried off and Dev sighed. He'd bet his next paycheck that nobody ever messed with the All-American Princess's knives. When she put a paring knife on the counter, she wouldn't come back from makeup to find that it had disappeared. Cathy Mallory struck him as being blessed with one of those warm, sunny personalities that had people falling all over themselves to keep her happy. He, unfortunately, was much too intense and driven to share her amiable manner.

"Okay, people, are we ready?" Still obsessing about the wallpaper, Scott made a final adjustment to one of the overhead lights. "Then let's do it. In five, in four, in three, in two..." He nodded his head and pointed at Dev.

"Hello and welcome," Dev said, feeling the familiar rush of adrenaline as he smiled into the camera. "I'm glad you could join me for another evening of 'Dining With Devlin.' Tonight we're going to take a journey to Vienna, a city that rivals Paris in its claim to be the perfect destination for lovers. Nestled on the banks of the River Danube, it was once the seat of power for the Hapsburg empire, and a melting pot for dozens of ethnic groups. Centuries later, the legacy of these diverse cultural roots is the city's abundance of wonderful music, good wine and rich food."

As he talked, Dev expertly peeled potatoes, then cut them into paper-thin slices with the precision drummed into him during his apprenticeship in a famous Brussels restaurant. For an entire year, he'd been allowed to do nothing but prepare vegetables according to the rules laid down by the terrifying chef who ruled the kitchen. As he finished cutting each potato, he slid the perfectly aligned slices off his cutting board into a bowl of ice water.

"A hundred years ago, Vienna was considered the most exciting city in the world, the glittering center of Europe, as well as its fast-beating heart. Richard Strauss composed his famous waltzes there, and Sigmund Freud developed his theories concerning human psychology at the renowned General Hospital. And while aristocrats danced through the night in gilded ballrooms, ordinary Viennese citizens found new ways to enjoy themselves in their city's famous cafés and restaurants. One of the many contributions Vienna has made to the world's cooking was Wiener schnitzel— Vienna cutlet—which is a thin slice of milk-fed veal, lightly seasoned and coated with soft bread crumbs, then deep-fried in butter."

Dev gave a shrug and grinned. "Yes, you're right. Tonight we're definitely not preparing a low-fat, heart-healthy meal, but believe me, Wiener schnitzel is worth an extra ten minutes' running on your treadmill. One of the dishes the Viennese loved to serve with their schnitzel is called potatoes Anna, and most of the packaged instant-potato dishes that you can find on the shelves of your supermarket these days are a variation of this famous Austrian dish. Tonight, we're going to see how to make the original recipe, and once you've tasted the real thing, I'm sure you'll agree with me that there's no going back to the imitations."

Moving slightly to one side so that Bill could zoom in and get a close-angle shot, he stirred the potato slices so that the ice in the glass bowl clinked. "I've peeled four mature baking potatoes, and as you can see, I've dipped them in ice water to remove the loose starch on the surface of the slices. This prevents the potatoes from sticking together and tasting gluey. Drain the potatoes and dry them on paper towels." He went through the simple steps of explaining how to melt butter and layer the potatoes in a pan with salt, grated onion and freshly grated Parmesan cheese.

"This is actually a very simple recipe and there are all sorts of shortcuts you can take in making it," he explained. "But for each substitution, you take away something from the final result. For example, if you decide to buy grated Parmesan cheese, the recipe will still work, but you'll lose the wonderful tang that really fresh cheese gives. You'll lose even more if you substitute freeze-dried chopped onions. What you'll taste in the end is the artificial preservatives, not the satisfying sensation of real onions, with their flavorful juices released by baking that mingle with the butter and permeate the potatoes."

He put the potatoes Anna into the oven, and stared into the camera, so intent that he forgot to smile. "You might be thinking that I'm taking a long time just to make a few potatoes, and you're right. Obviously, this isn't a recipe for every day. In our tight economy where both partners in a marriage usually need to work, we can't come home from the office and expect our spouse and the kids to wait around while we spend the next couple of hours slicing potatoes and grating onions. But the weather forecasters are predicting snowstorms this weekend, so maybe this is the perfect time to think about taking a few hours out of your busy schedule and spending them in the kitchen, cooking a really special meal.

"Does that still sound like hard work?" Dev reached

for another slice of veal, and pounded it briskly with his mallet. "Maybe you should try thinking of it as a way to work out your frustrations. I've learned over the past decade that the secret to great cooking is the same as the secret to life: the journey is the destination." He grinned. "Which means, roughly speaking, that the fun you get preparing a truly great meal is every bit as important as the pleasure you and your friends get from eating it."

He seasoned the veal, adding the lightest possible dusting of bread crumbs and explaining how important it was not to let the delicate flavor be destroyed by overcooking, or drowned by a heavy batter. To keep the audience entertained, he chatted about the Wiener schnitzel he'd eaten last summer at a restaurant tucked away in the Carpathian mountains that ring Vienna.

"It was raining that night, but there was no wind and the air was warm, so my friend and I decided to sit at a table outside on the covered balcony, where we could enjoy the view of the hills. As we ate, the sound of the rain and the Viennese wine mellowed our moods. It almost seemed that the world around us faded away, leaving just the two of us. That was the last time I ever saw my friend, and it was a wonderful way to say goodbye to her. A final great memory to add to all the good times we shared."

Dev added the veal to a pan of foaming butter. The kitchen was already filled with the heady aroma of cheese and onion from the potatoes Anna. The warm butter added another layer of fragrance and Dev took in a couple of deep breaths, thinking how lucky he was to earn his living doing something he enjoyed so much. Sometimes he felt guilty taking a paycheck for cooking and chatting about the world and its cuisines, his two favorite subjects. The half hour flew past.

"Okay, that's a wrap," Scott said. "Great show, Dev. No technical problems, anyone? Nothing we need to repeat?"

"No problems at my end," Bill said.

"Sound was good," Penny reported.

"Now can we eat?" Bill asked.

Penny had already helped herself to a serving of potatoes. "God, Dev, these are truly heavenly. Way better than sex. Tell me the worst. How many million calories am I eating? Two million? Three?"

"Something like that." Dev grinned. "Next week, I'll plan something low-fat."

Penny grimaced. "I should be grateful, but these potatoes are to die for."

"Speaking of sex," Bill said, around a mouthful of veal. "Who was that poor woman you dumped over a meal in the Viennese mountains?"

"I didn't dump anybody. What are you talking about?"

Bill put his hand to his heart and tried to look soulful. *"It was a wonderful way to say goodbye...a final great memory..."* he intoned. "That's what I'm talking about, Dev. Although I can't duplicate your bedroom eyes and husky voice very well."

"The friend I was talking about happened to be an eighty-five-year-old woman," Dev said dryly. He moved off the set so that the cleanup crew could get started. "She ran a restaurant that had been in her family for three generations, and she gave me my first job as a sous-chef. Sorry to disappoint you, but the memories we shared were strictly about cooking."

"I believe you." Bill shrugged. "But nobody else would. I'm through here. How about you?"

"I'm through. Let's go home."

Scott ran to catch up with Dev and Bill as they left the studio. "Wait up, you guys!" He tucked the inevitable clipboard under his arm. "Dev, you know that Paul Lyman's agreed to chair this year's culinary contest—"

"Yes, I knew. It'll be good publicity for the station."

"Very good, especially if you win. I was talking with Paul yesterday, and he asked me what you were planning to cook. I told him I had no idea and he pointed out that the money that's raised is going to support the new wing at the children's hospital. Since he's also on the hospital's board of directors, he's putting a lot of promotional backing behind the contest. Naturally, he's hoping for big things from you."

"Trust me, so am I." Dev frowned. "Make sure you control the number of copies of that tape floating around, Scott. We don't want everyone in town knowing what I'm going to cook for the contest. Surprise and novelty give you a competitive edge."

"Sure, no problem." Scott scribbled a note on his clipboard. "Don't worry, we have the copies under strict security control. I don't want the tape to leak any more than you do. I happen to know Paul has some major expansion plans for the station in the works, and we want to guarantee that 'Dining With Devlin' is included. Winning that contest would generate a hell of a lot of good publicity for you, Dev."

"Yes, sure, I understand." Dev had been around KDID long enough to know that shows never remained static in the ratings. They either went up, or they went down, usually with brutal speed. Scott was ambitious, and he had a big stake in Dev's continued success.

They parted company at the main entrance, with Scott rushing off to a meeting. Dev and Bill crunched through the light dusting of snow to the parking lot. It was only the third week in November, but Denver had already shivered through two major snowfalls, as well as three days when the high had hit the midseventies. After so many years of living in Europe, Dev was still trying to get used to the vagaries of Colorado weather.

Being a native Denverite, Bill barely seemed to notice the cold. "You heard anything yet from American Universal Syndication?" he asked.

"No." Dev shoved his hands deeper into the pockets of his jacket. "I should hear something soon. When I went to Atlanta for the interview, the marketing director said they would make their decision before November 23. That's this weekend."

"You're going to get the job," Bill said. "I feel it in my bones."

Dev gave his friend an affectionate punch. "Yeah, right. Just like you felt in your bones that the Broncos were going to win the Superbowl last year. Your bones cost me twenty bucks."

Bill appeared uncrushed by this reminder. "You're the best, Dev, and you're going to get this job."

Bill was the only person at KDID who knew about Dev's dealings with Universal Syndication. Every local television celebrity hoped for national syndication, and AUS was about to offer one lucky chef a shot at the brass ring. Ever since his initial interview with Universal Syndication executives in Atlanta, Dev had been dreaming about future cookbook deals, endorsements, and the chance to find a production company for the line of cookware he'd designed. He'd warned himself not to get carried away with too much pie in the sky, but his mind spun with the possibilities.

"See you next week," Bill said, climbing into his car. "Try not to break too many hearts this weekend, Dev."

Dev smiled. "I'll limit myself to two a night," he said, stepping into his car. He wondered what Bill would think if he realized that Dev would actually spend the entire weekend in his kitchen, testing recipes for his restaurant, Chez Dev. At the highest levels, being a chef meant hours of hard work, followed by a few rare moments of excitement and glamour.

He drove home to the condo he'd bought last year on the penthouse floor of a new downtown building. After years of living on an apprentice's wages in Europe, he relished the space and privacy he could finally afford. He loved the clean, bright walls, the thickly carpeted floors and the luxury of a bathroom bigger than the total square footage of the apartment he'd rented in Paris. Best of all, he loved the kitchen, with its long, bare counters, its two oversize ovens, the huge sink and the efficient overhead lighting.

Ramses was waiting for him in his favorite straight-backed chair by the front door. Dev had found Ramses on the back steps of the restaurant in Milan where he'd been working. The cat had been filthy, a ragged ball of fur, too weak and emaciated to jump into the garbage can in search of food. Responding to the imperious gleam in the cat's starving eyes, Dev had taken him home, nursed him back to health, bought him a kitty bed lined with acrylic fur, and generally spoiled him rotten. Ramses rewarded his savior by ignoring this fur-lined bed and sleeping with Dev, preferably draped over Dev's feet. He did not approve of the women Dev occasionally brought home, and had various methods, all highly embarrassing, of making his disapproval known.

Dev scratched Ramses behind his battered left ear, then made straight for his answering machine to check for messages. He'd had half a dozen calls, but nothing from Universal Syndication. Hoping against hope, he went into the bedroom he'd converted into an office and checked his fax machine.

There was a letter waiting for him, and the header showed that it had come from AUS.

He saw the word *Congratulations,* and his stomach vaulted in relief. Despite all his daydreaming, he hadn't quite realized how badly he wanted this shot at syndication until he read that word. His parents—solid Irish immigrants, who'd worked hard and lived decent lives—had never understood what drove him, but he knew they would bust their buttons with pride if they could boast to their neighbors that he had a show on nationwide TV. He discovered that he very badly wanted his parents to feel proud of him.

He put the letter down, wanting to savor this moment of triumph. He had a bottle of Viennese wine that he'd put in the fridge to chill before he left to tape his show. It was one of the full-bodied Rheinrieslings that came from the Heiligenstift monastery at Thallern, and it was the perfect wine for celebrating.

Glass of wine in hand, he put a George Winston CD into the player. The disc was called *Winter,* and the subtle, impressionistic melodies were the perfect accompaniment to the falling snow that he could now see out the wide, uncurtained expanse of his windows.

He sat in a comfortable chair, took a long sip of wine,

then smoothed out the fax and started to read. American Universal Syndication's president congratulated him on being one of two finalists for their new show. He wished to share his excitement about the plans already being formulated, and assured Devlin that AUS was prepared to invest heavily in production, packaging and promotion.

Two finalists? Dev stared at the letter, brows furrowed. *Two* finalists. When had they decided there were going to be two finalists? How was AUS going to make the final selection? How much longer would it be before he knew that he had the job?

He took another sip of wine and settled down to read the final paragraph of the letter. The president of American Universal Syndication was pleased to inform him that the company's Vice President of Planning, Annette Dunning, would arrive in Denver next week to interview both finalists and make the selection. Devlin should expect a phone call from Ms. Dunning to set up an appointment.

The president wished Devlin good luck and signed the letter with warm regards.

Shock left Dev paralyzed. He stared at Annette Dunning's name, trying to convince himself that it must be another Annette Dunning. He crumpled the fax into a ball and threw it at the wall. Ramses, delighted with the game, leaped into the air, crash-landing on the credenza and sending papers and magazines flying.

Dev barely noticed the mishap. Annette Dunning. Her name danced mockingly inside his head. There must be hundreds of Annette Dunnings in America, Dev told himself. This couldn't be the same woman he'd known in Paris. Fate surely wouldn't be so cruel as to dangle the brass ring in front of him, then snatch it away by handing the final decision to Annette Dunning.

To Dev's knowledge, there was only one person in the universe who hated him.

And that person was Annette Dunning.

Chapter Three

*She said: The recipe for success is one cup of
hard work plus one cup of commitment. Stir
well with half a cup of ambition and add three
cups of luck.*

THE LIGHT SNOW was starting to thicken when Cathy left
the house, and she wished she'd canceled her weekly
date with Jean at the health club. She had a half-dozen
errands to run, but already the roads were icing up.

"Did you catch the weather report?" she asked Jean
when they met in the locker room. "Is it going to snow
all day?"

"According to our weather forecaster, it shouldn't be
snowing right now." Bending at the waist, Jean leaned
into a warm-up routine, dark hair swinging past her
cheeks. "I wish I could get Bill interested in exercise.
He's put on twenty pounds since he was assigned to
Devlin's show."

"It's no wonder," Cathy sniffed. She adjusted the
sweatband on her forehead and began a series of
stretching exercises. "God forbid that His Highness
would alter his haute-cuisine recipes to make them
healthy. I don't think he ever considers calories. I don't
know why Devlin Gilpatrick doesn't weigh three hundred pounds."

"He must work out. I only wish he'd take Bill with him."

Of course Devlin Gilpatrick worked out, Cathy decided. Most on-camera celebrities did. There wasn't an ounce of fat on the man. Frowning, she followed Jean into the equipment room and they climbed onto stationary bikes.

"You know," Jean said, smiling, "for someone who professes to dislike Dev, you talk about him an awful lot."

"Today I have a good reason," Cathy said, pumping her legs. In fact, she'd been thinking about little else other than Devlin, wrestling with an enormous moral dilemma. After a moment's debate, she decided she had to share her quandary, and who would understand it better than Jean?

"Jean? A strange thing happened yesterday." She stopped pedaling, leaned back, and pushed a wave of hair back from her cheeks. "Does sea bass with lemongrass mean anything to you?"

Jean laughed. "Nope. Now if you want to talk about Hamburger Helper—there I can relate." She adjusted her mileage counter and looked at Cathy. "So what's with the sea bass and lemongrass?"

Cathy looked at her. "That's going to be Devlin Gilpatrick's entry in the Chefs' Culinary Contest."

"What?" Jean stopped pedaling, shock widening her eyes. "Cathy, how could you possibly know what Dev is planning for the culinary contest?"

Cathy's frown deepened. "You know how we taped an extra show to be aired after the contest? The show where I prepare my contest entry for our audience? Well, Dev made the same kind of tape for his audience."

She lifted her head and gave Jean a troubled glance. "Someone sent me a copy of Dev's tape."

"Oh my God!" Jean's hands flew to her mouth.

"The thing is, I'm not sure what to do." Tilting her head back, she blinked at the high ceiling of the gym. "I'm ashamed to admit it, but for several hours I actually considered doing nothing." A sigh lifted her chest. "It's a tremendous advantage, knowing what my only real competition is going to prepare."

"Cathy, this is terrible. If anyone finds out about that tape...they might think Bill sent it to you as a favor to me or something like that, and it's not true!" Jean shook her head for emphasis. "We're in a delicate situation, with me working on your show and Bill working on Dev's show. Right from the beginning, Bill and I agreed not to talk about the actual shows—and we don't—because we don't want you or Dev to think we're sharing secrets or carrying tales." Her eyes widened. "If anyone finds out about the tape you received, Bill is going to be the first suspect. Damn, that isn't fair. I'd stake my life on it that he doesn't know anything about this. Bill's one of Dev's best friends and he'd never betray him any more than I would do something like that to you!" She stared at Cathy. "Do you have any idea who sent you the tape?"

"I don't know. There was no return address on the package."

Jean pressed her lips together. "This puts me in a tough position. I feel like I ought to tell Bill that someone copied the tape and sent it to you. Cathy? What are you going to do about this?"

"I'm going to tell Devlin about it," she said with great reluctance. She'd already made the decision. Jean's reaction only confirmed it. "I think I have to tell him."

"Absolutely," Jean said promptly.

"If someone sent one of the other chefs a copy of *my* tape revealing my contest entry, I'd sure as hell want to know about it. I'd be furious." She sighed. "As much as I'd like to have a leg up going into the contest, it wouldn't be fair. Plus, I hate it that someone thinks I'd keep quiet about this and take advantage of knowing Devlin's entry in advance. I don't need to cheat to win. I can win fair and square."

"That's right," Jean said loyally, her expression still disturbed. "I just know you'll win. Venison is a difficult dish to prepare well. You'll blow the judges away."

"I can't concentrate on pedaling. Let's move to the weights, okay?"

After they'd settled in on side-by-side machines that worked both legs and arms, Jean said, "On a different subject...I'm dying to know what AUS said in their fax to you. Tell me about the syndication possibility."

"There are two finalists." Cathy puffed with exertion. "Their vice president is coming to Denver next week to interview me."

"Wow, that's great! How can you sound so calm about it?"

Cathy stopped pushing and pulling at the machine. "Because it's a done deal. There's nothing to think about, nothing to get excited over. I know there isn't one chance in ten million that I'll get the position."

"You don't know that."

"Yes, I'm afraid I do." She rolled her head on the headrest and gave Jean a look of anguish. "The vice president is a woman named Annette Dunning. I knew her in college." She closed her eyes. "Annette blamed me because she was pressured to leave school. The last thing she said to me was: I'll get even with you if it takes a lifetime. Well, now she has her chance. No way is she going to select me for syndication."

Jean stared, then swung her legs out of the machine. "That's it, I'm through exercising. I want to hear this story and I don't want any distractions. Come on, let's hit the juice bar."

Cathy wasn't sure she wanted to talk about Annette and one of the most painful experiences in her life. Already she regretted mentioning it.

"I've never told this story before," she said when she and Jean were seated at a table with frothy orange drinks before them. "I wish we hadn't gotten into this."

"Maybe it's time you talked about it," Jean suggested gently. She waved a hand in front of Cathy's eyes. "Cathy? Yoo-hoo. You're slipping away, girl."

"Sorry." She gave her head a shake. "When I was a sophomore in college, some friends asked me to share a large house they were renting off campus. We were all undergrads except Annette. She was in graduate school." Looking down, she stirred her drink with her straw. "I usually make friends easily, but—I don't know—Annette and I just didn't hit it off. She used to call me 'Kansas.' She'd draw the word out like it was a joke, like I was the world's greatest, most naive hay-seed." She sighed heavily. "The thing is, she was right. If you think I'm gullible now, you should have seen me twelve years ago."

"I take it Annette Dunning was not naive?"

"Lord, no. Annette was born street-smart. She knew all the angles and knew how to play them. I don't know about the others, but five minutes with Annette always made me feel like the dumbest rube who ever came down the pike. I worked for grades—she finagled them. I saved to buy clothes—she borrowed them. When we ordered out for food, everyone chipped in except Annette. With her, it was always 'I'll pay you later.'"

"But she never did." Jean nodded. "I know people like that. So what finally happened?"

"Look, I'd really appreciate it if you didn't tell anyone about this."

"If that's what you want...."

Cathy nodded, hesitated, then continued the story. "One of my best friends was caught cheating. She turned in a paper that the professor recognized because he'd seen it before. It turned out that Annette had sold her the paper. Annette had a very lucrative business selling term papers, theses, course notes, book reviews. If you were willing to cheat," Cathy said bitterly, "Annette was happy to profit from it."

"How does this involve you?" Jean asked.

"When Annette was brought before the college disciplinary board, she told them the only thing she'd done wrong was to trust *me*." Cathy was so deep in painful memories that she didn't hear Jean's gasp. "She said *I* was the person selling term papers, not her. All she did was give my friend an envelope as I'd instructed her to do, and she collected the money for me. For all she knew, the two events were not related. She thought my friend owed me the money for something else." Cathy shrugged. "You get the picture."

"Surely the college didn't take her word for this. Didn't your friend tell them who sold her the paper?"

"Eileen dropped out the minute she was accused of cheating. I think her parents sent her to Europe, but I don't know. I only know she wasn't there to help clear things up."

"Wasn't there anyone—?"

"I had a lot of friends, including professors and counsellors, who spoke on my behalf, but Annette proved that it was me who bought reams and reams of copy paper, not her. The envelopes she delivered the papers in were the green-and-white oversize envelopes that I used. The papers were typed on a computer, not a typewriter, and in those days, I was the only one among the roommates who had a computer...." Cathy shrugged. "I thought I was doing her a favor by picking up supplies for her, and by letting her use my computer. I never questioned the errands she asked me to do for her, not once."

"And all the time, she was setting you up."

"Playing the angles. That was Annette. She thought it all out before there was even a hint that she might get caught."

"So, how did you prove you were innocent?"

Cathy pulled a hand down her face. "I didn't. Since the disciplinary board couldn't reach a conclusion as to who was the guilty party, they pressured both of us to leave the college."

"God!"

She nodded. "It was devastating. I had to tell my parents...." Her hand formed into a fist on the table. "I felt so stupid! This was going on right under my nose, and I was so busy dating, studying, having a ball, that I didn't notice a thing. Nothing. Pollyanna, that's me. It never entered my mind that some students were cheating or that Annette was helping them do it. On *my* computer." She shook her head. "Talk about naive."

"And then Annette blamed you. Did you ever figure out why?"

Cathy shrugged and frowned. "I think that the hayseed from Kansas was popular and she wasn't. Certainly she seemed to resent that so many people later came to my defense while no one spoke up for her. It might also be that she believed I turned her in, in an attempt to help Eileen, the friend who was caught cheating. Anyway, when it became obvious how the hearing would end, one of my professors moved heaven and earth to get me into the Culinary Institute of America, one of the best things that ever happened to me. Annette was furious that I came out smelling like a rose, as she put it." Cathy returned her gaze to Jean. "I can only tell you that at the end, Annette had convinced herself that she was an innocent victim and I was totally to blame for her having to leave school in disgrace. She was good at twisting things around."

"Oh, Cathy." Sympathy filled Jean's large, dark eyes. "Now she turns up as the person who could grant you the plum opportunity of a career. Or deny it. I'm so sorry."

Looking down, Cathy watched the orange drink blur. She blinked hard. "So am I," she whispered. "The other finalist doesn't know it, but he or she is a shoo-in. There's no question who Annette will select for syndication. It sure won't be me."

They sat in silence for several minutes, then Cathy lifted her head and pulled off her sweatband. "Well, I've got a million things to do today. I need to stop by the catering office, then I have to take my car in—there's a funny knock in the engine—I have to run by the grocery store, need to pick up some dry cleaning. And I want to practice a bit more with the sauce for the venison. I wasn't thrilled with the way it turned out on the tape we made."

Jean made an obvious effort to look cheerful. "We didn't talk about Dustin. How's the romance progressing?"

"About as well as my last big romance." Cathy burst into laughter. "I keep telling you, Dustin and I are just friends. Believe me, there's no romance."

They power-walked toward the locker room, squeezing in a last bit of exercise.

"Well, I don't believe you," Jean said, grinning. "You've been seeing a lot of him. Are you telling me that you can resist a guy that good-looking? That attentive? That crazy about you?"

"Yep, that's what I'm saying. Jean...Dustin is gay."

Jean stopped dead in her tracks. "You're kidding. My God. I'm the worst matchmaker in history!"

Cathy laughed again. "There's a lesson here, my friend."

"And I'm starting to get it," Jean admitted with a weak grin.

"But don't stop trying just yet. A wonderful man would be a terrific consolation prize for losing the syndication opportunity."

Jean gave her a long appraising look in the locker room. "You know, of course, who's just the perfect man for you."

"Don't even say his name," Cathy groaned. "He's the competition, the enemy."

"If you'd just give Dev a chance...."

"Jean, it would never work. Take the Chefs' Culinary Contest. There are going to be—what? Ten or twelve master chefs competing? But the only one I care about is Devlin Gilpatrick. I want to win the contest, but what I really want most is to beat Devlin." She sighed. "That's why receiving the tape revealing his entry was such a dilemma for a while. I'd love to knock off a little of his arrogance. Believe me, no matter how it turns out, if I place ahead of him, I'll walk away from the contest a winner. It will just kill me if he places higher than I do!"

"You know I'm rooting for you."

"I know. Thanks."

She wanted to win the culinary contest so badly she could almost taste it. It wouldn't be the same as getting the syndication offer from AUS, but at least she would have something to hang her pride on.

FEELING A LITTLE LOW, Cathy didn't stay long at Just Like Home, her catering business. Seeing that everything was running smoothly without her didn't improve her spirits as it usually did. Wondering if it was time to sell, she hurried to the car dealership for her appointment.

"But I'm only five minutes late," she protested when the manager informed her they had begun work on another car since she hadn't arrived on schedule. "The streets are awful out there. I tried my best, but it's like driving on a mirror!"

"Sorry." The manager shrugged. "We'll get to you in about an hour. We've already started work on Mr. Gilpatrick's car."

"Mr....?" Whirling around, she spotted Devlin through a window looking into the waiting room. Oh, no. It was too late to escape—he'd spotted her, too. He nodded pleasantly and she nodded back. Then she stared at the vehicle the mechanics had up on the rack. "Is that Devlin's car?"

The classic red-and-white Corvette had been perfectly restored. "It's a beauty, isn't it?" the manager said, beaming.

Indeed it was. Slowly, Cathy shifted her gaze to her car. Devlin drove a classic Corvette; she drove a practical, unexciting minivan. It figured. Shoving her hands into her coat pockets, she stared at a grease spot on the garage floor. "When you finally get to my van, how long is it going to take to fix the knock in the engine?"

"Won't know until we get to it," the manager said. "But plan on at least an hour. Hope you brought something to read. The waiting-room magazines aren't exactly current."

"Just like a doctor's office," Cathy commented with a forced smile. When she couldn't hang around the bay area any longer without feeling foolish, she stiffened her shoulders and made herself walk into the waiting room. The room was small, stuffy and overly warm.

"Hi," she said to Devlin. They were the only people in the waiting room, but it felt crowded. "Getting your car worked on?" Oh, terrific. That was a brilliant thing to say. *Duh.* She felt a rush of embarrassing pink flood her cheeks.

Setting aside a tattered magazine, he gave her one of his dazzling smiles. "Needs new spark plugs. Is yours the minivan?"

"I bought it a couple of years ago when the catering business started to really take off and I needed space to..." Letting her voice trail off, she glanced at a tumble of magazines on a table that looked as though it would collapse if someone sneezed. "The engine's making a funny sound."

When she realized how girly that comment sounded, she grimaced. He knew exactly what was wrong with his car; all she could say was that hers was making a funny noise. Well, so what? He probably didn't know a pleat from a tuck.

"I just realized," he said, standing, looking svelte and handsome in a pair of jeans, a black turtleneck and a corduroy jacket. "You're the customer who was late, the one whose place I took."

"No problem. These things happen." She shrugged. "I would have been on time, but there was an accident on Wadsworth."

"Now you're going to have a longer wait than you expected. The least I can do is buy you a cup of coffee. There's a place across the street...."

Cathy could smell the lemony scent of his cologne in the small room, and she suddenly remembered that she'd dashed out of the health club planning to shower at home after her errands. It was daunting to consider spending an hour trapped in this small, stuffy room worrying if she smelled sweaty while trying to think of a way to tell him about the tape she had received.

"Thanks," she said. "Coffee sounds great." She couldn't imagine how she would introduce the subject.

On the way across the street, ducking her head against flying snow that stung her face, she remembered that she wasn't wearing any makeup. And beneath her coat, she still wore her exercise leotards and tights. Damn. It was just her luck to run into Devlin Gilpatrick when she looked her worst. And he looked...fabulous.

Frowning, she stepped up on the curb and responded to a light touch at her elbow that directed her toward a coffee shop. Inside, it was warm and redolent with the rich aroma of coffee beans and freshly baked cinnamon rolls.

Devlin seated her at a table and smiled. "Shall I take your coat?"

"No thanks." No way was she going to reveal that she was braless, wearing a leotard. She'd feel like a total goof.

"What would you like?"

"Mocha latte if they make it with German chocolate," she decided. "With skim milk, please."

"Skim?" His eyebrows lifted as if she'd said a dirty word.

"Less fat and calories," she explained, unnecessarily in her opinion. So, he was a purist even with coffee. *Oh, pu-leeze.*

"If you insist. Single or double espresso?"

"Single," she answered, guessing by his frown that she'd uttered another dirty word.

"Back in a minute."

Some days it just didn't pay to get out of bed. She hadn't gotten a good workout because she and Jean had talked about Annette Dunning, which had upset her and left her feeling depressed. Her own catering business didn't need her anymore. The dry cleaners had lost her second-favorite sweater. She was going to waste an extra hour waiting for her car. And while looking like something that Romeo had dragged home, she'd run into Devlin and he didn't approve of her coffee choice. Floating above all this like a sour top note was knowing that she had to tell him about the tape.

Chin cupped in her hand, she glumly watched him talking and laughing with the girl behind the counter. And she thought about how fabulous he'd been on the tape she'd received. He had a wonderful presence on camera—commanding, actually. And, although she hated to admit it, sea bass with lemongrass was an inspired choice for the culinary contest. She'd watched the tape three times and knew he would be tough to beat.

Damn. The only thing to do when you were feeling as inadequate and bummed out as she was feeling right now, was to square your shoulders and pretend you were sitting on top of the world. That's what her mother had always advised.

"*Grazie,*" she said when Devlin placed a foamy mocha latte in front of her.

"*Parla Italiana?*" he asked, smiling in surprise.

"Only a few words." Embarrassment heated her throat. "I don't know why I said that. I visited Italy a few years ago, but I only learned enough Italian to order a meal and request directions, that kind of thing."

"Ah," he said politely.

She couldn't come up with any small talk. All she could think about was her guilty knowledge of what he was going to prepare for the contest. She had to tell him about the tape. If an opening didn't present itself, she'd just have to blurt it out.

"I liked your soup-and-corn bread show," Dev mentioned after tasting his coffee. She couldn't tell what he had ordered. It didn't have any foam on top of it.

"You watch my show?" This shouldn't have surprised her—after all she watched his—but it did. And it secretly pleased her. She would have been devastated if she'd learned her archrival was indifferent to her as serious competition.

"Occasionally."

"I watch your show, too. Occasionally. The Bulgur Wheat Dressing was…interesting."

He had a wonderful laugh. His eyes twinkled when he asked, "What did you think of the fried cucumbers?"

Despite the twinkle, this was not a frivolous question, not between two cooks, and Cathy didn't offer a frivolous answer. "I wouldn't have thought of the sumac," she admitted after a pause. "Dill would be too obvious, of course. Celery seed too common."

Suddenly she was burning to go home, fry up some

cucumbers and try the sumac. Except she was positive she didn't have any sumac, and she wasn't sure where to buy any. She didn't use exotic ingredients on her show.

Because that seemed like a failing at this moment, her chin rose defensively and she blurted, "I trained at the Culinary Institute of America."

"Very impressive," he said with a long look that suggested he meant the compliment.

"You're Cordon Bleu?" Stupid question. Of course he was.

"It's a euphemism for years of drudgery," he said with a grin.

She couldn't decide if he was being condescending or if he was charmingly self-effacing. But it confused her that she'd inadvertently handed him an opportunity to display some crushing arrogance and he'd sidestepped it. She hadn't expected that.

Certainly she hadn't expected they would trade anecdotes about their training as they did for the next thirty minutes, or that she would laugh and thoroughly enjoy herself. She would have sworn that she'd detest every minute spent with Devlin. Instead, she began to see why everyone lauded his charm.

"You know," she commented after emptying her second cup of mocha latte, "I think this is the first time you and I have really talked."

"We usually run into each other at social events when we have other people in tow."

She thought about some of the women she'd seen with him. Without exception they had been beautiful, sexy film-star types.

Self-consciously recalling her own scrubbed face and skinned-back hair, she consulted her watch. "Well, they should be about finished with your car...." It was now or never. She had to tell him about the tape. "Dev, there's something—"

"Cathy, wait a minute." Leaning forward, he folded his hands on the table and gazed into her eyes. "I was glad to see you when we ran into each other in the waiting room because there's something I have to tell you. I've been looking for an opening, but..." A frown drew his eyebrows together. "I guess there's no way to lead into this except to state it straight out. Someone sent me a tape of your show, the show where you prepare the same venison dish that you're going to prepare for the culinary contest."

Cathy fell back in her chair and stared at him. Something very weird was going on.

"Sea bass with lemongrass," she whispered.

Dev's frown deepened and shock darkened his eyes.

Four

*He said: Nothing keeps a memory so
alive as an intense wish to forget it.*

DEV STARED at her, more surprised by her revelation
than he should have been. "If you know what I'm cooking for the culinary contest, somebody must have sent
you a tape, too."

"Yes." She drew in a visible breath. "It arrived this
morning in one of those padded mailing envelopes. No
return address on the envelope and no message on
the inside. Not even a label on the cassette."

"That's exactly how the tape of your show was sent
to me." Dev frowned, his mind racing with possibilities,
rejecting them almost as fast as they formed. "Why
would anybody do something so pointless? What
would they hope to gain?"

"I don't know. I can't imagine." Cathy shook her
head. "The contest is important to us, but it's not exactly an earthshaking event to the rest of the world."

"There has to be a reason why somebody would go
to all the trouble of bootlegging tapes. Neither of the
shows has been aired yet, so it can't have been easy
to get copies. And from two different studios, as well."
Dev got up, absently tugging Cathy to her feet. He took
her scarf from the back of the chair and wound it

around her neck, his thoughts still miles away. He came back to earth with a bump when his knuckles accidentally brushed against her cheek.

She has the softest skin of any woman I've ever met. Dev let out a sharp breath, surprised by the speed and intensity of his reaction to such a slight physical contact. He looked down at Cathy, his gaze arrested, the mystery of the tapes forgotten. How had he managed to watch a dozen of her shows without ever noticing that she had the most kissable lips he'd seen since…he couldn't remember when.

She colored under his scrutiny, then turned away and walked swiftly toward the door. Dev grabbed his own scarf and chased after her, disconcerted to feel this sudden flare of sexual attraction for a woman he'd previously thought of only as a professional rival. There was one rule Dev had never broken: he never dated a woman who was a chef. In his experience, chefs didn't make good romantic partners. Far from spending cozy nights amiably swapping recipes for coq au vin before tumbling into bed, professional chefs who became sexually involved were more likely to end up squaring off with meat cleavers at twenty paces.

You're supposed to be talking to her about the tapes, he reminded himself, holding open the door of the coffee shop and following Cathy outside into a flurry of snow and wind. He needed to focus on the mystery of the tapes, and not on the intriguing fact that when he tucked her scarf around her neck, he'd noticed that she was wearing almost nothing at all beneath her thick woolen overcoat.

She spoke while he was still trying to get his thoughts back on track. "Could it be that someone's playing a joke and we're missing the punch line?" she asked.

"I don't think so," he said. "Whoever mailed these tapes must have realized that they were doing something unethical. As I see it, there are most likely at least two people involved in this deal—someone at your studio as well as at mine. The problem is, it's hard enough to imagine one person with such a warped sense of humor, never mind two. One working for KDID and the other coincidentally for KBAB? What two people would go to this much trouble for a joke that's so feeble neither of us gets the point? And that could get them fired if they were found out."

She shifted uneasily, and didn't look at him when she answered. "It seems so unlikely...but if you're right, and two people are involved, then Bill and Jean Sadler are going to be the most logical suspects."

Bill and Jean might be logical suspects, but Dev couldn't believe either one of them would have pulled this stunt. He'd only met Jean socially, but he'd been working with Bill for over a year, and knew him well enough to say with conviction that something like this just wasn't his style. If Bill wanted to bootleg a tape of Cathy's show, he'd hand it to Devlin in person, with a pithy comment to go right along with it. Besides, he would never get involved in anything as unethical as revealing Dev's contest recipe to the competition.

The traffic lights finally changed and they crossed the road. "Jean and Bill have better professional ethics than this," Dev said, trying not to get distracted by the captivating sight of snowflakes melting on the end of Cathy's lashes. "And although they know the contest is important to us, they also know we want to win because we're the best, not because we cheated."

"I didn't really think it could be them, either. They'd never get us mixed up in a situation like this."

Dev help open the door to the repair shop. "And leaving aside the issue of their ethics and their sense of humor, why would two people risk their jobs to do something so silly? Because we shouldn't lose sight of the bottom line, which is that the people who did this are likely to get fired the moment they're found out."

He got the distinct impression that Cathy was thinking something she didn't want to reveal. What the hell did she know that he didn't? Dev walked into the waiting room, taking Cathy's hand so that she was forced to follow him. "Look, Cathy, if you have any ideas on this, you need to share them with me. Remember Big Bird's lessons on "Sesame Street"? Cooperation is the magic word if we want to clear up this problem before it escalates into something really nasty."

She smiled at his mention of Big Bird, just as he'd hoped. But she removed her hand from his clasp and shifted her gaze to the workshop, just visible through the glass door panel of the waiting room. "Your car looks as if it's ready. Mine, too."

"To hell with the cars. What is it that you don't want to tell me, Cathy?"

She shrugged, but in the end she decided to answer him. "There's only one reason I can think of why Jean and Bill might have sent the tapes. Jean's always had this crazy notion that the two of us would make a great couple. You've probably noticed that she and Bill have invited us out on quite a few double dates."

He'd not only noticed the invitations, he'd noticed that Cathy had turned them all down with a speed that might have given a guy a complex—if he hadn't been equally determined to avoid getting involved, of course. "Yes, I've noticed," he said stiffly. "What does that have to do with bootleg tapes turning up in our mailboxes? I'm sorry, Cathy, I'm not getting the connection. You need to spell it out."

"I just wondered if Jean and Bill might have decided that this was a way to bring us together," she said. "Even if we hadn't happened to meet today, I'd have called you tonight for sure, and you'd most likely have done the same, wouldn't you? Jean and Bill know us well enough to guess how we'd react. It's the perfect way to guarantee a meeting between the two of us."

"And then what was supposed to happen?" he demanded. "Are you suggesting that Jean and Bill expected us to take one look at each other and realize what we'd been missing all these months?" He gave a sarcastic laugh, to cover the fact that he was starting to think that was precisely what had happened, at least in his case. And he was feeling damned uncomfortable about it, too.

"Well, when you put it like that, it does sound ridiculous...."

Her cheeks had turned scarlet, and Dev felt a twinge of guilt for having protected his own feelings at the expense of hers. He conquered the crazy urge to take her into his arms, kiss her kissable lips, and suggest that they continue their discussion in his apartment, over a glass of burgundy—with the door to his bedroom open if they should happen to feel a sudden overwhelming need for a bed.

"It wasn't ridiculous at all," he said contritely. "Any man thrown into your company would be bound to notice that you're extremely attractive, Cathy. But this stunt isn't the Sadlers' style. Bill's a direct, go-for-the-jugular kind of guy, and Jean is the same way. If they wanted to mastermind a plan for getting the two of us together, we wouldn't be left in any doubt about their intentions. They for sure wouldn't waste time doing something that we might totally misinterpret and that is unethical to boot."

"You're right," Cathy said. "Jean's a good friend of mine, and I know she and Bill couldn't be involved in this. Which leaves me fresh out of ideas, Dev. What do you suggest we do next? Forget about it? Report it to our respective producers next time we're taping a program?"

"We certainly can't forget about it," Dev said slowly. "In fact, I'd say we need to take the tapes to our producers today, as soon as we leave here."

"Contact our producers at home, over the weekend?" Cathy looked less than thrilled by his suggestion. Then she sighed. "I guess you're right. We can't afford to have any questions raised about how we handled this. Although, in the end, I'm still willing to bet we'll discover this was nothing more than somebody's very bad idea of a joke."

"I hope you're right," Dev said. An image of Annette Dunning sprang out of the dark reaches of his subconscious and took shape in his mind. His stomach tightened with a premonition, his suspicion of Annette's meddling touch all the more powerful because it wasn't entirely rational. If Annette was behind the sudden arrival of the bootlegged tapes, Dev knew one thing for sure: she intended nothing good for him.

He chose his words carefully, wanting to impress Cathy with the potential for harm to both their careers, but not wanting to reveal facts about his past to someone who was his most direct competitor in the Denver area.

"It's no secret in this town that the two of us are rivals," he said. "Suppose there was someone who wanted to make trouble for either one of us. We'd look pretty bad if we kept quiet about these tapes and word got out that we had them, but we'd never reported receiving them. If the story was presented to the organizers of the culinary contest, we might be disqualified— and you can imagine how that would go over with management at the TV stations."

Cathy winced. "Like a lead balloon," she said. "At worst, we'd look like sleazeballs. At best, we'd look as if we were so uncertain of our own talents that we'd been reduced to sneaking previews of each other's programs."

He was a little surprised when Cathy didn't dismiss his theorizing out of hand. But instead of telling him he was building mountains out of tiny molehills, Cathy seemed lost in thought. It was a full minute before she turned to look at him, her eyes troubled.

"Dev, would you mind telling me something? You must have heard about American Universal Syndication's plans to put together a new cooking show—gossip about the show has been all over town for weeks. And all over the Internet, too."

"Yes, I'd heard about their plans." And why the hell was she mentioning AUS right now, almost as if she'd been reading his thoughts about Annette Dunning?

She hesitated again, then spoke rapidly. "They have two finalists still in contention for the top spot on the show. It's crazy to think that with all the great chefs in this country both of the AUS finalists might come from the same town, but I wondered...are you one of the finalists, Dev?"

"Yes," he said, holding her gaze, a lot of things suddenly becoming clear. "And are you by any chance the other?"

"Yes, I am."

HALF AN HOUR of lifting weights left Dev sweating and tired, but no better tempered than he had been when he arrived at the health club. Scowling, he toweled off and made his way to one of the treadmills, setting the speed to eight miles an hour, the resistance to maximum. Bill came in five minutes later and climbed onto the treadmill next to Dev's, sighing as he adjusted the electronic controls for a pace and incline less than half of what Dev was tackling.

"You're late," Dev said shortly.

"I know. I had a hard time getting away."

"I don't understand why you can't tell Jean the truth about what you're doing."

Bill shook his head, already panting. "Not until I've lost fifteen pounds and lowered my blood pressure ten points. I want this to be a surprise for her." He grimaced, giving his friend a wry grin. "What's up, Dev? A lesser man might be intimidated by that ferocious scowl you're wearing."

Dev wiped sweat out of his eyes with the back of his hand and tried not to frown. "You remember that tape of Cathy's show I told you about?"

"The one mailed to your house? Sure, I remember. You only told me about it this morning."

"I think Annette Dunning sent it to me. I'm trying to work out what the hell she's up to, and precisely what she hopes to achieve by sending it to me."

"Gee, that's amazing, Dev." Bill sucked in a strangled gasp of air. "It would be even more amazing if I knew who Annette Dunning was."

"She's the vice president of American Universal Syndication. The woman who's going to decide which chef will be the star of their new cooking show."

"Oh, boy! *That* Annette Dunning." Bill stumbled and regained his stride. "And you think she's the person who sent you a tape of Cathy's show? Why the blazes would she do something so odd?"

"In general terms, because she hates me. In specific terms, I don't know." Dev was finally starting to pant. "That's what I've been trying to work out for the past couple of hours…with a spectacular lack of success."

"Er…for what it's worth, Dev, Jean told me that Cathy was sent a tape of your show, too. I wouldn't mention it, but Cathy apparently told Jean it was okay to pass word to you."

"I know about Cathy's tape." Dev made no effort to enlighten Bill as to how he knew. For some reason, he was less than willing to get into a discussion about Cathy Mallory.

"Do you think Annette Dunning was also the person who sent the tape of your show to Cathy?"

Dev hesitated. "I guess so. Although I can't begin to imagine why."

"Well, by your reasoning, it must be because she hates Cathy, too."

Dev turned to look at his friend, so shocked that he lost his rhythm and almost fell off the treadmill. He stumbled, then regained his pace. Good grief, talk about being too close to a situation to see it clearly. He'd been so damn busy obsessing about his own relationship with Annette that he'd failed to make the obvious logical connection that Bill had made instantly. Could Annette possibly have reasons—personal reasons—to dislike Cathy Mallory?

Dev dismissed the idea as stretching the long arm of coincidence much too far. There were a bunch of reasons why Annette might have sent a tape to Cathy other than the fact that they were already acquainted. Annette disliked young and attractive women on principle, so she would be quite happy to get Cathy into trouble as a side benefit of whatever convoluted scheme she'd devised for punishing Dev.

"You're awful damn quiet," Bill puffed. "Are you having a heart attack, or have I said something that shocked you into silence?"

"You shocked me," Dev said dryly. "Unfortunately, Annette Dunning and I have a history, and it isn't a pleasant one, and knowing the sort of person she is, I can't help seeing her sticky fingerprints all over this videotape mess."

"You can't be sure she's involved," Bill said. "If you've got a history, you might be letting that color your judgment."

"Possibly, but I'll tell you one thing that's guaranteed. There isn't a snowball's chance in hell that Annette's going to recommend me for the new syndicated show, so Cathy Mallory is a shoo-in for the job. I might as well call Universal Syndication and tell them I want to withdraw my name from consideration…in fact, I may do that first thing on Monday morning. It's likely to save me a lot of grief in the end."

Bill sighed and turned off the treadmill, mopping his profusely sweating forehead. "Look, Dev, I'm not Mr. Macho like you. I can't think and exercise at the same time. You want to come and drink some carrot juice? That sounds revolting enough to be low-cal and healthy."

"Right now, I feel more in the mood for a vodka

straight up," Dev said gloomily. He switched off the machine, and grabbed a clean towel from the basket by the door, slinging it around his neck. "You know, Bill, ambition's a strange thing. When I was slaving away as an apprentice, all I wanted to do was make my rent payments each month, and have enough money left over to take the occasional date out to dinner and a movie. Now I have my own restaurant, and I'm making as much money in a month as I used to make all year in Europe. To cap it all, I really like living in Denver. It's a great city, full of interesting activities and attractive women, plus I have the Rocky Mountains and the world's greatest skiing right on my back doorstep. So who cares if I don't get the chance to work my ass off as the chef on Universal Syndication's new program?"

"Right on." Bill gave him an encouraging thump on the back. "I'm glad you feel that way, Dev."

"But I don't feel that way," Dev said wryly. "I want a shot at that AUS job so badly I can taste it. I've spent most of my spare time for the past two months planning the first package of shows. I hadn't realized how much I was looking forward to the chance of syndication until I heard that Annette Dunning was in charge of the final selection process. Which was as good as hearing that I hadn't a chance in a million of making the cut."

They'd arrived at the juice bar. Dev ordered fresh-squeezed white grape juice. Sighing, Bill ordered chilled carrot juice. "This doesn't taste any better than I remembered," he said, taking a sip and pulling a face as he led the way to a corner table in the small room, away from the other customers. "If anybody had told me four years ago that I'd give up beer and hot dogs for a woman, I'd have laughed in their face. It's humiliating what falling in love will do to a man."

"Yeah, you look real downtrodden and miserable."

Bill grinned. "There are compensations to married life, you know."

"I'll take your word for it. Personally, I don't see what any wife provides that I can't get from a date with far less hassle."

"Companionship?" Bill suggested. "Commitment. Someone to watch TV with."

"I have Ramses. Trust me, that's about as much companionship and commitment as I can handle. A wise man knows his limitations." Oddly enough, it was Annette Dunning who was partly responsible for his reluctance to get involved in a long-term relationship. Dev found himself wondering if there wasn't something seriously out of kilter with his life if he was allowing the person he most despised in the world to have so much influence over his behavior.

"Cut to the chase, Dev. You're so tense you're making me nervous." Bill pushed out a chair and patted the seat. "Sit down and tell me about this Annette woman, and why you're so sure she's determined to destroy you. What did you do? Leave her at the altar or something?"

"Just about," Dev said, sitting down reluctantly, not sure he wanted to talk about an episode that he considered one of the more painful experiences in his life.

Bill's eyes widened. "My God! You're not kidding, are you?"

"No, I'm not kidding. Unfortunately." Dev stirred the ice in his juice, reluctant to confront memories that he'd never managed to get into any sort of comfortable perspective. To this day, he hadn't decided how much responsibility he bore for the debacle that had ended his affair with Annette. But over the past few years, he'd gradually come to the painful conclusion that the blame wasn't—couldn't be—exclusively hers. If she'd been a predator, he'd been more than willing prey. Cocksure and overconfident, he'd walked open-eyed, yet blindly, into the trap Annette had laid for him. Then, when he finally saw what was happening, and realized that her tentacles were closing in around him, he'd fought back ruthlessly.

He became aware that Bill was waving a hand in front of his eyes. "Dev? Are you with me, man? Where did you just disappear to?"

"Sorry." He shook his head, deciding to give Bill a pared-down version of what had happened with Annette. Some things were too intimate to share even with a good friend. "Annette Dunning and I met in Paris, more than six years ago," he said. "I'd been working in Europe from the time I finished high school, but I waited until I had eight years of experience under my belt before I had enough confidence to tackle Paris. It took me months of searching, but I finally landed a job as first cook at the Grand Maritime restaurant—"

"Wait a minute. You were in charge of one of the world's most famous restaurants before you hit age thirty? Hot damn, Dev. I knew you were good, but that's unbelievable."

"Yeah, it's unbelievable all right." Dev gave a rueful smile. "First cook doesn't mean I was in charge of the restaurant, Bill. It means I was rated slightly above the other peons in the kitchen. Five sous-chefs and the executive chef were all above me in the pecking order."

Bill grunted. "There seem to be more darn ranks in a French restaurant than there are in the army."

Dev grinned. "That's because the French decided several centuries ago to treat food and cooking with the seriousness they deserve. They consider the two great driving forces of civilization to be the hunt for food and the desire for sexual conquest. And any Frenchman will tell you that advanced civilizations devote more attention to food than to sex. According to my former chef, Americans are self-evidently primitive because we spend way too much time worrying about sex and not nearly enough time worrying about what we eat."

Bill pushed aside his empty glass. "Speaking as a man who's just finished eight ounces of carrot juice, my sympathies right now are with your chef. But back to business. It's six years ago, and you're first cook at the Grand Maritime and you've just met some woman called Annette Dunning...."

"Yeah." Dev sighed. "We met at a party. Annette was a couple of years older than I was, very sexy, very enticing. Way out of my league, but I was young and crass and full of my own importance.... After years of bumming my way around the kitchens of Europe, first cook at the Grand Maritime sounded pretty fancy to me, a title to impress."

"What was Annette doing in Paris? With a name like Dunning I assume she's American?"

"Yes, she's American, although she had some French relatives...maybe a grandmother? Anyway, she spoke pretty good French, which I admired because so many Americans spend years overseas without ever learning the language of the country where

hey're living. She was working as the sub-agent for a
big New York literary agency, selling American books
o French publishers, and she ran with an interesting
crowd of people. I was dazzled. And to add to her other
attractions, she was the first American woman I'd
lated in years. We started seeing a lot of each other.
For a while, it was pretty intense between us." A hell
of a polite way to describe the dark, driving sexual ob-
session that he'd experienced the first few weeks he
knew her.

"But your relationship didn't work out?" Bill said, rat-
ling his empty glass.

"No, it didn't work out," Dev agreed, sliding over
three months of increasing bitterness and mutual dis-
lusion. "In fact, it ended so badly that Annette swore
'd ruined her life and that she'd never forgive me for
the way I'd treated her. Her parting words to me were
something along the lines of 'I don't forget or forgive.
I get even.'"

Bill winced. "I must say, it doesn't sound too good,
Dev. Still you may be making too much of something
that happened a long time ago," he said. "Your life's
moved on, and so has Annette's. People say a lot of
things they don't mean when they're breaking up. Look
at all the couples you know who've been at the point
of committing murder when they get divorced. A few
years later they meet at their kid's college graduation,
or a wedding, and they can't even remember why they
once cared. Life's moved on, and so have they."

HE SURE AS HELL hoped that Bill was right, Dev thought,
driving home through the rapidly gathering darkness.
He was an optimist by nature, but he couldn't quite

convince himself that Annette Dunning was the sort of woman to let the tides of life wash over her in a cleansing wave. Annette was a woman who needed to be in control, and Dev couldn't believe her character had undergone a fundamental transformation in the years since they'd separated.

For the first few weeks of their relationship, Dev had been so mesmerized by Annette's sexual skills that he'd made no attempt to analyze what was happening, he'd simply let himself drown in the pleasures she evoked. After a while, though, Dev had regained sufficient control of his wits to realize that something major was missing. Although Annette's body might be on the bed, coiled around his, inventing amazing new ways to make love, a part of her always stood aside from what was happening, not so much participating as manipulating him, analyzing his reaction and tempting him to ever more exotic sexual adventures. However hard he tried to give her pleasure, she always seemed to remain an observer when they made love, never a participant.

For weeks Dev struggled to change her attitude to sex, to touch her heart and her emotions, and to make her a true partner in their lovemaking. When he realized that she was incapable of trusting him enough to let herself go, even for a few seconds, he'd given up on their relationship. He finally understood that the one-sided sex was simply a metaphor for everything between them. Their relationship was physically explosive, but spiritually empty, with Annette so desperate to remain in control that she was willing to sacrifice every other pleasure.

After five months as her lover, Dev still hadn't understood what motivated Annette. However, he was quite sure she wasn't in love with him, so he'd felt no compunction about inviting her for a final dinner in his tiny, one-room apartment. Over dessert, when she was getting ready to lure him into bed, he told her bluntly that their affair was over and that he wanted her out of his life. It was then that Annette had told him she was expecting his baby.

The phone was ringing as Dev let himself into his apartment. He tossed aside his scarf and gloves, gave Ramses an affectionate scratch behind his chewed-up ears, and let the answering machine pick up.

"Hello, Devlin, long time no see." Annette Dunning's throaty voice filled the living room. "I'm due to arrive in Denver on Tuesday, the second of December, and I was hoping that the two of us might be able to get together for a quick dinner...."

Dev was so disconcerted by the brisk friendliness of Annette's tone that it took him a couple of seconds to gather his wits and decide how to react. "Hello, Annette," he said, picking up the phone. "This is Devlin."

"Devlin, how nice to hear your real voice instead of a recorded message. Isn't life strange? I'm sure you never expected to hear from me again, and yet here we are, quite likely to end up working for the same company."

"I didn't expect you to sound so cheerful at the prospect of my becoming your colleague, Annette. We didn't exactly part on friendly terms."

She gave an audible sigh. "Devlin, nobody could regret what happened between us more than I do. The best excuse I can find for the way I behaved is that I was young and incredibly foolish. Either that, or too

much French wine had induced a temporary fit of in-
sanity." A soft ripple of laughter made its way along
the phone lines, the sound nostalgic and almost
tender. "Oh, Dev, you have to agree we had some
good times together before it all fell apart."

"Yes, we did." If Annette wanted to reshape her
memories of the past into something false but more
agreeable, Dev saw no reason to discourage her.

Annette resumed a more businesslike tone. "I can
assure you, Devlin, that when I arrive in Denver on the
second, I intend to remember the early days of our
relationship when we were both so happy together, not
the last few weeks when we both managed to make
each other thoroughly miserable. I also want to assure
you that I have no intention of allowing our past mis-
understanding to affect my professional judgment
about who is the most qualified chef to take the starring role in Universal Syndication's new cooking show.
I'm making no promises, of course, but if you're the
more qualified candidate, Dev, then you're the man I'll
recommend to my boss."

"It's good to know that you're willing to be so objec-
tive," Dev said, striving to keep all trace of sarcasm
out of his voice. Annette had always been masterful at
sounding like the soul of sweet reason until the very
second that she delivered a blow aimed to cut her victim off at the knees. He might be maligning her, of
course, but Dev was older and a lot more cynical now
than he had been when he'd known Annette in Paris.
This time, it wasn't going to be quite so easy for her
to deceive him.

Annette Dunning was about to discover that he had no intention of allowing himself to become roadkill on her one-way single-lane highway to success.

Chapter Five

She said: Tradition is as soothing as warm oatmeal on a cold morning.

WHILE CATHY SHOWERED, she considered what an odd day it had been. A day of frustration had been interrupted by the startling revelation that Devlin Gilpatrick could be as charming as everyone insisted he was. And incredibly sexy. When he had draped her scarf around her neck, his fingers had brushed her nape and, for a moment, she'd felt paralyzed, hot tingles shivering down her body.

It had been a long time since a man's touch had stopped her in her tracks. Longer still since she had gazed into gorgeous dark eyes and forgotten what she was talking about.

Sighing, she toweled off, then pulled on a plaid-flannel nightgown and her favorite green robe. She'd make an omelette for dinner then spend the evening catching up on the bookkeeping for Just Like Home. Another exciting Saturday night in the life of Cathy Mallory. Undoubtedly Dev had a hot date tonight, probably a tall, leggy model who wouldn't be caught dead wearing a flannel nightgown.

Bending, she scratched behind Romeo's shaggy ears.

"Well, we like flannel, don't we, big guy? Flannel is fashion's version of comfort food."

One of the secrets for a great omelette was to omit salt, as it broke down the egg whites if added before cooking. There was great pleasure in knowing these small secrets, Cathy decided, feeling marginally better.

When the phone rang, she frowned. The butter had reached exactly the proper temperature in the skillet, and it was crucial to pour in the eggs immediately after whisking. But on the forth ring, she realized she'd forgotten to turn on the answering machine.

Damn. Moving the skillet off the burner, she turned off the stove, wiped her hands, then picked up the kitchen phone.

"Hi, Kansas, it's Annette Dunning." Annette Dunning's throaty voice sounded exactly as it had years ago—confident, amused, slightly mocking. "I hope you received Gene's letter telling you to expect my call."

"Hello, Annette," Cathy answered cautiously. "Yes, I received Mr. Montford's letter."

"Congratulations. You're headed for the big time, kiddo." Annette laughed. "You're not in Kansas anymore."

"I haven't been in Kansas for a very long time."

Hearing Annette's voice pitched Cathy back in time. Suddenly she felt like a naive sophomore again, viewing the world with cheerleader optimism, awed and slightly intimidated by grad-student Annette's savvy cynicism and sophistication.

"I'll be arriving in Denver in a couple of weeks, on Tuesday the second. Are you free for lunch on December third?"

Cathy hesitated. Cynicism would never form part of her personality, but she wasn't the wide-eyed innocent

she'd been in college, either. Thanks to Annette's lies
and accusations, she would never again be that gullible.

"I'm available for lunch next Wednesday...but...what
exactly will the interview process entail?"

"It's nothing for you to worry about. In your case, the
interview is just a formality. I can't make any promises,
but...well, there have to be some perks between old
friends, right? I'm sure you understand what I'm saying."

Old friends? Cathy's mouth dropped and she blinked
in astonishment.

"We'll have lunch and chat about your plans for the
syndicated shows. And we'll get together off and on
throughout the week I'll be in Denver. Naturally, I'm
interested in the Chefs' Culinary Contest and Benefit.
I'll attend to cheer you on."

"But you'll also be interviewing Devlin Gilpatrick?"

"Him? Oh, yes, I'll be speaking to Mr. Gilpatrick."

Was Cathy imagining things or did she detect a sudden chill at the mention of Dev's name? If so, she
couldn't have been more surprised. This conversation
was not unfolding at all as she had imagined it would.

"I just realized that I phoned during the dinner hour,"
Annette said apologetically, "so I won't keep you. We'll
have plenty of time to catch up next week. For years
I've wondered who framed us in college, not that it mat-
ters anymore. Actually, it appears whoever set us up did
us both a favor. We're doing very well in our respective
fields. Still, I've always wondered who disliked you and
me enough to get us kicked out of college."

Speechless, Cathy stood rooted to her kitchen floor.
Annette thought they had been framed? That was how
she remembered lying, cheating, selling term papers,
then accusing Cathy? A setup had existed all right, but

it was Annette setting up Cathy to be the fall guy in case she got caught.

After hanging up the telephone, Cathy poured a glass of Chablis and sat at her breakfast table, staring out at the frigid night. Romeo padded across the hardwood floor and plopped down on top of her slippers.

Something was very odd here. A person like Annette Dunning didn't forget wrongs, real or imagined. Certainly she would not have forgotten her promise to get even. And now was the perfect opportunity. She could deny Cathy the dream of syndication, just as she had blamed Cathy for denying her the dream of graduating. The Annette Dunning that Cathy had known would see poetic justice in doing just that.

Instead, Annette had rearranged the past, making them old friends, and she'd hinted that her decision had already been made in Cathy's favor.

One thing was certain. Annette did nothing without a reason. And the reason always benefited Annette.

Cathy sipped her wine and wiggled her toes beneath Romeo's warm bulk. If Annette gained something by selecting Cathy for syndication instead of Dev...

A frown creased her forehead. She would have preferred that the rivalry between herself and Devlin Gilpatrick be decided objectively without prior preference or prejudice. But it appeared the selection would be based on Annette's hidden agenda.

Annette's phone call had certainly turned things around. Minutes ago, Cathy would have sworn that she didn't have a snowball's chance in hell of winning the syndication. Now, it appeared that the job was as good as hers.

Actually, she felt a twinge of sympathy for Dev. The

poor guy didn't know it, but Annette was refereeing a race that had already been won. And Dev had lost.

USUALLY, Cathy spent Mondays at Just Like Home. She particularly needed to be there today as they had a heavy schedule this week, catering at least a dozen Thanksgiving parties. But she swung by KBAB first.

The instant Mike Millican spotted her, he started wringing his hands. "You never come by on Mondays. Is something wrong? Something's wrong, isn't it? You can't come in tomorrow and tape the Thanksgiving show?"

Laughing, she patted his hands. "Nothing's wrong, and I'll be here tomorrow. But we should have taped the Thanksgiving show last week instead of waiting until hours before airtime."

"We had the extra show on your contest recipes last week. No way could we have managed the Thanksgiving show, too."

"Actually, that's why I'm here, Mike. The contest show. Do we send out review tapes of my show?"

Giving her a curious look, he shrugged. "Sure. Viewers can order transcripts or tapes."

"Do we send any tapes out before the show is aired?"

"Policy prohibits sending pre-air tapes to anyone local, but we mail out of state, I believe."

"Who would know who gets copies of the tapes of my show?" Then she told him about her and Devlin each receiving a copy of the shows featuring their contest entries.

Mike swore. "That's terrible! I'm sorry, Cathy. Will you change your contest entry?"

"You bet I will. And so will Dev. That's a given."

"We'll have to retape that whole show." He thought

a minute. "Whoever sent our tape to Gilpatrick...I'll have his head on a platter, by God! Give me half an hour and I'll know which member of our crew has been using the copier."

Cathy nodded. "Thanks, Mike, but I just can't believe a member of our crew would do something like this."

"How else could it have happened?"

"I don't know," she said, frowning. "But I'd like to see a list of everyone who receives copies of our tapes."

It required an hour to follow the threads. The tape of her show was copied immediately after editing. Then the copies went to cool storage, ready to fill viewer requests. Cathy eventually wound up in the mail room, speaking to an assistant named Rory, the person who prepared the tapes for mailing.

The only interesting name on the list of locals who automatically received tape copies was Paul Lyman, owner of Dev's station.

"It's a professional courtesy," Rory explained when she questioned Paul Lyman's name. "We exchange tapes with all the local stations. But only after the programs have aired," he added hastily. "Never before airtime, of course."

"Is there a list for out-of-state mailings?" she asked, determined to cover all bases.

"Sure." Rory rummaged around his desk then handed her a list. "The tapes are sent out automatically to everyone on this list."

"When are the tapes mailed to this list?"

"Since all the names here are out of state, the tapes go out immediately after taping."

"Pre-air," Cathy murmured.

"Unless it's a delayed airdate, like a holiday special or your recent contest show."

The name Universal Syndication jumped off the page. Cathy stared at it and thought: *Annette Dunning.* "Rory, could a mistake happen? Could you have sent a tape of my contest show to someone on this list?"

"No way," he said promptly.

"Are you very sure?"

"Well...pretty sure," he said defensively.

Biting her lip, Cathy stared at a point in space. Instinct told her that sending a copy of her contest show to Dev had Annette Dunning's stamp all over it. And AUS's name was on the mailing list. But that didn't explain how Annette would have gotten a copy of Dev's contest show.

Cathy spent the rest of the day cooking turkeys and making cranberry sauce at the Just Like Home kitchen, but her thoughts continually strayed to the problem of the bootlegged tapes and Devlin.

She needed to speak to him.

INITIATING A CALL to a man had never been easy for Cathy. She possessed a streak of old-fashioned traditionalism that insisted men called women, not vice versa.

After tossing her Just Like Home apron into the washing machine and then sorting the day's mail, she made herself look up Devlin's phone number in the phone book. Then, fortified with a glass of sherry, she leaned against the kitchen counter and dialed his number.

"Gilpatrick here."

"Oh. I was expecting a machine." What a dumb beginning. "Dev, it's Cathy Mallory."

"I was just thinking about you. You're on my list of calls to make this evening."

He was thinking about her? And had planned to

phone her? A liquid weakness spread through her stomach.

"The reason I called is that I've discovered that Universal Syndication has been receiving pre-air copies of the tapes of my shows."

"That's why I intended to phone you. I stopped by KDID this afternoon and did some sleuthing. We send pre-air tapes to Universal Syndication, too, but the guy in charge of the mailing swears that he never sent out a copy of my contest program. He showed me the log of everything he's sent out over the past week, and the tape of my show isn't there."

"That doesn't prove it wasn't sent," Cathy pointed out. "Just that it didn't get written up in the log."

"True. But apart from that, there was supposed to be a security hold on all the tapes for the contest show. Unfortunately, my producer's on location in Durango for the next couple of days, so I can't double-check any of this with him."

"The connection to AUS gives us a common link. The woman who'll interview us next week, Annette Dunning, could have gotten our contest tapes."

"The same thought occurred to me," he agreed after a short pause. "But, frankly, it seems unlikely. And even if she got the tapes, why would she have mailed them to us?"

A good question, Cathy thought ruefully. "I don't know. But—" she drew a breath "—I can't shake the feeling that somehow Annette Dunning had a hand in this."

"Cathy? May I infer from what you just said that you and Annette Dunning know each other?"

"We knew each other in college, a million years ago. Despite what you may be thinking," she added hastily, "that doesn't give me an advantage." If Cathy held any advantage in the final competition for the chance at syndication, it was based on Annette's private plans and certainly not on their prior acquaintance. "I haven't talked to Annette since college, and I didn't know she was a vice president at AUS." She hesitated. "Annette and I didn't like each other in college."

Straining to interpret his silence, she experienced a rush of guilt. She was trying to persuade him that she had no advantage, when in fact Annette had made it clear that she did.

Searching for a way to change the subject, she impulsively inquired, "I wonder...do you have plans for Thanksgiving dinner?"

His silence continued for another beat but there was a different quality to it now, sharper and more intense.

"I'm having a few friends over," she continued hastily, "and I thought...if you didn't have anything else to do..."

Scarlet flooded her cheeks and she was thankful that he couldn't see her standing there feeling like an utter fool. What was she thinking of? Of course he had plans. She deserved the rejection that was coming.

"What time are you planning dinner?"

At least he was trying to spare her feelings. Whatever time she mentioned, he would say he was busy. "I'm telling people to arrive any time after six-thirty. We'll eat around eight," she said, pressing a hand to the agonizing heat flaming her cheeks.

"Excellent," he said with what sounded like genuine enthusiasm. "Thanksgiving is one of the busiest days of the year at Chez Dev, but things should start to slow down by seven. I think I could safely leave by then. I'd love to come."

His restaurant. She'd forgotten. Of course he would be at his restaurant on Thanksgiving Day. Her insecurities were showing big-time, she thought with a grimace.

"Is this a couples event? Should I bring a date?"

"I don't think anyone else is bringing a date, but if you're seeing someone regularly, of course you're welcome to bring her." She surprised herself by holding her breath while she waited to hear how he would respond.

"There's no one special at the moment," he said evenly. "What can I bring?"

Slowly she exhaled, not pausing to analyze why she should feel so pleased that he wasn't seeing anyone. "You could bring a vegetable dish if you like, but it really isn't necessary."

"A vegetable dish it is. How about a dessert wine?"

She laughed. "Despite all those lectures in cooking school, I've never believed there's any wine that goes with pumpkin pie. Thanks, but I'll probably serve coffee with the pie, followed by Amaretto if anyone wants an after-dinner drink."

"Amaretto? Actually Armagnac strikes me as a..." He paused and cleared his throat. "As an equally good choice. Not as sweet as Amaretto."

She sensed that he'd been about to say, "a better choice." A little steel firmed her voice when she answered coolly, "I'll consider your suggestion."

"Well, then...I'll see you about seven on Thursday night. Thanks again for the invitation."

After she hung up, Cathy stared balefully at Romeo. "Oh, boy. There's nothing worse than cooking for a cook." Suddenly her other guests were forgotten. There was only one opinion that would matter when she served Thanksgiving dinner. Devlin Gilpatrick's.

TUESDAY SHE TAPED her Thanksgiving show for KBAB, doing a traditional and relatively easy meal. Wednesday, she spent all day cooking pies for Just Like Home. After she filled her minivan with pies and delivered them to the catering kitchen, she returned home, then set the table using her grandmother's lace tablecloth over linen, and the Royal Doulton china that her mother had prized so highly. Only the crystal wineglasses were new. Everything else on her table represented the best of Thanksgiving tradition, happy memories of past gatherings.

For the first time she didn't kick herself for inviting Devlin. Including him brought the number of guests to ten. Even numbers made for a balanced and beautiful table.

Still, because Devlin was coming, she saw things with fresh eyes, striving to see everything as he would. With a sinking heart, she suspected he would dismiss her home as too folksy, too unsophisticated. Biting her lip, she gazed at the comfy, well-worn furniture. She had tried for a come-in-and-sit-down look, but suddenly she wondered if all she had achieved was a this-junk-needs-to-be-replaced look.

"It's too late to run out and buy new furniture," she said to Romeo, who sat on a braided rug beside her, wagging his tail.

Then she laughed at herself. Her guests included a multipublished author, a top-rated D.J., an advertising whiz, and the owner of a cooking-supply company, among others. But the only guest she worried about was Dev, her rival and nemesis.

How in heaven's name had Devlin Gilpatrick gotten to be so important to her so swiftly? She thought about him all the time.

Blushing, she gave her head a shake and returned to the kitchen to bake her pies.

THANKSGIVING MORNING Cathy rolled out of bed before dawn and rushed over to Just Like Home to see if she could offer any last-minute help. It was almost one o'clock before everything was firmly under control and she could dash home again.

Working smoothly and swiftly, she made a Waldorf salad, using an old family recipe, and unmolded an aspic. Next she cut tiny baskets out of oranges and carefully filled them with whipped and seasoned sweet potatoes. She arranged the baskets on a cooking sheet, ready to pop into the upper oven.

If Devlin hadn't been a guest, she might have cheated and used frozen corn for her authentic Indian baked corn and squash dish. But since he was coming, she pared the kernels from ears of fresh corn, not cutting any corners. The dish was time-consuming and a pain to make, but worth it, she thought grimly. He couldn't help but be impressed. She hoped.

At two-thirty she rubbed salt and pepper inside and outside the turkey, then dusted the outer skin with flour. The flour was a step that most people skipped. Finally she stuffed the bird with her famous lemon-and-ham stuffing—using real suet was the secret here—and formed the leftover stuffing into balls that she would cook separately and use to decorate the turkey platter along with sprigs of parsley and purple grapes.

Glancing at the clock, she slid the turkey into the oven, reminding herself to do the first basting in an hour. Turning in a fluid motion, she placed the giblets on the stove to simmer then sat for a minute to catch her breath. She had been on a dead run all week and was starting to feel the weariness of late nights and early mornings. Hopefully, a shower would perk her up.

Afterward came the decision of what to wear. Wrapped in a fluffy white towel, she stood in the doorway of her closet and considered. If Devlin hadn't been expected, she would have worn the dusty-blue pants set that matched her eyes. But...

After discarding half a dozen possibilities, she decided on her best knee-length cashmere skirt, paired with a gold silk turtleneck. A green-and-gold silk scarf worn like a wide collar and tied in front set off the outfit. Striving for a sophisticated effect, she brushed her hair back— she had just enough length to manage a twist—and pinned it in place. Finally, she added elaborate bead earrings.

She didn't look quite like herself, but she looked polished, as coolly cosmopolitan as the women she'd seen on Devlin's arm. She didn't let herself wonder why she was dressing to please him. Instead, hurrying, she focused firmly on all she had to do yet.

Later, when the bell rang announcing the arrival of her first guest, everything was organized. There were a dozen last-minute tasks, of course, but the stuffing balls were in the oven and so were the sweet-potato baskets. The rolls were rising, the gravy mellowing, and the white potatoes would be ready for mashing at the proper moment.

She drew a breath, straightened her shoulders, arranged a smile on her lips and opened the door. "Hi, Mary! Oh, good, Rick, you remembered to pick up the centerpiece!" More people were coming down the sidewalk, a car pulled to the curb. "Everyone is arriving at once," she said, laughing.

By seven o'clock, when her doorbell rang again, the

party was happily under way, the hors d'oeuvres vanishing at a flattering rate. Cathy smoothed her palms over her hips, then opened the door with a casual smile as if she invited famous cooks to dinner every evening of her life. Sexy, gorgeous famous cooks.

"Hi," she said, glancing from his smile to the grocery sack in his arms. "Glad you could make it. Come in and meet everyone."

Dev wore charcoal slacks and a cream-colored turtleneck beneath a navy blazer. As she introduced him to her other guests, he managed to charm them in two minutes flat, modestly acknowledging a multitude of compliments about his show. The formalities out of the way, he grinned and pointed to the grocery sack.

"Time for work." Heading toward the kitchen, he flashed Cathy a smile that turned her knees to straw. "I didn't think of this until I was pulling up in front of your house, but I'm planning a carrot dish. I hope that doesn't conflict with anything you're doing?"

"Not at all." Cathy took his blazer, watching him push up his sleeves, then she hung his jacket in the hall closet and followed, leaving her guests to entertain themselves while she rushed through the last-minute preparations. Until this moment, it hadn't occurred to her that she and Devlin would be working around each other. She'd expected him to hand her a covered dish, not appear with a sack of ingredients. "Glazed?" she asked hopefully. Glazed would be relatively quick.

He didn't sneer, but it was a near miss. *"Flan aux carrots,"* he said lightly, removing an apron from the sack. Charcoal stripes. Very masculine, very elegant, very...well, sexy.

"Ah, *flan aux carrots,*" Cathy repeated, her mind racing. Not a simple, fast dish. "Would the cook like a drink or a glass of wine?" she asked, scanning her kitchen. It hadn't been designed for two cooks.

"White wine would be nice." A springform pan came out of his sack, and a round paper mold. And his knives, of course. "You look wonderful, by the way." He stared at her a moment, as though considering her appearance. "Your hair is different," he stated, sounding thoughtful. Out came the carrots and a jar of consommé. "I'll need the Cuisinart, salt, sugar and butter." He thanked her for the wine and tasted it. A tiny frown puckered his brow. "A California Chablis?"

"I hope you enjoy it. Californian wines are underrated, don't you think?" Bending, she brought out the Cuisinart and a sieve, which he would also need.

"I see you have a dog."

"Romeo." Who was, of course, directly underfoot, happily drooling and thumping his tail at Devlin, who didn't look particularly flattered by Romeo's instant devotion. "Did you make the crust in advance?"

If he hadn't, she would have to push back the time they ate by at least half an hour. Trying not to worry, she glanced at the clock, then opened the oven door and peeked at the turkey. Almost perfect. She'd take it out in thirty minutes, let it sit for another twenty minutes. *If* the crust was already prepared.

"Of course," he said, producing a Tupperware bowl out of the sack. "The paste is right here."

Cathy almost laughed. The idea that she was wildly attracted to a man who owned his own Tupperware helped settle her nerves. "I have a dozen things I should be doing right now. Is there anything else I can do for you?"

"Don't worry, if I need something, I'll find it myself," he said, commandeering the cutting board with a smile.

"The turkey smells wonderful. Please tell me you aren't one of those people who cooks it in a brown paper bag." He toasted her, then set down his wineglass and started washing carrots in the sink.

"No paper bags," she said absently. Well, if she needed a cutting board, she had another one. Somewhere. And surely he'd be finished with the sink in a few minutes. "How did it go at the restaurant today?" she asked, opening the refrigerator door. Time to assemble the relish tray. Naturally, Romeo stuck his nose in the fridge and when she pushed him aside, he left a damp line of drool near the hem of her cashmere skirt. She stared at it in dismay.

"Busy." His knife flew over the carrots, spinning out perfect slices. "A saucepan?"

"In this cabinet," Cathy said, stepping out of the way so he could get to the pans. "Oh, you needed salt and butter."

He snapped his fingers. "And a colander."

The minutes were flying past, and she needed to set up the buffet, baste the turkey, check on the rolls, shred the cheese for her corn dish, mash the potatoes, heat the gravy. *And what else? Something else.*

"The colander is...wait, it'll be easier if I just get it for you. Excuse me, I need to get in the cabinet right in front of you." *Tick, tick, tick.* She heard the clock in her head while she watched Dev stumble over Romeo to get out of her way.

Obviously trying to avoid Romeo's affectionate nudges and ignoring the drool on his pant legs, Dev asked about her guests while the carrots cooked on the stove and he pressed the paste around the springform pan. Then he placed the ring of paper inside and carefully filled the pan with uncooked rice to hold the paper firmly against the crust.

Cathy moved his grocery bag aside for the tenth time to see into the pan. "I always use split peas," she said. "I guess everyone does it differently. Oh, lord. You need oven space to bake the crust." Spinning, she stared at the double ovens. "All right. I can remove the sweet-potato baskets, but not the corn dish. Then I can put the baskets back in to heat right before serving. Excuse me," she said again as she tripped over Romeo and caught Dev's arm for balance. She quickly released his arm with a blush.

They bumped into each other, brushed against each other, waited impatiently for the sink, and murmured, "Sorry," a dozen times. Cathy cleaned up after each hurried task; Devlin simply moved to the next step, leaving carrot tops in the sink, his knives on the cutting board, the Cuisinart coated with pureed carrots. Cathy ground her teeth.

He didn't criticize what she was doing, but he watched her. And she imagined that *he* would have mashed the potatoes by hand instead of using a mixer. *He* would have decorated the turkey platter with sprigs of watercress instead of parsley.

"Excuse me," she said yet again, needing him to move so she could reach the butter. *He* would have jellied his cranberries instead of making a sauce. *He* probably would have flown to Greece and picked his own damned olives for the relish tray.

Blowing a wave of hair out of her eyes, she turned and leaned against the countertop, reaching for the nearest glass of wine. That it was his didn't matter. She drained it in a gulp.

"Devlin?"

"Yes?" He leaned past her, filling her nostrils with an exotic aftershave, and dumped the rice out of the spring-form pan into the disposal. She watched him pour the puréed carrots into the pan and artfully arrange whole slices on top.

"I hope you won't take offense at what I'm about to say...but...get out of my kitchen before I kill you."

His dark eyebrows lifted, then he burst into laughter. "Go mingle with the guests. Go pour yourself another glass of wine. Go fill the water goblets if you want to. But go!"

Grinning, looking impossibly tall and handsome, he stepped over Romeo and grasped her shoulders, then he leaned down and astonished her by placing a kiss on her nose. "I'm going. But only because this is your house, and only because I've been fantasizing about strangling *you* for the last fifteen minutes."

She returned his grin and tried to pretend that his kiss hadn't rattled her. "Before you go, would you take the turkey out of the oven and set it on the platter?" Stepping away from his hands on her shoulders, self-conscious from the tingle that they caused, she tossed him the oven mitts.

Even with Romeo glued to his side, he made it look easy. "Smells wonderful. Ham in the stuffing?" he asked. She nodded. "Put the carrots in the oven five minutes before you're ready to serve."

"Thanks." She caught the oven mitts he tossed back to her. Because he didn't know about the extra stuffing balls, he started arranging the parsley and grapes she'd set out, placing them on the platter around the turkey. Even though she knew the motion was as automatic as breathing to him, it annoyed her. "Out!" Grasping his shoulders, feeling the muscle beneath her fingertips, she turned him toward the door. "Go! You have seconds to live if you don't get out of here."

Laughing again, he untied his apron and handed it to her, backing away with his hands raised. "I'm going, I'm going." Then his gaze sobered. "Cathy, there are a couple of things we need to discuss. Do you mind if I stay for a little while after your other guests leave?"

Her heart rolled over in her chest, and she suddenly realized that she had hoped he would stay. "I'd like that," she said in a husky voice. They looked at each other for a long moment, then she flung out a hand and pointed over his shoulder, trying to make the gesture amusing. "Goodbye!"

It wasn't until she heard the voices swell in the living room that she realized she was holding his apron. *Well, damn.* Wasn't that just like a man? To hand a soiled apron to a woman? Turning, she scanned her wrecked kitchen. Even cleaning up as she went along, it was impossible to prepare a holiday feast without the kitchen looking like a tornado had blown through. This particular tornado had left a lot of carroty debris.

She would have sighed, but smothered a shriek instead when she caught sight of herself reflected in the window above the sink. Her sophisticated hairdo was disintegrating; wisps of blond hair floated around her flushed cheeks. When she looked down, she discovered that her spiffy scarf, the scarf that made her outfit, had worked out of the top of her apron and the ends were damp with turkey gravy. Lines of dog drool ringed her hem.

"Well," she muttered after a moment, "that's what you get for trying to be something you're not." Earlier, she'd gotten the impression that Dev hadn't thought her new look quite suited her, either.

Once all the dishes were set on the buffet and she had called her guests, she ducked into her bedroom, hastily smoothed her hair, wiped at the drool, and found another scarf. Then she dashed back to discover Devlin standing at the buffet, cheerfully carving slices of turkey and placing the slices on plates.

"White or dark?" he asked Nancy, the writer.

Nancy batted her eyes. "White. Aren't we lucky to have the two best cooks in Denver preparing our Thanksgiving feast?"

"Nothing to it," Dev said graciously before he asked Marv the perennial holiday question, "White or dark meat?"

Cathy narrowed her eyes. *Nothing to it?* Hours and hours and hours in the kitchen and there was nothing to it? All right, it was a cordial and automatic response. But he might have mentioned that the only dish he'd prepared was the carrots. Which looked and smelled fabulous, she thought with a sigh.

After everyone had passed through the buffet, Cathy took a plate and handed one to Dev. But he stopped her as she reached for a spoon.

"I like your friends, and the food is as lovely as our hostess," he said gruffly, gazing into her eyes. "I sampled the dressing. You used real suet, didn't you?"

Her knees went weak. There was something incredibly erotic about a man who could spot real suet. God, he was sexy. She didn't think she knew another man who would detect the difference.

"Yes." She wet her lips, gazing at his mouth. "Thank you for carving and serving the bird. I had to change my scarf."

"The gravy." So he'd noticed her flinging the scarf

out of the way, trying to deal with it. *Damn.* "A touch of Marsala?"

Oh my God. Cathy stared into his dark eyes. He'd tasted the wine in the gravy. "Too much?" she whispered.

"It's perfect."

She didn't know how long they would have stood in front of the hot trays, gazing into each other's eyes, aroused by the sexy talk about suet and Marsala if Rick hadn't called for them to hurry up. A toast was waiting, and the feast.

Moving in a daze, Cathy filled her plate, then walked into the dining room. Ten minutes ago, she'd been irritated with Devlin. Now, her pulse was beating wildly at her throat and wrists. There was something intimately familiar about the way he had covered for her and begun slicing the turkey.

She took her seat at the head of the table and reached for her wineglass, smiling at her guests. Rick stood to propose a toast, but waited until Devlin had seated himself. The others had automatically left him a place at the foot of the table. Cathy gazed at Dev down the length of the table, suddenly realizing they were seated as host and hostess. Her eyes widened.

Good heavens. Her guests saw them as a couple.

His gaze met hers and he sent her a high-voltage smile.

"To our lovely hostess," Rick said, raising his glass. "One of the two best cooks in town." He sent a diplomatic smile toward each end of the table.

Cathy murmured something, her gaze locked to Dev's.

She wished her guests would hurry up, eat their dinner, and go home.

Six

He said: The hardest thing to learn in life is which bridges to cross and which to burn.

DEV WISHED the other guests would hurry up and drink their coffee and go home. Cathy's friends seemed congenial people, and in other circumstances, he'd have enjoyed getting to know them. But tonight, he was impatient to be alone with Cathy, and not just because he needed to discuss Annette Dunning. Without any apparent effort on her part, Cathy was managing to drive him crazy. On camera, she always appeared too pretty and too friendly to be real. In person, she was twice as pretty and twice as good-natured. She was flushed with pleasure at the success of her meal, and her eyes sparkled with so much naive enjoyment that he wasn't sure whether he wanted to shake her or kiss her. No, that was a lie. He knew damn well that he wanted to kiss her.

Dev sipped his coffee and brooded. How the hell did you break up a party when the guests were slumped in their seats, nearly comatose with stuffing and mashed potatoes, chattering happily about football and Christmas shopping?

Inspiration finally struck. "Cathy, we should help you

clean up," he said, springing to his feet and stacking dishes almost at random. "After all the hard work you did preparing such a great meal, we can't go home and leave you with this huge mess. No, no, Cathy, don't get up, it's our turn to do some work. We'll take care of everything, won't we, guys?"

"Sure we will," Marv said heartily, although he didn't actually move. He shifted on his chair and stared at the bowl of whipped cream as if afraid it might jump up and force more of its contents down his throat. He lumbered to his feet. "Tell me what to do, Dev. I'm not much use in a kitchen, but I'll do my best."

The other guests stood, obviously feeling obliged to echo Marv's offer of help. Nancy actually went so far as to start collecting the crystal water glasses. "Would you like me to take these into the kitchen?" she asked Cathy, two goblets perched precariously in each hand. "Or maybe I should clear some counter space first." She smiled brightly. "I pride myself on being pretty good at finding my way around other people's kitchens."

Cathy's mouth was opening and shutting in silent horror. Dev grinned to himself, pleased that he'd guessed right. She couldn't tolerate the idea of her well-meaning guests stumbling around her kitchen, getting underfoot and putting everything away in the wrong drawers. There was nothing like a bunch of helpful amateurs to set a professional chef's nerves on edge, and Dev had counted on it.

She smiled weakly. "Oh, no!" she exclaimed. "It's quite all right, thanks. I'll have everything taken care of in a jiffy once you've gone." She appeared to realize that might not be quite the right thing to say and got up, quickly grabbing a couple of liqueur bottles from the buffet. "Please sit down, Nancy, and enjoy your coffee. More Amaretto, anyone? Or some of the cognac Dev brought? Rick, I know you love a good cognac. Have some more."

Good grief, she was going to get them all to sit down again! Dev rescued his plan before she had them lolling around the table, sipping another round of after-dinner drinks, and rambling on about the prospects of a winning season for the Colorado Avalanches. "Tell you what," he said. "Why don't you folks carry the coffeepot into the living room and relax around the fire? Meanwhile, Cathy and I will take care of the kitchen." He grinned at her down the length of the table. "I survived the threat of death by paring knife before dinner, so I'm counting on my good luck holding. What do you say, Cathy? I'll help you clean up, and in exchange, you'll refrain from murdering me. Do we have a deal, honey?"

She stared at him as if he'd suddenly sprouted a crop of turkey feathers on top of his head, and he realized what he'd called her: *Honey.* The endearment had slipped out unintentionally, but it suited her very well, Dev thought. Like honey, Cathy was sweet and natural, with a shy charm he was beginning to find damn near irresistible. But perhaps it was just as well that she didn't reciprocate his feelings. In life, as in cooking, there were very few surefire, never-fail recipes that Dev knew of, but getting sexually involved with a fellow chef was as close as you could get to a guaranteed recipe for disaster.

As he'd expected, the other guests took his offer of help as a signal that it was getting late and the time was approaching for them to leave. What he hadn't expected was the amused glances that shot among the people grouped around the table. Hell, had he made it that obvious he wanted to be alone with Cathy?

Obvious or not, his ploy worked. The guests gathered coats and gloves and purses and made their way to the front door, murmuring effusive thanks for a great dinner. While Cathy said her goodbyes, Dev headed straight for the kitchen and got started on the cleanup chores with a speed acquired during his years as a lowly apprentice. After his first few weeks spent ducking to avoid missiles thrown by irate chefs, Dev had learned how to transform chaos into order at a breakneck pace that kept even the most demanding chef happy.

Well, perhaps not happy, Dev thought, as he added detergent and closed the dishwasher on the first load of dishes. In his experience, most master chefs had temperaments slightly less cheery than that of a Marine Corps drill sergeant presented with a batch of new recruits. In fact, marine recruits probably had an easier time of it than apprentices training in a fancy European eating establishment.

Cathy's kitchen was as well organized as Dev would have expected, and he was able to work fast. In addition to setting the dishwasher, he had the stove top scrubbed, the trash tied up in a plastic sack, and one counter wiped clean before Cathy had closed the front door behind the last guest. He was starting to sponge off the small appliances when she walked into the kitchen.

"Dev, I'll take care of this later. You said there was something you wanted to discuss with me...." Her voice trailed off, and she stared around her. "Good heavens, I thought I could clean a kitchen quicker than anyone else in Colorado. This is amazing, Dev."

He shrugged, ruefully aware that she sounded more admiring of his cleaning skills than she had been of any of his other talents. "You'd be astonished at how fast a twenty-two-year-old kid can learn to clean up when he wants to close the kitchen and go meet his date."

She smiled, taking her apron off the hook by the door and putting leftover food into plastic storage containers with swift, economical movements. "The training for a chef is so hard, isn't it? But sometimes I think the actual cooking was more fun back in those early days when we were still learning the fundamentals. Nowadays, I expect everything to turn out right, so I only pay attention to the disasters. Every so often I have to remind myself of the thrill I felt the first time I actually prepared a perfect chocolate soufflé—light, crusty, with just the tiniest trace of moisture right at the heart of it. It gave me such a wonderful sense of accomplishment."

"Ah, Cathy, darlin', looking at you is enough to make a man weep."

She shot him a questioning glance, and Dev gave an exaggerated sigh. "If you could have seen the dreamy expression in your eyes just now, the helpless longing, the lips parted in breathless anticipation. And all for the memory of a chocolate soufflé."

She laughed. "Well, it was my *first* successful chocolate soufflé. I've become a lot more blasé since then."

She had a soft, warm laugh that made Dev think not just of how enjoyable it would be to take her to bed, but also of how good it would feel to wake up in the morning with her still lying beside him. He shook his head, dismissing the image as a dangerous one to have in regard to Cathy Mallory. Best to keep firmly in mind the fact that they were rivals in a highly competitive industry. Rivals, moreover, who had very different ideas about what constituted great cooking.

"Remember how your granny used to tell you that the way to a man's heart is through his stomach?" he asked lightly. "Well, she was dead wrong. Men will go for a sexy body over domestic skills every time. It's women who turn into a puddle of liquid desire at the mere mention of macadamia-nut cookies or white-chocolate mousse with raspberry sauce."

She shut the fridge door and turned to him, her eyes bright with laughter. "You make white-chocolate mousse with raspberry sauce? That's one of your specialties?"

He nodded. "My signature dessert."

She sighed, feigning rapture. "What a man! Be still my heart."

He flung the towel he was holding onto the counter and walked over to her. "Raspberries are the way to get to you, huh?"

"Absolutely. Add a dash of Cointreau and my resistance is reduced to zero."

"I'll keep that in mind for future reference." Dev's voice was husky. "No more coming to your house armed with cognac and carrots. From now on, it's strictly Cointreau, chocolate, and luscious fresh raspberries."

She rolled her eyes and held her hand to her heart. "Help! I'm a lost woman."

"Not lost. Just very beautiful." Dev hadn't meant to say that, hadn't meant to find himself standing this close to her, hadn't meant to reach up and skim his fingers over the delicate curve of her cheek. Her color deepened, and her skin became hot beneath his touch. She was so fair-skinned that he could imagine her whole body flushed pink in the aftermath of making love. The image packed an unexpected erotic punch and desire burned in him with sudden fierceness.

For a long moment, they stared at each other in tense silence, gazes locked, not moving. Then Dev let his hand drop. He turned and walked away, stepping back physically and mentally from the brink. Earlier, during dinner, he'd wanted to kiss her. Now he realized that wasn't a good idea. Cathy Mallory wasn't a woman that you could take to bed and forget about half an hour later, and Dev was at the wrong point in his life to be getting seriously involved.

"Okay, what next?" He spoke with deliberate briskness. "I've finished all the pots and pans. Do you want to wash the crystal by hand?"

After a slight pause, she answered, her voice as brisk as his had been. "Yes, I do. But I have no intention of doing any of that now. I don't have to be at work until tomorrow afternoon, so I have the whole morning to take care of cleaning up here. There's nothing more we need to do tonight."

"Are you sure?"

"I'm positive. Thanks, Dev, I really appreciate your help, but let's get out of this darn kitchen. Right now I'd like to go into the living room, throw another log onto the fire, and listen to whatever it is that you wanted to talk to me about."

Annette Dunning. Dev grimaced. He didn't *want* to talk about Annette, especially to Cathy, but he recognized that they needed to swap stories about their previous encounters with the woman if they were going to contain whatever mischief she was brewing. He followed Cathy into the living room, which felt pleasantly cool and fresh after the steamy heat of the kitchen. Cathy had furnished the room in a way that was the antithesis of the sleek, uncluttered look Dev usually preferred, but there was something unexpectedly appealing about the knickknacks on the bookshelves, the overstuffed plaid armchairs grouped next to the fire, and the puffy sofa cushions that seemed to invite you to lean back and relax.

A stone jug stood on the coffee table filled with branches of pine and eucalyptus, the dark green leaves enlivened by the scarlet splash of holly berries. Dev sat down and Cathy moved the jug out of their way, setting it on an end table by the sofa and giving a quick tweak to adjust the arrangement. At her touch, the scent of winter evergreens mingled with the smell of wood smoke coming from the fire, and a wave of nostalgia washed over Dev. It had been a long time—too long—since the holidays had meant anything to him except a killing pace of work at the busiest time of the year. Thinking back, he couldn't even remember when he last had eaten turkey and all the trimmings, as opposed to cooking some variation of the meal for other people.

Cathy sat down in one of the chairs, then immediately jumped up again. "I forgot the brandy," she said. "I'll be right back."

"Forget the cognac." Dev grasped her wrist and tugged gently until she sat down next to him on the sofa. Next to him might be an exaggeration, he conceded with regret. Cathy left an entire seat cushion of space between them. Then she crossed her legs primly at the ankles and held her back ramrod straight, making sure that her body language underlined the message that she had no intention of allowing this situation to develop into anything intimate. Contrarily, instead of being grateful that she shared his own reluctance to get involved, Dev was gripped by an intense desire to topple her backward, kiss her senseless, and discover just how great sex between the two of them could be.

The tension was getting uncomfortable when Romeo saved the day. He wandered in, ambled over to the sofa and stuck his head onto Cathy's lap, nudging her clasped hands with his nose until she relented and rubbed in a circular motion under his chin. He drooled in instant ecstasy, giving her the occasional reproving nudge when she dared to stop stroking.

Dev laughed. "I can see Romeo has you well trained," he said.

Cathy kept stroking. "My friends call him a benevolent dictator. He's a dictator, all right. I'm just not sure about the benevolent part."

"I have a cat," Dev told her. "He's a straightforward dictator, and nobody would be foolish enough to call him benevolent. Last night he knocked over a stack of papers on my desk, and while I was on my hands and knees picking them up, I actually apologized out loud for having put them in the place where he likes to sit."

She sent him an amused glance. "Did he accept your apology?"

"Not until I'd spent a considerable amount of time doing penance by scratching his favorite spot behind his left ear."

She chuckled and gave the dog a final pat, dismissing him to the rug in front of the fire and refusing to succumb to his reproachful gaze. "I've only had Romeo since I moved to this house, but he's known exactly how to manipulate me since week one of our acquaintance."

"Where did you get him? Or maybe that's the wrong question. I should probably ask how Romeo selected you to be his owner."

"He was sitting on my front porch the day I moved in, almost as if he'd been waiting for me to arrive."

"He probably was. Animals can scent a sucker from miles away."

She smiled, but absently, and he sensed a renewed tension in her. "As a matter of fact, in an odd sort of way, Annette Dunning is a large part of the reason I kept Romeo."

Dev looked up, startled. "I didn't realize you'd met Annette so recently. For some reason, I jumped to the conclusion that you were old acquaintances who hadn't seen each other in quite a while."

"You're right, I haven't seen Annette in years, not since I was in college. Actually, until I received the letter telling me I was one of the finalists for Universal Syndication's new cooking show, I hadn't even heard her name mentioned for at least a dozen years. But some people manage to cast a long shadow over your life."

"For good or ill," Dev said.

"I'm not sure how much good there was in my relationship with Annette. Although I guess she forced me to do a lot of growing up in a very short time." Cathy stared into the leaping flames of the fire, her expression shuttered. She hesitated a moment, then turned to meet Dev's gaze. "I've never told anyone this before, not even my parents when they were alive, but one of the things I regret most about my relationship with Annette is that she had this horrible knack for making me behave badly. She brought out all my insecurities and always seemed to know just what to say in order to coerce me into doing my worst instead of my best. It's hard to explain how someone could have the power to do that...."

"You don't have to explain," Dev said wryly. "She had exactly the same effect on me."

Cathy expelled a long, slow breath. "You know Annette Dunning," she said flatly. "I wonder why that doesn't come as even a small surprise to me?"

"Yes, I know her," Dev acknowledged. "And we aren't friends."

"Are you...enemies?"

It was his turn to hesitate. "That's a strong word, but I guess Annette would say that we are." As soon as he'd spoken, Dev recognized how big a risk he was taking by confiding in Cathy Mallory, his most serious professional rival. Strangely, he didn't regret his confession, even though on a rational level he knew he should.

Cathy picked up a throw pillow and threaded her fingers through the silk tassel. "Based on my experiences with Annette, I suspect she has a long list of enemies. And I don't know why I'm telling you all this, seeing as how we're both going to be competing to impress her during the next couple of weeks."

Dev leaned forward. "Let's take this a step at a time," he said tersely. "And let's spell everything out so that there are no misunderstandings. I want that job with Universal Syndication. I want to beat the hell out of you in the culinary contest next week, and I want to cremate you in the Denver television ratings. But I also want to have the satisfaction of knowing that I beat you because I cook better, because my recipe for the contest was more original and because my show for KDID is more entertaining than your show for KBAB. I don't want to win because I found some way to screw you over with Annette Dunning. You can trust me on this, Cathy. Nothing that you say here tonight will be repeated to Annette. Not for any reason."

"You don't have a chance of beating me in the contest," she said hotly. "And last week, my show for KBAB was higher in the ratings than yours."

"For the first time in four weeks."

She glared at him. "But I was two points up, and 'Dining with Devlin' has never been more than a single point higher in the ratings than 'Cooking with Cathy.'"

"Wait until next week."

"Hah!" She tossed her hair out of her eyes. "I'll beat you by three points at least."

She really looked enchantingly hot and bothered, which made it quite difficult to focus on what they were actually arguing about. "Want to make a small bet on that?" Dev suggested, recovering.

"Sure I do. Ten bucks says 'Cooking with Cathy' is up by three points over 'Dining with Devlin.'"

"You're on." God help him, but he almost hoped she'd win.

Cathy scowled, then drew in a deep breath. "All that aside, what I'm trying to say is that I agree with you, Dev, about not repeating this conversation to Annette Dunning. I want to beat you fair and square, then sit back and watch you grovel...."

On television, Cathy appeared too relaxed and cheerful to be consumed by the same sort of ambition that nipped relentlessly at his heels. Dev found himself intrigued by this unexpected glimpse of her competitive spirit. "I don't grovel well," he said. "But indulge your fantasies while you can, sweetheart."

Her glare intensified, and she huffed at the endearment as he'd known she would. Dev hastily backtracked to safer ground. "You were going to tell me how Annette was connected to your decision to adopt Romeo."

"It was a very indirect link." Cathy laced and unlaced her fingers. "When I was in college, I shared an apartment with Annette. She was five or six years older than me, a graduate student when I was a sophomore, but I always felt at least a hundred years younger than her in terms of experience."

"I suspect Annette Dunning was born a hundred years more sophisticated than the rest of us."

"Maybe. But the truth is that I wanted to be like her. I envied her with the sort of intensity only a naive country girl could feel for a worldly woman who'd grown up in a sophisticated urban environment. A few weeks after a group of us moved into a large old house off campus, I found a puppy wandering around. He looked so lost and hungry and—lonely—that I walked him back to the house with me, planning to keep him for the rest of the semester and then take him home to my parents' farm. Annette happened to be at the house when I brought him back, so she saw him before I had a chance to bathe him and make him look a bit more cute and cuddly. She was entertaining some of her ultrasophisticated male friends, and when she saw the puppy, she squinted down her nose at him in that superior way she had that always made me feel about two inches high. She tossed off some cutting remark to the effect that he was just the sort of mongrel she'd have expected me to adopt. 'No breeding there,

Kansas. You'll make a perfect couple,' she said. That was the nickname she'd given me: Kansas."

Cathy stopped talking, and Dev took her hand in silent comfort. She must have been badly in need of reassurance, because she didn't resist. "Nothing you've said reflects badly on you," he said. "The opposite, in fact. It simply shows what an unpleasant person Annette could be when she set her mind to it."

"You haven't heard the rest of the story," Cathy said. "It gets much worse. Annette's friends were making rude comments about the puppy, joking about how I could groom him for a dog show where he could win the prize for ugliest mongrel. Somebody even suggested I should call him Romeo, as a joke because he was so unappealing. I was insecure enough in those days that instead of ignoring them, I turned around, walked out of the house, and took the puppy straight to the pound."

She fell silent, staring at their linked hands, although Dev suspected she wasn't seeing anything from the present. "I expect someone adopted him," he said.

Cathy looked up, meeting his gaze. "No, nobody ever adopted him. I called the pound ten days later. That's how long they gave the strays to find homes, and Romeo hadn't. He'd been euthanized."

Dev grimaced, his hold on her hand tightening. "Cathy, it wasn't your fault that he died."

"Of course it was. And what I hate so much about myself is that the puppy lost his life for the stupid reason that I couldn't stand to be called Kansas." She drew in a shaky breath. "Anyway, when I saw Romeo sitting on my porch, looking even more battered and scruffy than he looks today, it was as if I'd been offered a second chance to do things over, and to do them right."

Dev didn't insult her by offering any more false reassurances. In the grand scheme of things, allowing one stray dog to go to the pound wasn't a monstrous crime, but he understood why the incident haunted Cathy. It was always disconcerting to realize that another person had the power to provoke you into behaving badly. He should know, since Annette had provoked him into behavior that was a hell of a lot worse than Cathy's.

Dev got up and walked over to the fire to throw on another log. He'd planned to give Cathy the same truncated account of his relationship with Annette that he'd given to Bill Sadler, but that seemed insulting after her honesty. Besides, she'd given him the perfect opening to broach the subject of his suspicions about Annette's intentions. From the small sampling he'd heard about Cathy's past dealings with Annette, Dev wasn't willing to believe that—by sheer coincidence—the two finalists for the new show happened to be two people Annette Dunning seriously disliked.

"I understand your regrets, Cathy, because I have several of my own in regard to Annette. And I can't excuse my behavior on the grounds of being young and naive, like you. I was twenty-six, and I'd lived in half the capital cities of Europe when Annette and I met in Paris. She still managed to manipulate me almost as easily as she manipulated you."

Cathy looked doubtful. "With your background, how could she possibly make you feel like a hick?"

"She didn't even try. Instead, she set out to convince me I was a world-weary cynic, who needed her to show me new and more exotic ways to entertain myself. We started out going to poetry readings in smoky coffee houses, and watching Chinese movies with French subtitles at art cinemas. That was the beginning. Then, before I really noticed what was happening, Annette had introduced me to an entire Parisian subculture that I'd only half guessed existed."

Perhaps because she'd seen Annette at work, Cathy understood at once. "She took you to places and persuaded you to do things you're ashamed to remember."

"Yes." He drew in a harsh breath. "There's absolutely nobody more stupid than a young man who thinks he knows everything. And Annette homed in on my stupidities with razor-sharp precision. She homed in on them, and then she exploited them."

Cathy frowned. "Dev, this is a personal question, so I'll understand if you don't want to answer, but when you and Annette split up, were you the person who walked away from the relationship? Or did she decide it was over?"

"I guess the decision was well and truly mine." Dev lifted his shoulders in an embarrassed shrug, remembering his fury when he found out on the morning of their wedding day that Annette had tricked him, and that she was no longer pregnant. "We were due to get married, and I left her literally standing at the altar."

Cathy gasped, then smiled. "Oh, my. Don't think me an evil person, Dev, but I can't tell you how much I enjoy hearing that."

She was so far removed from being an evil person that Dev felt an unaccustomed urge to protect her. Nobody as basically nice as Catherine Mallory could possibly grasp the full vindictiveness of Annette's personality, and he needed to warn her to be prepared for the worst.

"Cathy," he said softly. "Don't you think it's a very odd coincidence that out of all the chefs in this country, the two finalists for the Universal Syndication project not only live in Denver, but are two people Annette Dunning has good reason to dislike?"

Cathy stared at Romeo. He wagged his tail hopefully, then settled his nose back down on his paws when he realized that she hadn't even seen him. Frowning, Cathy brought her gaze back to Dev. "Yes, I think it's very strange," she said. "But it must be a coincidence, despite the long odds. Annette has to choose one of us to be the star of Universal Syndicate's new show; that's her job. It's the reason she's coming to Denver. Ultimately, when she's enjoyed tormenting us for a few days, either you or I will be AUS's new celebrity chef. In view of what's happened between us in the past, I'm sure Annette would never have set herself up to make such a difficult choice. She's just found herself in this position and she's making the most of it."

The choice wouldn't be so difficult, Dev thought gloomily. He was willing to bet all the leftover turkey in Colorado that Annette Dunning would walk naked across the Sahara Desert before she would select him for a shot at national stardom. Cathy Mallory might have offended Annette in various minor ways during the time they roomed together in college, but she couldn't have done anything that came close to the offense Dev had committed. In truth, he had to admit that leaving a woman standing at the altar, with fifty guests watching her humiliation, would provoke more generous souls than Annette Dunning to fantasies of revenge. And Annette wasn't the sort of woman to admit the lies, trickery and betrayal that had forced Dev to run out on her.

The fire sputtered in the grate as the log crumbled into ashes. Dev suddenly remembered that he'd been up since five that morning, and realized that he felt weary to the marrow of his bones. He sensed Cathy's eyes resting on him in a silent question, and he leaned forward, kissing her on the forehead with a casual friendliness that was fifty-percent fake, fifty-percent sheer willpower. Cathy Mallory was an attractive, desirable woman. The more he saw of her, the more he liked her, and the more he wanted to take her to bed. Unfortunately, he knew their relationship had no place to go. Dev prided himself on keeping his masculine ego under reasonable control, but there was no way he'd be able to pretend that he wasn't hurting when Cathy landed the job with Universal Syndication. If they were merely friendly rivals, the situation would be tough. If they became lovers, it would be unbearable.

He snapped his fingers and, by happy chance, Romeo chose to amble over to his side. Thank God, he now had something to do with his hands. Dev stood up, scratching the top of the dog's head and moving pointedly toward the front door. "Cathy, it's been a terrific evening, and I'm really glad you invited me. It's been much too long since I enjoyed a traditional Thanksgiving dinner."

She looked up at that, but whatever she saw in his face caused her smile to congeal into something stiff and formal. "You're welcome," she said, her voice cool. "I'm glad you could come."

He wanted to explain how much he liked her, how much he wished they could explore the possibilities of their relationship. Hell, he even wanted to say how much he'd enjoyed clearing up the kitchen with a woman who really knew what she was doing. Instead, he gritted his teeth and searched his repertoire of trite good-night phrases.

Cathy handed him his scarf and gloves. "You can send me my ten dollars in care of KBAB," she said. "Good night, Devlin."

As a blow-off, it was a damn sight more effective than anything he'd been able to come up with. Dev found himself torn between rueful laughter and a renewed desire to take Cathy into his arms and kiss her. A hot, openmouthed kiss, with his tongue thrusting against hers, and her breasts pressed against his chest.

Dev realized he'd closed his eyes. He opened them, and was struck by a bolt of mental lightning. Of course! How had he and Cathy managed to spend the better part of an hour discussing Annette Dunning without grasping such an obvious truth?

"Annette doesn't intend either of us to get the job with Universal Syndication," he said. "Somehow, she plans to screw us both."

Chapter Seven

She said: Falling in love is like making a soufflé—the risk of failure is very high.

CATHY GUILTILY considered Dev's last words the next morning as she finished cleaning her kitchen. He didn't know about Annette's hints that the decision had already been made in Cathy's favor. He thought Annette intended to work her dirty tricks on both of them.

Actually, even though she'd made a flip comment about it last night, she couldn't really blame Annette for hating Devlin. Now that Cathy had spent some time with Dev and had gotten to know him better, he didn't impress her as the type of man cruel enough to humiliate a woman by jilting her at the altar and leaving her vulnerable to unthinkable humiliation. But that's what he had done.

Surely something devastating must have happened between the evening before the wedding, when he presumably believed he loved Annette, and a few hours later when he simply didn't show up at the church.

Had Annette known why he didn't show? If she had known, why had she arrived at the altar, believing it was her wedding day?

These and other questions troubled her about Devlin, clearly a man of contradictions. Among her Thanksgiving guests, Dev had been the only one thoughtful enough to bring a dish; yet he'd seemed oblivious to the difficulty he caused by preparing his dish while she was frantically trying to complete her final chores. He was considerate enough to cover for her while she changed her scarf and freshened up; yet he'd invited everyone to help clean up her kitchen when he had to know the suggestion would offend her. At least twice, she had believed he was about to take her into his arms and kiss her; then he had backed off and become brisk, almost cool toward her.

After putting away the last of the crystal, she took a coffee break, propped her chin in her palm, and looked down at Romeo.

"He's a dangerous and complex man," she decided, thinking out loud. "Remember his last show? He said he dumped some poor woman over Wiener schnitzel. And he left another standing at the altar...and those are just the ones we know about." A sigh lifted her chest. "So why am I sitting here feeling disappointed and wishing he'd kissed me good-night?"

Romeo placed his head in her lap and happily echoed her sigh when she scratched behind his ears. "Here's the problem as I see it, pal. Make that plural. Problems. Dev and I are serious rivals. There are our cooking shows, the upcoming Chefs' Culinary Contest, and we're both contenders for the AUS opportunity of a lifetime. And we're so different. He's uptown, I'm downhome. He's cognac, I'm Amaretto. And listen, you won't believe this, but he owns a c-a-t." She sighed again and gazed out the window at the kids next door playing in the snow. "He's penthouse, I'm picket fence. He's restaurant, I'm catering. I'll bet he even uses fresh tarragon. So why aren't I running away as fast as I can?"

Part of the reason, she suspected, was her growing fascination for a type of man who lay outside her experience. The men she usually attracted, and usually found attractive, were her counterparts, All-American Boys grown up. Now that she was brooding on the subject, she realized the men in her life could be clones of one another. Tall, golden, handsome in a straightforward manner, climbing the corporate ladder one rung after another. They were nice men who remembered birthdays and favorite colors or favorite foods; moderate men who were not extreme in word or thought. Men who were in no way her direct competitors. They were safe men. Predictable. Dull.

Now she was discovering there was something secretly thrilling about dancing close to a dangerous flame. She hadn't previously realized why a moth flirted with fire. Didn't the heat singe the moth's wings? Didn't the moth recognize its danger?

She suspected it did, just as she had felt the heat last night between herself and Devlin, just as she had sensed the danger. Yet, bedazzled, the moth courted the flame, perhaps thinking it would be the one to conquer the beautiful, seductive light.

"Good heavens," she said, blinking down at Romeo. She laughed out loud. "He'll have me quoting sonnets next!"

Springing up, she finished straightening the kitchen, gave her house a quick once-over, and checked in with the catering service. The last call on a long list was to Dev.

She drew a breath and listened to his smooth voice invite her to leave a message on his machine. "You don't have to be a moth," she told herself irritably just as the machine beeped. Forcing a cheerful note into her tone, she said, "Hi, Dev. It's Friday about noon. You left your springform pan at my house last night. I'm going to be running a few errands tomorrow, and I thought I'd drop the pan at your restaurant. You can pick it up there. Thanks again for the carrot dish. Everyone raved. 'Bye."

Oh, jeez. She dialed his number again, feeling like an idiot, and inwardly groaned when this time he picked up the phone.

"Dev?"

"Cathy? I didn't get to the phone quickly enough to pick up, but I heard the message. I think I got all of it except the first part. Were you telling me not to be a moth?" His laugh sent a ripple of desire down her spine.

Pink poured into her cheeks. "I was talking to someone else. Never mind the moth. I called back because I realized I hadn't left my name on the message."

"I recognized your voice," he said softly. Before she recovered from that nice piece of flattery, he continued, "I'm glad you called again because I'm not going to be at my place tomorrow. I'm driving up to Vail to look at a restaurant that's for sale up there."

"Are you thinking about expanding to another location?" she asked in surprise. He must be very certain that Annette wasn't going to select him for the syndication shot. She didn't blame him, but she felt a pang of sympathy.

"Let's just say I'm hedging my bets." Clearly he'd guessed her thoughts. "If this plan works for you, I'll swing by your house on my way back into town and pick up the pan." He hesitated a beat. "I'll be returning about six o'clock. Would you like to go out for dinner?"

She considered a minute, trying not to think about

moths and flames and dangerous men. "Actually, we could have turkey leftovers...."

His laugh made her smile. "Like you, I can whip up a dozen dishes using leftover turkey. The problem is, I'm not enthusiastic about leftovers. There's a wonderful Chinese restaurant not far from your house—"

"Su Lin's."

"Right. How does that sound?"

Chinese food while the fridge was filled with fabulous holiday leftovers? "It sounds great," she said in a faint voice.

"Good. I'll pick you up around six-thirty."

Slowly Cathy hung up the telephone. "I'm a lunatic," she said solemnly, gazing at Romeo, who thumped his tail and grinned at her. Romeo didn't care; she was *his* lunatic.

Laughing, already thinking about what she might wear tomorrow, she hurried back to the kitchen. Today, she planned to practice her new entry for the culinary contest. She had chosen duck this time, a difficult dish to prepare properly. The fresh rhubarb sauce could also be tricky.

So, not only would she have leftover turkey in the fridge, but at least one roast duck and possibly two. Well, it didn't matter; she would see Dev tomorrow.

The thought lifted her spirits and her heart sang. He was her rival, he was dangerous, and he was the worst possible man to get involved with.

Maybe her new Liz Claiborne pant suit...

"SORRY I'M LATE," Dev apologized as she opened the door. "It's not only a weekend, but a holiday weekend. I-70 was bumper-to-bumper traffic all the way to Vail and all the way back down the mountains."

For once, he did indeed appear a little frazzled. His dark hair was tousled as if he'd been pushing his fingers through it, and he looked tired.

"Why don't you call Su Lin's and delay our reservation? Give yourself a few minutes to relax."

"Good idea," he agreed, giving her a grateful look as he handed her his topcoat and scarf. "Where's the nearest phone?"

She almost suggested her office, but she couldn't recall what papers lay on her desk. The menu for her next show? Notes regarding the culinary contest? "There's a phone in the kitchen. May I fix you a drink?"

While Dev telephoned Su Lin's, she poured Scotch into two crystal glasses, sobered by her hesitation over letting him see her desk. This was a good reminder, and one that she needed. His dark eyes, beautifully shaped mouth and personal charisma too easily made her forget about their rivalry.

They settled on stools in front of the kitchen counter. Dev touched the rim of his glass to hers, saying, "cheers," and tasted his drink with a sigh. "You look lovely, by the way. I like your hair natural like that."

Cathy ran a hand through her curls self-consciously. "Was the Vail restaurant what you expected?" she asked, sliding a bowl of cashews toward him. His hands were slender, the fingers tapered and artistic. Dev had the hands of a pianist, a surgeon, a master chef…or a sensitive and skillful lover. Cursing herself for an easy propensity to blush, she lowered her gaze and sipped her drink. She had to get a grip.

"The layout is good but there isn't enough seating," Dev said, pulling his fingers through his hair. "The kitchen also needs to be expanded and updated. On the plus side, the location is excellent. In the Village. On the downside, there really isn't space to allow for the expansion the place needs." He took a long swallow of Scotch, then shrugged. "Another opportunity will come along if this one doesn't work out. Have you ever thought about owning a restaurant?"

She laughed, covering a flustered moment when their hands collided above the cashew dish. "My parents owned a small restaurant for about three years while I was growing up. They were up before dawn and fell into bed exhausted around midnight. What I remember about holidays during those years was working at the restaurant, helping out in the kitchen. Thanksgiving, Mother's Day, New Year's Eve...they weren't holidays, they were big days at the restaurant. Eventually my father returned to farming and my mother went back to teaching." She smiled. "So, no. What I learned from that early experience was that I was fascinated by the preparation of food, but not by the restaurant business."

Interest warmed his eyes and she noticed that he was beginning to relax. "Isn't the catering business equally demanding?"

"It was until a couple of years ago. But now that Just Like Home is a success, I've hired a good manager and reduced my own involvement. I help out as needed and I do the bookkeeping, but it's nothing like the daily, hands-on demands of owning a restaurant."

He shook some cashews in his hand, studying her expression. "What will you do with Just Like Home when you win the AUS syndication?"

"*When* I win the AUS syndication?" Her eyebrows lifted and she shifted on the stool to face him.

"I had a lot of time to think while I was creeping along in traffic, Cathy." He gazed into his drink, then lifted his eyes to hers. "There isn't a chance that Annette

Dunning is going to select me for the syndication slot. I left her standing at the altar...you and Annette had a squabble over a dog that probably ended the way Annette wanted. So you tell me—which is the worst offense? Therefore," he said with a painful grin, raising his glass to her, "congratulations. I think you're the clear-cut winner."

Cathy stared, a frown forming a crease between her eyes. His resiliency and realistic approach were admirable, but also sad. This wasn't fair.

"There's more to it," she said in a low voice. God, she hated to tell him what had really happened.

"Oh?" Curiosity flickered in his sexy, dark eyes. "Shall I freshen your drink? We still have an hour before we need to be at Su Lin's."

Silently, she handed him her glass and watched him move around her kitchen as if he knew it as well as she. When he returned to the stool, he touched her hand lightly. "Look, if you don't want to talk about this..."

But he had confessed to jilting Annette, and it must have been difficult to admit. She owed him more than she had given. Drawing a deep breath, she gazed at the old-fashioned cooking utensils decorating the back wall as she told him the full truth about her relationship with Annette.

"I wasn't the person who blew the whistle on her," Cathy said at the end of her story. "But I could have been." Frowning, not looking at him, she added in a whisper, "I had thought about exposing her for profiting from students willing to cheat. I *wanted* to hit back at her in some way. Annette always brought out the worst in me."

"But you didn't," Dev said quietly. Lifting a hand, he brushed a strand of hair off of her cheek.

"I might as well have. Annette certainly believed that I was the one who turned her in to the authorities. And she hit back twice as hard. In the end, she placed us both under suspicion and in disgrace. We both had to leave college. But lying and taking me down with her wasn't enough for Annette. The last thing she said to me was, 'You'll pay for this.'"

Scowling, Dev gazed at a point in space. "She must have gone to Europe after leaving college. But I could swear she said she had finished grad school." He shook his head. "I don't know why I'm surprised by another lie. Truth is whatever Annette wants it to be."

"Anyway, I wanted you to know the playing field isn't as lopsided as you thought it was. For about a year, I was hurt and angry. Then I realized Annette's lies had turned my life in a direction that opened worlds of opportunity for me. In an odd twist, I guess I could say that I owe my present success to Annette Dunning. If it hadn't been for her lies and accusations, I'd probably be working in hotel administration now instead of doing what I really love to do. Cooking. With my own business and my own television show."

"Cathy, thank you for telling me this. I know it wasn't easy."

She gave him a pained smile. "You can't even imagine. I never talk about why I left college. It's embarrassing and humiliating. Only someone who knows Annette would believe me or understand how I could have been manipulated so easily."

Suddenly she was aware of how close they were sitting, aware that they were gazing into each other's eyes with speculative expressions, wondering if they shared other things. They had Annette in common, and cooking, and their TV shows. They knew many of the same people, attended many of the same social events, seemed to laugh at similar things.

She wondered if he felt as wildly attracted to her as she did to him. Swaying slightly toward the magnetic tug of his warmth and his gaze, she inhaled the faint, vanilla scent of his cologne.

"Well," she said abruptly, flustered. "It's good that Su Lin's is nearby or we'd be late." Sliding off the stool, she gave him a bright smile. "This way to the coats, Mr. Gilpatrick."

"After you, Ms. Mallory," he said, following her lead.

The red-and-white Corvette parked in front of her house was splashed with mud and slush, but she'd wanted to ride in it ever since she spotted his car at the mechanic's shop.

"Nice," she stated with a sigh of pleasure after slipping inside. "I always wanted a car like this."

Dev revved the engine for her benefit then laughed. "Why don't you buy one?"

"A practical nature, I guess," she said, smiling. "I look at a car like this and wonder how many grocery sacks I could fit in the trunk, or how many pies I could deliver to Just Like Home." She gazed at his handsome profile by the light from the dashboard. "Some people walk on the wild side...and some of us were cursed with practicality. Darn."

As he pulled away from the curb, he winked at her. "Would it surprise you to learn that I also own an Oldsmobile? A big boat of a car that will carry exactly twelve sacks of groceries?"

Cathy blinked, then laughed. "It would astonish me."

"The Corvette was an extravagant and impractical gift I gave myself when I landed the show at KDID. I felt it was more in keeping with the bachelor-about-town image." Reaching, he squeezed her hand. "Or maybe it's just a wild fantasy, left over from my teenage years, of tooling around Chicago in a flashy Corvette with a beautiful blonde in the passenger seat. The envy of all."

She joined in his laughter, but her thoughts had turned inward. How could she have believed he was all arrogance and no substance? Her surprise that he didn't take himself too seriously shamed her. Far from what she had assumed, Dev was a man firmly grounded in reality. Yes, he had a healthy ego, but if she were honest with herself, his high regard for his talent and skills was completely justified.

"You, by the way, are doing a fine job of being a beautiful blonde tonight," he said with an admiring glance. "We're going to create exactly the impression my superficial teenaged self longed to impart. If we can find a parking space out front, that is."

"I'm happy to do my part in fulfilling your teenage fantasy," she said, laughing. "But it looks as if we'll have trouble finding a parking space at all." He cruised past Su Lin's, then turned to circle the block.

"Must be busy tonight," he murmured, scanning the curb. "I guess I'm not the only one with an aversion to turkey leftovers. I'll let you out in front of the door, park, and catch up with you."

There it was again, the unexpected thoughtfulness and courtesy. And a sudden flash of hot electricity when he leaned and kissed her lightly on the mouth before she slid out of the Corvette to wait for him.

Frowning, her fingertips on her lips, she watched him slowly drive away, searching for a parking place. She didn't know what was happening between them, but something definitely was. If she needed confirmation of the obvious, then she had only to remember telling him about leaving college. That was a story so humiliating that she had shared it with only a handful of people. Two weeks ago she wouldn't have been able to imagine any conceivable circumstance in which she would have confided the experience to Devlin Gilpatrick. Nor would she have imagined that a light kiss could make her heart pound and her fingers tremble.

Her thoughts were so firmly focused on Dev and the thrill of his lips on hers, that she didn't immediately realize that she'd been watching a couple standing beside a nearby car. Smiling at the potent body language they were conveying, she walked toward the entrance to Su Lin's. Then, she stopped suddenly, whirled and stared back at the couple, her knees shaking with shock.

She hadn't seen Annette Dunning in years, but Cathy recognized her at once. Annette's shining dark hair was longer than she had worn it in college, swept into a stylish chignon right out of *Vogue* magazine. She wore a forest green cape over silk evening slacks and carried a Chanel bag, which she stroked along the coat sleeve of her escort. It was this oddly seductive gesture that had caught Cathy's attention and had caused her to smile indulgently at a man and woman whose posture and attitude suggested they were lovers.

Now the smile vanished from her lips and she stared in stunned surprise. Even after all these years, the jolt of seeing Annette sent a burst of adrenaline through her system. When Annette leaned into the man and kissed him, Cathy flinched and felt as if she were spying, witnessing something Annette would not want her to see. Confused by such a peculiar thought, she ducked her head and hurried into Su Lin's, all but collapsing into the nearest chair in the waiting area. At once, she felt angry with herself for reacting to Annette by giving in to an instinct to flee. Some things didn't change.

By the time Dev swung through the door, she had begun to calm down and regain her equilibrium. But her distress must have shown in her expression because when she stood to greet him, he frowned and grasped her shoulders.

"Cathy? What's happened? Are you all right?"

"You won't believe this, but I just saw Annette Dunning outside." She stared into his eyes. "Dev, she was with Paul Lyman. They were kissing."

Dev's eyebrows shot upward. "Annette and Paul?" Paul Lyman owned KDID, and was Dev's employer. He was also the chairman of the hospital board that was sponsoring the culinary contest.

Dropping his hands from her shoulders, Dev stepped to the maître d's lectern. "Excuse me. My friend and I were supposed to meet Paul Lyman. We're terribly late, but...could you direct us to his table?"

The maître d' ran a finger down his reservation list then glanced into the restaurant. "I'm sorry, sir, Mr. Lyman has already left."

"Would you recall if there was a woman with him?" Dev glanced at Cathy as she stepped forward to describe Annette.

"She was wearing a green cape...."

"Ah, yes. I remember her."

"You're right," Dev said quietly. "They were together."

Cathy turned aside then took Dev's arm and gazed up into his eyes. "Suddenly I have no appetite, none at all. Please, could we go home?"

Without a word, he placed a hand at her waist and led her outside. He didn't attempt to change her mind, didn't bring up their reservation, didn't mention any platitude about how she had to eat something. He simply did as she asked.

For a moment she thought what she was feeling was gratitude. But in fact, that was the instant that Cathy realized she was falling in love.

SHE DID WHAT she always did when she was upset. Or happy. Or depressed. Or elated. Or feeling blue. She tossed her coat over a chair and headed for the kitchen, bending to remove the platter of turkey from the refrigerator. While Dev opened a bottle of wine, she sliced turkey for Romeo, who watched with great interest, and she sliced turkey to make a sandwich for Devlin.

While Cathy assembled the sandwich, Devlin found the leftover salads and placed them on the countertop. Cathy had forgotten that he didn't care for leftovers. When his plate was ready, she set it on the countertop then sat beside him, turning her wineglass in her hands.

"Dev...when did Annette tell you she would be in town?"

"She said she would arrive on Tuesday the second. She suggested we have our first interview that evening over dinner."

Cathy nodded. "I'm positive she also told me that she was arriving on Tuesday." Propping her chin in her hand, she watched him bite into the turkey sandwich. "She didn't mention her dinner with you, of course. She suggested that she and I have lunch the next day."

"Cathy, I'm sorry. The food is wonderful, but I'm not hungry, either." Putting down his sandwich, he reached for his wineglass and took a sip. "She lied about when she would arrive in Denver."

"I wonder if Universal Syndication knows that Annette is in Denver. Or maybe they think she's scheduled to meet with you or me before she actually is?"

Dev toyed with his glass. "So why did she lie about when she would arrive? What is she doing here that she didn't want us to know about?"

Although the question was rhetorical, she offered a possibility. "Maybe it doesn't have anything to do with us. Maybe she's here to—I don't know—see some friends? Take care of other business?"

Dev reached for her hand and held it between his. "Cathy," he said gently, "whatever Annette is doing, it's about us. We're part of it. There are too many co-incidences to be a coincidence. Do you understand what I'm saying? Of all the competitors for the AUS syndication, the two finalists just happen to have a history with the person who will make the final selection. We receive pre-air tapes of each other's shows and AUS just happens to be on the distribution lists. Annette says she'll arrive on the second, but she just happens to turn up earlier. These occurrences are not accidents."

She looked down and watched his thumb stroke her palm, feeling a resultant tingle race along her skin. A sigh lifted her chest. "You're right, of course. I'm one of those people who tries to put a positive spin on things."

"That must get you into trouble sometimes."

"Often I'm up to my ears in trouble before I even recognize it," she agreed with a weak grin. "Dev, can you think of any reason why Annette and Paul Lyman would be having dinner together? Did you know they knew each other?"

The question concerned him enough that he released her hand and reached for his wineglass. "No, I didn't. Paul and I are friendly, but I wouldn't say we're close.

We don't share confidences, and certainly we've never discussed women in specific terms."

Cathy drew a deep breath and gazed into his eyes. "Is it possible that Annette has decided to award you the syndication slot and she's announcing it to your employer before she tells you?"

Suddenly she understood what she should have comprehended from the beginning. Annette's hints about having decided in Cathy's favor meant nothing at all. Annette was capable of building up her hopes just for the pleasure of crushing her later.

Dev was right. Annette could be planning to put the screws to both of them.

"Informing Paul before me would be unethical," he said flatly. Then he stood, laughing. "As if ethics ever mattered to Annette Dunning." He gazed at Cathy. "That isn't the solution. Annette isn't going to give me a chance at syndication. Would you hand a plum to a man who left you at the altar?"

She considered the question, striving to be fair. "I'd try very hard to separate personal feelings from professional considerations...but it would be difficult." After hesitating she added, "And it would be equally difficult to hand a plum to someone I blamed for losing my graduate degree."

Slipping off the stool in front of the counter, she followed him to the door. "I'm sorry this evening didn't work out—" She almost said, "As I hoped it would," but caught herself in time. "I didn't realize that seeing Annette again would be so upsetting."

After donning his topcoat, he looped his scarf around her waist, letting it drop to her hips. Slowly he pulled on the ends of the scarf, drawing her close. "I owe you a dinner. Rain check?"

The heat of his chest and thighs seeped through her skin to her bones. Helplessly she gazed at him and recognized desire smoldering in his dark eyes. Her breath caught in her throat and her cheeks grew hot. She wondered if he felt her shiver where their bodies touched.

"Rain check," she agreed in a whisper, her eyes dropping to his mouth. And suddenly she realized he was going to kiss her, really kiss her, not a teasing kiss dropped on her nose, or a light brush across her lips, but the kiss they had been building toward for what seemed like aeons. She read his intention in his gaze, felt it when his thighs tensed against her.

The scarf slid to the floor and his hands framed her waist. For a long moment they stood together, not moving, hardly breathing, gazing into each other's eyes as if searching for answers to unspoken questions. They were about to take a step from which there would be no going back.

For one trembling moment, Cathy considered stepping away, considered evading the bright, hot flame that Dev represented. But she inhaled the dizzying scent of him, felt his tense heat, and she could not move away. Her lips parted helplessly and her head tilted up. The tiny sound of yearning that came from deep within her told her that she was lost.

At this moment, it didn't matter that they were fierce rivals. She longed for his kiss, wanted his arms around her, needed to feel the hard heat of his body pressed tightly against her.

As if in a trance, she watched her hands slide up his shoulders and encircle his neck. When her fingers brushed his nape, he groaned and the low sound kindled a blaze in her lower stomach.

Then she did something she had never done before.

In a turnabout that she wouldn't have believed, she became the aggressor and pressed hard against him, guiding his mouth to hers.

The sensation of his lips against her mouth exploded through her body like lightning. Her skin caught fire and her eyes fluttered closed. His arms tightened and she was no longer the aggressor. They embraced with the same raging desire, wildly ardent in their exploration of lips and tongues and darting touches. One kiss demanded another and another, until they were tangled in each other's arms, gasping for breath.

Leaning back in his arms, Cathy placed a hand against her racing heart and fought to breathe normally.

"Good lord," Dev whispered, staring at her.

"I never felt like...I..."

He touched her cheek, his fingertips gentle. "I think we just added an interesting complication to our relationship."

"I didn't realize you were prone to understatement," she said in a shaky voice, trying to smile.

Laughing, he kissed her again, a lingering kiss they ended reluctantly. "If I don't leave right this minute..." he said gruffly, his eyes dark. "I'll call you tomorrow."

Dazed, Cathy leaned against the doorjamb, welcoming the cold air against her hot skin. She watched until the taillights of the Corvette disappeared around the corner before she returned inside.

This was going to be a tense and crazy week, she thought, walking into the kitchen.

On Tuesday she would be at the station all day, taping her regular TV show and the replacement for the contest show. On Wednesday she would meet Annette for their interview lunch. On Saturday she would compete against Devlin and the other master chefs in the culinary contest.

And no matter where she was or what she was doing, she would be thinking about him. She knew that already and wondered if she had fluttered too close to the flame. It didn't matter anymore. He had kissed her, and now it was too late to do anything but fly forward.

Eight

He said: I don't have time for romance.
Maybe next year.

DEV REACHED for the bottle of olive oil to add to the garlic and shallots he was sautéing for this week's TV show. He tilted the bottle and gave a quick shake, the movement calibrated by experience so that he knew he would add exactly a teaspoonful. Except that the pouring spout broke and oil gushed into the pan, drowning the food, and splattering all over Dev's shirt.

"Cut!" Scott Mortimer yelled. He rushed onto the set, grabbing a cloth and rubbing at the grease on Dev's shirt, only making the stains larger and more visible. He waved his clipboard in a familiar sign of impending panic. "Dev, what's going on here? So far we've spent three hours trying to tape a half-hour show and all we have is a series of disasters."

"What's going on is that people are messing with my equipment," Dev snapped, pulling off his shirt and tossing it into the darkness surrounding the set. "There's no way the pouring spout on that oil could have come off by itself, any more than the eggs could have been rotten, or the faucet could have suddenly started spraying water because the valve *just happened* to stick."

Scott turned pale. "What are you suggesting? That somebody's sabotaging the show? That's impossible—they'd never get access to the set." Despite his vehement denial, Scott grabbed a towel to mop his sweating brow and scurried around the kitchen, shaking bottles and pulling open cupboard doors in a frenzy of impromptu testing.

Was he being paranoid? Dev wondered as he wiped up spilled olive oil, cleaning off the stove elements so that they wouldn't smoke next time he used them. Annette Dunning's unexpected arrival in Denver had him on edge…with reason, in view of the fact that she'd told both him and Cathy that she wouldn't be arriving until today. But just because he and Cathy had discovered that she'd had dinner with Paul Lyman, forty-eight hours before she was due to get into town, was that grounds for leaping to the conclusion that she was sabotaging his TV show for KDID? Maybe. Dev wasn't sure how far Annette's thirst for revenge might stretch, but he feared the worst. On the other hand, accidents did happen, and he shouldn't let his suspicions run away with his common sense.

He had just finished talking himself into a more reasonable state of mind when Scott let out a howl, and marched over to Dev's side, his face twisted into an expression of such exaggerated dismay that in other circumstances it would have been comic.

"The oven's not working!" Scott delivered his line with enough tragic overtones to do justice to Hamlet's death scene. "I switched it on, and nothing happened! Oh, boy, are we screwed! We're going to run out of studio time and lose the production crew before we've finished taping. We'll be left with no show for this week. Oh my God!"

The oven not working made four minor, but time-consuming disasters in the space of fifteen minutes. Dev gave up trying to persuade himself that the mishaps were coincidence. He could see Annette's manicured fingerprints all over the afternoon's troubles.

"Don't worry," he said to Scott with determined calm. Damned if he was going to hand Annette the victory of being put off stride by her machinations. "I don't need the oven today, that's why it wasn't turned to preheat. And we can get it fixed long before next week's show. No big deal, Scott. Providing there are no more accidents, we can finish the taping on time."

Scott whirled across the set and shut the oven door with a bang. "I'm gonna give maintenance an earful," he growled, his alarm changing to self-righteous anger. "They're supposed to check the equipment right before we start taping. The idiots never do their jobs properly, then I get hauled over the coals when the production costs escalate."

Dev hesitated for a moment, then decided to say nothing. Since Scott had chosen to blame the maintenance department, there was no point in upsetting him by suggesting somebody else might be responsible. Besides, it would be smarter to mention his suspicions of sabotage when the entire production crew wasn't listening. If Annette had already bribed somebody to wreak havoc on the set, Dev would spot the culprit more easily if he pretended to have no clue about what was going on. In fact, for all Dev knew, Scott Mortimer himself might be Annette's accomplice. Unfortunately, she'd always been able to recruit the most unlikely allies. And although Scott was prone to exaggerated highs and lows, wasn't his behavior today a bit too extreme to be genuine? Could he be acting outraged to cover up his guilt?

Dev followed Scott's progress around the studio, then stepped out of the circle of lights illuminating the kitchen to scan the faces of the production crew, searching for signs of complicity. When he realized what he was doing, he turned abruptly, strode back onto the set and tossed the pan of grease-soaked shallots into the trash, sickened by the thread of his own thoughts. Damn it, he wasn't going to start down the slippery slope of suspecting his friends and colleagues of treachery until he was left with no other choice. He wouldn't let Annette's insidious brand of poison trickle back into his life, seeping into his subconscious until every one of his relationships was tainted by doubt.

Banishing Annette from his thoughts, Dev triplechecked everything he would use to prepare this week's menu. Right now, the most important task was to get the show taped and in the can before his concentration broke completely. Scott was screaming orders and showing renewed symptoms of impending panic. Dev drew in a deep breath and refused to speculate on the reasons for Scott's erratic behavior. He wiped the interior of his sauté pan with a paper towel, and resisted the temptation to brain the producer with his own clipboard.

Experience had taught Dev that Scott often calmed down best in the face of specific requests for action. "Any chance we could rustle up another clean shirt?" he asked. "I've already used the spare I brought with me."

One of the young interns spoke up. "We don't have

anything in here," he said. "I'll try makeup. They should have something on hand for the newscasters."

"Or you could borrow mine." Bill Sadler stepped out from behind the camera and held out his arms so that everyone could get a good view of his oversize shirt, striped in a virulent combination of purple and orange. He grinned. "Think you can handle the hordes of women who'll come chasing after you once you put this on, Dev? This shirt's sexual dynamite, you know. I can vouch from experience—you'll have to fight off the women. Look at Penny...she can hardly take her eyes off me."

"That's certainly true," Penny said dryly. "I can't believe what I'm seeing. Wherever I turn, I'm confronted by acres of purple and orange."

Everyone in the studio laughed, and Dev returned Bill's grin, grateful for the way his friend had managed to lower the level of tension. "Thanks for the generous offer, Bill, but that shirt would be false advertising on me. Everyone knows I'm not half the man you are."

"Here's a clean shirt, Dev." The intern returned to the studio at a run, holding out a forest green, stud-collar shirt in a silk-and-linen mixture. "Bernadette says to tell you she's sorry, but this'll have to do. She doesn't have anything else in your size."

Dev took the shirt. The damn thing had so many tabs, flaps and pockets that he looked as if he was going on safari. Or auditioning for a photo shoot in *GQ* magazine. He smothered a groan and reminded himself it wasn't Bernadette's fault that he'd messed up two shirts in one afternoon. He even managed to mutter a brief word of thanks to the intern as he shoved his arms into the sleeves and rolled up the starched cuffs.

Bill peered into his viewfinder and gave an appreciative whistle. "My, my, Dev, your new shirt looks real pretty on camera. That color's just darling on you."

Dev directed a glare at his friend that was ferocious enough to fell a gorilla. Bill gave him the thumbs-up sign.

"Okay, people. Back to work," Scott called. "The shirt's great, Dev. That dark green looks terrific against the yellow background of the kitchen walls."

Dev wasn't reassured to know that he was color-coordinated with the wallpaper, but his show was about cooking, not fashion, so he ordered himself to stop worrying about the way he looked, and walked quickly around the kitchen. After running yet another equipment check to satisfy himself that the set held no more surprises, he moved back to his position between the sink and the stove, and glanced briefly at his notes.

As a relief from the hearty traditionalism of Thanksgiving, he'd decided to prepare one of his favorite seafood recipes, a cioppino *Mediterraneo,* with scallops, mussels and shrimp sautéed with garlic, shallots, white wine and plum tomatoes, served on a bed of homemade linguine. While he cooked, he was going to talk about the ancient town of Ancona, on Italy's Adriatic coast, and the restaurant where he'd first learned to prepare this particular dish. The cathedral in Ancona dated back to the fourth century, and the owner of the restaurant insisted that there were records at the local museum proving that the Romans had been eating a similar seafood dish in the time of Caesar Augustus. Dev had always thought it was a great story, even if he didn't quite believe it.

It was especially important for this week's show to

go well, Dev reflected, as the technicians geared up to start taping again. Cathy Mallory might be sweet, talented and eminently kissable, but there was no way in hell he was going to let her win their bet. On the contrary, he planned to whip her cute, curvaceous butt. If Annette Dunning had hoped to fluster him to the point where he came across on camera sounding flat, or nervous, then she'd seriously misjudged him. There was a lot at stake this week, and Dev was more determined than ever to put on a top-notch show.

He smiled with satisfaction at the mental image of Cathy Mallory standing on his doorstep, ten dollars in hand, forced to concede that "Dining with Devlin" had swept past "Cooking with Cathy" in the ratings. Their comparative audience share had always been important to him, of course, but in the past, his rivalry with Cathy had been abstract and rather dispassionate. Now there was a new and intensely personal element to his feelings. He didn't just want to win the ratings battle, Dev realized. He very badly wanted Cathy to acknowledge that he was the best chef in Denver. The funny thing was that whenever he tried to visualize the moment when Cathy finally confessed that he cooked better than she did, they were always in bed, naked, and wrapped in each other's arms, replete after hours of passionate sex. The fantasy was both enticing and disturbing, since he'd never before experienced any confusion between his professional pride and his sexual desires. But with Cathy, everything seemed to be twisted into one tense, knotted strand.

"Okay. We're gonna take it from the top again." Scott held up his hand. "On my count. You have three...and two...and one." He pointed at Dev.

Dev took his cue and smiled into the camera. "Good

evening, everyone, and welcome to 'Dining with Devlin.' I'm so glad you're able to join me again tonight." The opening was similar to ones he'd spoken fifty times before, but this time he wasn't talking to the composite audience member he'd always had in mind for previous shows. This time, he was talking to Cathy Mallory, one-on-one. He felt her presence on the other side of the camera as clearly as if she'd been in the studio, as completely as if she was the only person in the world who would ever watch this program.

In the past, he'd always tried to emphasize that the demanding techniques of European cuisine could be simplified and adapted to fit the life-styles and kitchen equipment of ordinary American families. This afternoon, with Cathy for his sole audience, he was overcome by the urge to show off the skills he'd worked such brutally long hours to acquire. He chopped shallots with a speed that dazzled the eye and would probably have cut off the fingers of ninety percent of amateur chefs attempting to copy him. He discarded his spatulas and kept the contents of his sauté pan moving with almost indiscernible flicks of his wrist. He measured ingredients by sight, and whipped up a frothy dish of sweetened zabaglione while simultaneously simmering the cioppino. He demonstrated how to make linguine in one of the pasta machines people often got as wedding gifts, or as Christmas presents from spouses who were out of ideas. But then he couldn't resist adding an ad-lib segment, strictly for Cathy's benefit, in which he prepared the noodles faster than the machine, using nothing except his hands for kneading and a sharp knife for cutting the dough into strips.

This time there were no equipment failures during

the preparation of the food, and the finished dish looked and smelled wonderful. He piled the glistening scallops and mussels onto the loops of linguine and scattered chopped chervil over the enticing arrangement just as Scott signaled the final minute of taping.

Dev made none of his usual effort to tone down the hectic pace of the show with sixty seconds of soothing chitchat as he lit candles on the studio dining table. Coiled tight with the triumphant knowledge that this was the best cooking he'd ever done for a TV program, he stared at the camera with fierce intensity, willing Cathy to understand that he'd been cooking only for her.

"With Thanksgiving behind us, and Christmas still ahead, I know you've been busy planning wonderful meals to be enjoyed by all your friends. It's very rewarding to cook treasured family recipes for holiday parties, but don't forget that sometimes you need to take time out for the pleasure of preparing a special meal that's meant to be shared with only one other person."

Dev looked deep into the camera. "Have you ever cooked a favorite recipe to share with someone special? Someone whose mere presence adds a magic extra ingredient to the meal? If you haven't, I hope you will one day very soon."

He poured out a glass of Chianti, twisting the stem of the glass so that the wine swirled in a scarlet shimmer beneath the brilliant overhead lights. "I cooked this dinner tonight for you, the extraordinary woman who recently came into my life. I look forward to the next time we're together, when I can prepare my cioppino *Mediterraneo*...and the gift of your company will turn the meal into an enchanted feast for the two of us."

Scott dragged his hand across his throat, miming a cut. Dev raised his glass and 'took a long, slow sip of Chianti as the credits rolled.

"Okay, folks, that's a wrap." Scott finally put down his clipboard. "Wow and double wow, Dev! That was some windup you did there, even for you. I never understand how you manage to make eating food sound so sexy."

Dev smiled, covering a sudden fatigue. "Food and sex are the two most basic human needs. Why wouldn't they go together?"

Scott helped himself to a plate of cioppino and ate abstractedly. "You know, that's an interesting angle you introduced into this week's show."

"What angle's that?" Dev asked.

"The new and important woman in your life. It's worth developing." Scott was scribbling notes in between taking bites of pasta.

"I'm a chef, Scott, and this program's about cooking. I try never to confuse real life with what goes on in my show."

Dev's protest fell on deaf ears. "The more I think about it, the more I like it," Scott said. "Instead of producing the same old boring holiday menus—Two Hundred New Ways to Stick Silver Balls on Sugar Cookies—we can tease the audience with hints and suggestions that you have a great love affair going on."

"I never thought I'd hear myself defending sugar cookies, Scott, but at least you have to mix 'em and bake 'em. In case you haven't noticed, my love affairs, real or imagined, have nothing to do with cooking."

"Sure they have." Scott waved a forkful of pasta as a substitute for his clipboard. "We could lead up to Valentine's Day with a whole series of programs designed around the concept of recipes for lovers. Aphrodisiac appetizers, erotic entrées, and decadent desserts. Now, am I a genius to come up with an idea like that, or what?"

Dev gave a reluctant laugh. "All right, Scott, I admit the idea has possibilities. I'll work on some menu ideas, okay?"

"'Dining with Devlin', the new daytime soap," Bill said, sampling a shrimp. "Tune in and find out if Chef Gilpatrick succeeded in seducing his mystery lover with last week's recipe for Chocolate Sin."

Dev grinned. "If I do, Bill, you'll be the first to know."

Bill's eyes narrowed with sudden interest, but he simply helped himself to another shrimp and pulled on his jacket. "Can I bum a ride with you, Dev? My sister needed to borrow my car and Jean doesn't get off work for another two hours."

"Sure. I'll be right with you." Dev collected his two soiled shirts and stuffed them into his backpack. "Okay, I'm ready. See you next week, everyone?"

"I wanted to have a word with you alone," Bill said as they made their way out of the building. "Look, Dev, I've no idea what this means, but I happened to be in the studio earlier this afternoon when the maintenance guy came in to check all the equipment in the kitchen. That oven was working fine an hour before showtime, and so was the faucet that darn near flooded the set when you turned it on."

"What are you suggesting?" Dev asked quietly.

"I don't know. Except that you might want to arrive

early for next week's taping, and make sure that you check everything out yourself, personally."

"Yeah, thanks for the tip. I'll do that."

They trudged across the parking lot, collars turned up against the wind. "I heard you went to Cathy Mallory's house for Thanksgiving dinner," Bill said.

Dev shot him a sideways glance, then stared straight ahead. "Yeah. It—um—just kind of happened. No big deal. It doesn't mean anything."

"I'm sure it doesn't." Bill's voice was smooth as cornstarch. "And I guess that smoldering invitation at the end of today's show was sheer coincidence. No way Cathy Mallory could be the fascinating woman who's just come into your life."

"Of course not." Dev was rather pleased with the firm, no-nonsense way he issued his denial.

Bill didn't say anything, and Dev hastily filled the silence. "Cathy Mallory isn't my type. No way. Besides, it's a rule of mine never to get involved with a fellow chef. God knows, there's enough to argue about when you're married, without adding mortal combat over the amount of tarragon to use in stuffing a chicken breast."

It was quite dark in the parking lot, but Bill's air of satisfaction was unmistakable. "Interesting," he murmured.

"What? The amount of tarragon to use when you stuff chicken?"

"No. The fact that I asked you a simple question about Thanksgiving dinner and before I could catch my breath you were explaining why it would be a lousy idea to marry Cathy."

"I only said all that stuff because you and Jean are determined to marry us off!"

"Sure, Dev. Whatever you say."

Dev glared over the top of his car. "You can wipe that self-satisfied smirk off your face, big boy, or you're gonna be riding home in a cab."

"Okay." Bill levered himself into the passenger seat of the Corvette. "What's the latest on the AUS deal? Heard anything more from your old girlfriend?"

"I'm supposed to be having dinner with her tonight at the Westin downtown. I've no idea why she wants to pretend there's still a chance I could get the job, but I guess I have to go through the motions."

Bill thought for a moment. "Why?" he asked finally. "If you're really sure that you've got nothing to lose, why not call her bluff? Beats the hell out of sitting opposite her and allowing yourself to become her dupe."

"You're right," Dev said. "Except that Annette never makes it easy for a person to call her bluff. Before you can do that, you need to know what game you're playing. And in my experience, Annette doesn't let you know that until the game's over."

"Then change the game," Bill suggested. "Make her play by your rules…and watch her squirm."

BILL'S SUGGESTION was an excellent one, Dev thought as he handed his car keys to the parking valet and rode the elevator to the hotel restaurant. After all, he had nothing to lose, since in this chess match that Annette had concocted, he was sure that the endgame involved some elaborate scheme designed to cause Dev maximum personal and professional humiliation.

He was two minutes early, but Annette was already seated at a table by the window. She appeared to be admiring the nighttime view of the city, but she must have seen his reflection in the glass, because she rose to her feet as he crossed the room, and held out her hands in welcome.

The added years suited her, Dev thought. She'd always worn her hair pulled back into a chignon, and she hadn't changed the style, but she'd lost weight so that the bone structure of her face was now revealed with flattering clarity. Her eyes appeared larger than he remembered, her complexion smoother, her fashionably thin body shown off to perfection in a tailored satin evening suit. Everything about her appearance was elegant, low-key and businesslike, and yet Dev was intensely aware of the sensual aura that surrounded her, a shimmering cloud of potent sexual invitation. He hadn't expected to feel the pull of her sexuality, and he tensed, chagrined that he still needed to fortify himself against her allure.

Her eyes sparkled as she greeted him, and she appeared so delighted to see him that Dev felt momentarily dazed. "Devlin Gilpatrick!" she exclaimed. "My goodness, you look magnificent! Even better than I remembered…and that was pretty terrific!"

Laughing softly, she took his hands into hers and stood on tiptoe to kiss the air next to his cheek. She smelled of Chanel No 5, the same perfume she'd always worn. Up this close, he could see that her lips glistened as if she'd just moistened them with her tongue. Her teeth were small and very white and he remembered exactly how they'd felt nipping his skin. Shockingly, despite everything he knew about her, he felt a renewed tug of desire, a mind-blowing moment when he wanted to close the gap between them and kiss her. He froze, repelled by his own reaction.

"What is it, Dev?" Annette dropped his hands and stepped back, her gaze traveling over him in concerned and friendly appraisal. When her gaze lingered briefly on his mouth, Dev felt heat flare along his cheekbones. Annette lowered her eyes and turned away but not before Dev had seen her mouth curve into a tiny, satisfied smile.

That smile brought him to his senses. The confident smugness of it told Dev everything he needed to know about Annette's motives in coming to Denver. However much she might flatter him, and claim an eagerness to start afresh, that smile betrayed the truth. Annette hadn't forgiven him, and she never would. She was here to wreak revenge, and she thought he was too stupid to realize it. Dev's flash of physical desire congealed into revulsion.

Courtesy seemed the best option until he could get a better handle on what she was up to. "Annette, how are you?" he asked as they both sat down. "I hope I haven't kept you waiting?"

"Not at all. It's been a hectic day, so I was happy to relax for a few minutes and enjoy the view. The mountains are spectacular, aren't they? They make the Alps seem petty by comparison."

"The Alps *are* small in comparison to the Rockies."

"Yes, I guess they are." Annette gave a little sigh. "I miss Europe more and more as the years pass. Do you remember when we went to Gstaad and you taught me to ski? We had fun, didn't we?"

"Yes," Dev agreed, conceding the truth. "We had a great time." They'd made the trip to Gstaad in the early days of their relationship when he'd still been blinded by infatuation. Even with the advantage of hindsight, his memories of their time there were pleasant ones, of sunshine, fast runs down slick ski slopes, and long nights of passionate sex. Odd that he could remember how much he'd enjoyed himself at the same time as he realized how hollow that enjoyment had been. There'd never been any laughter between him and Annette. No shared jokes, none of the quiet sense of companionship he felt with Cathy.

"Have you skied the Rockies?" he asked, taking menus from a hovering waiter and agreeing with Annette that they should order a bottle of Merlot. "I try to get to Vail or Steamboat Springs at least a couple of times a year."

"No, unfortunately I don't have nearly enough time to play these days." Annette gave a self-deprecating chuckle. "Somehow, I seem to have turned into one of those single-minded career women I always used to despise."

It was easy to see what sort of a mood Annette wanted to create, Dev decided. She was taking every opportunity to show him that she harbored no resentment over the past, and that she could even laugh a little at her own younger self. Maybe it was time to remind her that—however pretty the picture she painted—he wasn't suffering from selective amnesia.

"Yes, that is a change," he said. "What happened to turn you against the idea of marriage?"

He wouldn't have been surprised if she'd thrown her glass of water straight in his face. But all she did was gasp quietly. "Oh, Dev, that was a low blow." She turned her head away, pressing her napkin to her mouth. Her eyes squeezed shut, as if she were overcome by the crush of memories.

Five years ago in Paris, Dev would have been guilt-stricken. Now, he simply looked at her, wondering how long it would take before she concluded this tactic wasn't working and switched to another.

The waiter provided a diversion by bringing their wine, and Dev asked Annette if she wanted to do the tasting. She gave him a brave little smile. "No, you have so much more experience with wine than I do, Dev. You're the professional, after all."

Impatient with her refusal to confront the reality of their past, he gestured to the waiter to pour a taste of the Merlot into his glass. When the little ritual was over and they were alone again, Annette was once more sitting up straight in her seat, her brave smile gone, her expression thoughtful.

Dev decided it was time to follow Bill's advice and take the initiative. Wherever Annette's thoughts were taking her, Dev suspected he wouldn't like the destination. He raised his glass. "A toast," he said. "I think we need a toast, don't you?"

"To old times?" she suggested.

Dev shook his head. "That doesn't seem quite right for the occasion. How about...to new opportunities?"

Annette smiled and took a sip of wine. "I'll drink to that."

Dev watched her, his expression grim. Then he put down his glass without drinking and leaned across the table. "Tell me about your friend Paul Lyman. Is he one of your new opportunities that we should talk about, Annette?"

The hesitation before she replied lasted a second too long, but she recovered quickly, as he'd expected her to. "Paul Lyman?" she said, sounding bewildered. "Is he someone I'm supposed to know?"

They'd played this game of lies, accusation and denial a hundred times before, and Dev discovered that he was heartily sick of it. He could have told Annette that he knew she'd been to Su Lin's restaurant with

Paul Lyman, but he'd learned from a dozen similar scenes in the past that she would simply deny everything to the point that he would end up doubting what he knew, whereas she would be left in no doubt at all as to how he had found out about their relationship.

He let his gaze rest on her, contemptuous of her machinations. "You don't lie as well as you used to, Annette."

She was flustered, but she was too old a hand at deception to lose her cool completely. "Dev, if I've met Paul Lyman, I don't remember the occasion or the reason for our meeting. Who is he, for heaven's sake, and why do you think I would be interested in him?"

"He's the president and general manager of KDID, the television station I work for. And there's only one reason I can think of why you would be interested in him."

Her fingers tapped once against her wineglass, then stopped. "What reason is that?"

Dev smiled without mirth. "You tell me, Annette. What role have you assigned to Paul Lyman in your grand scheme to screw me over?"

Chapter Nine

She said: Trust is the white sauce of all lasting relationships.

ALTHOUGH CATHY ARRIVED early for lunch, Annette was already seated. When Annette spotted her, she slid out of the banquette and stood with a smile. Cathy's heart sank. From the top of her shining dark chignon to the tips of her sleek Italian pumps, Annette was the picture of slender, tailored elegance. Astonishingly she managed to imbue stylish business attire with a hint of seductiveness that, Cathy noted, wasn't lost on the three businessmen lunching at a nearby table.

With abrupt insight, Cathy realized her secret desire to be a sophisticated fashion plate had originated during the brief time she had roomed with Annette in college. Annette had shaped her fantasy of glamour and cosmopolitan chic, an image she consistently failed to achieve. Instead of tailored subtlety, something in her nature unerringly guided her toward items like the flowing Carole Little outfit she wore today. Garments that were soft and feminine; no hard edges, no power suits.

If nothing else came of this lunch, she had just learned to stop fighting her own image. She did not want to pattern herself after Annette Dunning, past, present or future. Feeling a tiny spurt of wary confidence, she walked forward, encouraged when she noticed the long flattering stares from the nearby businessmen.

"Hi, Kansas. You look wonderful." Annette extended her hand.

Cathy hesitated, then pressed Annette's hand in a cursory shake. "You haven't changed a bit," she noted cautiously.

Annette slid into the banquette with a laugh. "I hope I *have* changed. Wouldn't it be awful if we remained the callow people we were in college? I'd certainly like to think that I've grown and matured since those crazy days." She shook her head with a look of affectionate dismissal then signaled the waiter. "Would you like a glass of wine?"

"I'd prefer coffee, thank you."

"A split of Pouilly-Fumé, please, and coffee for my friend." She returned her full attention to Cathy. "So. What have you been doing since I saw you last? I know your professional history, of course, but is there a husband? Do you have children?"

"I'm not married. I've come close once or twice, but…"

"Really?" One perfectly shaped eyebrow lifted. "I always saw you as the type who would marry the team quarterback right after graduation, move into a traditional two-story, and have two-point-five children."

If Annette hadn't been smiling, Cathy would have wondered if she'd just been insulted. The suspicion occurred anyway.

"How about you?" she inquired after the wine and coffee arrived. "A husband? Children?"

"Who has time for a family?" Annette said with a smile. "Right now, my career requires all of my energy."

"I can see how it would," Cathy agreed, speaking

slowly. "Being a vice president at AUS is quite an accomplishment." Whatever she thought about Annette Dunning, Annette had indeed risen to the heights. Or was it a job with more title than power and substance?

"Ah, but I've just begun."

And suddenly there it was. The smile. That unpleasant smile that Cathy remembered so well. A smile that combined cunning and secret knowledge, a Machiavellian smugness that called to mind plots and schemes and calculated manipulations. In the past that smile had signaled trouble for someone.

The only someone present was Cathy.

Shifting uneasily, she tried to think of a reply. "By that comment I take it you must have your eye on the presidency of AUS."

"Not exactly." Amusement and something predatory sparkled in Annette's eyes. Cathy had a startled thought that a cat must look at a mouse with a similar expression. "I can't go into details, but I'm putting together a deal that...well, let's just say the glass ceiling is about to shatter. Some hidebound executives are going to be very, very surprised, and some scores are going to be settled." This time her devilish smile didn't reach her eyes. Then, suddenly she looked at Cathy and laughed.

That was the moment when Cathy understood with absolute certainty that Devlin was right. Somehow, some way, Annette was going to avenge herself on both of them. Gut instinct told Cathy that Annette's revenge would occur as a side benefit of the deal she'd just mentioned. Revenge would be the icing on Annette's sweet deal.

While Cathy pondered this worrisome thought, the waiter arrived to take their luncheon order. Annette waved the menus aside. "If you don't mind," she said to Cathy, "I'll order for us both." She smiled at the waiter. "This isn't on the menu but I've made arrangements with the chef. We'll have fillet of sole *bonne femme*."

A flash of resentment heated Cathy's cheeks. She *did* mind. Annette was calling all the shots, rolling right over her. Annette was directing the conversation, Annette had selected the menu, Annette was making every decision based on her own private agenda.

It was time to exert at least a semblance of control. Cathy put her hand on her briefcase, resting on the banquette beside her. "I brought a concept sheet and some script proposals for the syndicated show. I don't know what you had in mind for the interview process, but perhaps you'd like to look over my material."

Annette shrugged and refilled her wineglass. "I'll look over the material if you like, but my decision is made." One eyebrow rose above a smile. "Of course, it would help me justify my selection if you'd win the upcoming culinary contest."

Cathy's heart rolled over in her chest and she found it hard to breathe. "You've definitely decided to award the show to me?"

"Just between us, I made the decision before I arrived in Denver."

A dozen emotions flooded Cathy's mind: elation, happiness, a twinge of sympathy for Dev, and suspicion. Annette's reference to her arrival reminded Cathy of seeing her and Paul Lyman outside Su Lin's restaurant. There was something very strange about that.

Suddenly she wondered how Dev's interview with Annette had turned out. She'd hoped he would call and share a few details, but he hadn't. Maybe sitting down to dinner with a woman he had jilted at the altar had been too painful to discuss. Maybe Annette had made it plain that he was not going to win the syndication slot. Dev and Annette's evening together was none of Cathy's business, of course...yet she was dying to know about it.

Abruptly it occurred to her that she was falling in love with the same man that Annette had intended to marry. She blinked and looked down at her lap. If Annette ever found out about *that*... A light shudder passed down Cathy's spine. She didn't want to even think about Annette's reaction if she learned that Cathy and Dev were seeing each other. Yet Dev was very much on her mind today.

"Annette...there's something I think we need to discuss." Frowning, she leaned back as the waiter served their sole with a flourish. "It looks and smells wonderful," she murmured automatically. Actually, she'd lost her appetite.

"What would that be?"

"I'm pleased and flattered that you've chosen me for the syndication show. I think you can guess what syndication will do for my career and how much this means to me. But I'm uneasy about being selected beforehand. I never thought I'd say something like this...but I wonder if you've made this decision for the right reasons."

She could not believe she was toying with fate like this. Looking a gift horse squarely in the mouth. Still, a strong sense of fair play rose stubbornly to the surface. She had wanted to win the syndication because she was the best choice for the position, not because Annette hated Dev more than she hated Cathy.

Annette's head came up sharply. "What are you talking about?"

"Annette, I know that you and Devlin Gilpatrick had

a relationship in the past." She drew a breath. "I understand it ended badly."

"Who told you that?" Annette demanded, putting down her fork.

"I'd rather not say." In fact, she would submit to torture before she admitted Dev had told her.

Annette tilted her head back and frowned at the ceiling. "It has to be someone I knew in Paris." She lowered a glare to Cathy. "We both knew Claudette Manning in college. It was Claudette, wasn't it?"

"The point is, I'd prefer to be selected because I'm the best choice for the new show rather than because you're carrying a grudge against the other candidate."

Annette blinked in astonishment. "Devlin Gilpatrick is your archrival. Everyone in town knows the two of you compete against each other, can't stand each other! Why on earth would you care why I picked you over him? It's enough that you won, isn't it?"

Cathy felt her stomach tense. "I'd rather have won fairly," she insisted quietly.

"Good God." Annette leaned against the back of the banquette and stared. "I didn't realize such naiveté still existed."

The comment triggered all Cathy's insecurities and made her feel foolish. Annette's expression and tone of voice made traditional values of fair play seem depressingly old-fashioned and hopelessly ingenuous.

"Kansas, it's you who hasn't changed. You're as gullible as ever. A sitting duck."

And there was that smile again.

CATHY HAD INTENDED to run some errands after lunch. But the interview with Annette left her disturbed and upset enough that she drove home instead, deciding she would calm herself by baking a sugar-and-cinnamon coffee cake. Comfort food for a cold day.

When she walked up her porch steps, she noticed a small package propped against her front door, accompanied by a note. Curious, Cathy turned the note right side up, then smiled.

Sorry I missed you. If the cioppino *Mediterraneo* sounds good, come to dinner tonight and sample it for yourself. My place, seven o'clock. Bring nothing but your sweet self.

                                                                Dev

Having forgotten about the coffee cake, the first thing Cathy did was open the package. Inside was a tape, which she immediately popped into the VCR. She watched it through twice, then made a cup of cappuccino and settled into a corner of the sofa to do some thinking.

She wasn't certain whether she was more elated by the wonderful comments directed at her on the tape, or more depressed by how genuinely gifted Dev was in the kitchen. Both emotions warred in her mind.

"What do you think, Romeo?" she asked absently, dropping a hand to scratch behind his ears. "Am I just feeling insecure after the lunch with Annette? Or am I looking a truth squarely in the eye? Is Dev a better cook than I am?"

Modesty was a lifelong habit, and self-deprecating remarks came easily to her. The danger lay in believing her own denials. Frowning, warming her hands around the coffee cup, she gazed unseeingly out the window.

She hadn't served an apprenticeship in Europe as Dev had, but her training was equal to his. She didn't have to take a back seat to anyone. The dishes she chose to present on "Cooking With Cathy" were simple everyday dishes because she believed her audience was composed of busy women more inclined to prepare a wonderful new meat loaf recipe for a weeknight dinner than they would be to prepare something like Dev's fabulous cioppino *Mediterraneo*. But had she chosen to do so, she could have prepared any dish that Dev did, and done it equally as well.

Couldn't she?

Or had her genuine interest in and passion for improving everyday meals eroded the skills required for preparing more difficult and complicated dishes? If so, did that make her a lesser chef than Dev, or merely a different kind of chef?

"The real question, of course," she murmured, "is which of us really and truly deserves to win the syndication?"

After a few minutes, she dropped her head and rubbed her temples. Annette had promised her the syndication. The only reason she still worried about it was...

Because she had hoped to win honestly and fairly. Coming in second would have been easier to live with than winning unfairly, as it appeared she had. Plus, she didn't know what winning would do to her budding romance with Dev. How would he take the news that he'd lost a fabulous career opportunity because years ago he had jilted Annette Dunning? He'd said he expected it, but how would he feel when it actually happened?

And there was the little matter of her side bet with Dev. Would his marvelous presentation of the cioppino *Mediterraneo* garner more ratings points than her show featuring turkey leftovers? It was a silly thing to worry about. But it was also a chance to win something honestly.

DEV HUNG HER COAT in the hall closet then brushed a light kiss across her lips. "Thanks for coming."

"You knew I would," she said in a husky voice, gazing into his eyes and trying to decide if they were gray or green. "The cioppino smells wonderful. And what a beautiful home you have!"

His penthouse condominium was situated on a high corner, with banks of windows overlooking the lights of downtown Denver. For a moment, Cathy stood still, awed by the view. "Can you see the mountains in the daylight? Of course you can. Stupid question." The terrace running beyond the living room windows would offer a magnificent sweep of the Rocky Mountains.

He'd furnished the interior in masculine tones of brown and cream with burgundy and blue accents. Her feet sank in thick carpet as she moved to the center of the living room and looked around at sleek lines and uncluttered vistas. "That's an impressive audio setup," she remarked. But the artwork took her breath away. Slowly, she moved around the room, admiring his selections. "The art is fabulous. Did you buy these paintings in Europe?"

"Most of them," he said, sounding pleased. "Would you like a drink?"

"Wine would be fine."

Aside from the artwork, his home looked oddly unfinished to her eye. Or maybe she was just accustomed to the homey clutter of her place. But his condominium struck her as rather impersonal. It might have been a show home. She didn't see any family photographs like those that covered the walls in her office, or collections like hers of antique utensils. The rooms impressed her as too perfect. She would have liked to see a couple of tacky but personal souvenirs, a jumble of papers or books somewhere. But about the only personal touch was Dev's cat, whom he had introduced as Ramses. Ramses had so far displayed a disdainful lack of interest in Cathy. She smiled, thinking about Romeo's slavish devotion to anyone who came into her house and paid him the slightest bit of attention.

Wandering, she walked through the dining room, appreciating the candles and flowers on the table, admiring the starlit view they would enjoy during dinner. Her practiced eye recognized Baccarat crystal and Limoges china. Following a wonderful fragrance, she found the kitchen. "Is there anything I can do to help?"

"Yes," Dev said, wiping his hands on a white muslin towel. "Sit there on the stool and inspire me. Your wine is on the countertop."

"Wonderful kitchen," she murmured, grinning because the layout was so similar to her own that she could have moved around it blindfolded. Then, watching him chop fresh chervil, her expression sobered. There was nothing sexier than a man moving confidently around a kitchen. Good Lord, he was handsome. Watching him made her stomach tighten and her palms feel moist. "Dev...thank you for the lovely things you said on your show..."

He paused at the cutting block and gave her a look that all but stopped her heart. "I swore I would never talk about my personal life on the show, except perhaps in the past tense. But I can't get you out of my mind," he said softly.

"Ah, 'past tense,' like the beautiful countess or the baroness you eased out of your life over Wiener schnitzel?" She tried to keep her voice light, tried not to stare at the wide, firm shape of his mouth.

A frown replaced his smile, then he laughed. "You thought...? Frau von Schadler was not a countess or a baroness. She was a delightfully acerbic eighty-five-year-old woman who gave me my first job as a sous-chef. I never worked so hard in my life, or learned so much. She was a remarkable woman." His knife flew through the chervil. "Frau von Schadler died last year, I'm sorry to say. I think of her often." Looking up, he grinned and winked. "I only wish I were as romantic a figure as people seem to think I am. Would it surprise you to learn that I haven't had a serious relationship in over three years?"

She considered the question. "A month ago, I would have been astonished. But now, I don't think so." Now she'd learned that he wasn't the frivolous man-about-town she had previously assumed he was. There was a seriousness about Dev, an intense commitment to his career, that argued against superficial attachments. "I think there's more to you than your public image suggests."

"My public image." He rolled his eyes. "I can thank the station's PR department for that carefully constructed fiction. If they had their way, I'd never be seen without a debutante or a model on one arm, and a cookbook or a Cuisinart in the other arm."

Cathy laughed. "Our PR department actually designed a gingham evening gown for me. Can you believe it? Their fondest wish is that I'll go to bed one night and wake up looking like Doris Day or Dinah Shore."

For a long moment they looked at each other, the word "bed" hanging suggestively between them. When

Cathy reached for her wineglass to get past the moment, she almost tipped it over on the countertop.

"So," she said brightly, "how did your interview go with Annette?"

"It started badly but ended rather well," he said, turning his back to her to fill a large pot with water. His answer puzzled her because of the frown she'd noticed before he turned to the sink. "How did your interview go?"

"The opposite of yours. It started well and ended rather badly."

He looked up immediately. "Cathy, I'm sorry."

The intensity in his voice and eyes surprised her. He turned off the water and gazed at her with what appeared to be sympathy beyond what was warranted. Tilting her head, she tried to conceal her curiosity. "It's all right. The interview was just a little upsetting, that's all. But then, I expected it would be."

After wiping off his hands, he walked to where she sat on the stool beside the countertop and lifted her chin so he could peer into her eyes. "You're being a good sport about this. I guess I knew you would be. Still, I wish it had been anyone other than Annette Dunning who'd been assigned to make the decision. It isn't fair, Cathy."

"I agree," she said, puzzled. If she hadn't known better, she would have thought that Devlin believed *he* had won the syndication and was offering comfort and consolation.

His thumb lightly traced across her lower lip and for a moment she thought he would kiss her. But he moved back to place the water on the stove top to boil, and set out a platter of homemade pasta. "I've been thinking about our situation." When he looked at her, his eyes were very serious. "Frankly, I was concerned about the syndication deal, but we seem to be handling that, thanks to you in large part."

From his words, Cathy realized that he meant she wasn't rubbing it in that she'd won. It was obviously his roundabout way of informing her that he knew he'd lost. This was a subject, she thought uneasily, that apparently neither of them were yet comfortable addressing directly.

"Something important is happening between us, and if you agree, I'd like to see where that something leads."

"I agree," she whispered, unable to look away from him. A kernel of relief opened in her chest. She'd been a little worried that she was imagining the powerful chemistry between them, or that she'd read more into what he'd said on his show than he had intended.

"You've become important to me. But the only way we can continue is if we're able to separate personal and professional concerns. The culinary contest and the AUS syndication put stresses on both of us, plus our cooking shows. But you seem to be handling, ah, everything remarkably well—"

"So are you."

"I guess what I'm trying to say is—" a smile curved his lips "—do you think we can have a relationship when we're trying like hell to best each other in our professional lives?"

She returned his smile. "I think we can try. But, Dev, I also think it's unrealistic to suggest that we ignore our shows and the culinary contest and—" she took a breath "—the syndication deal. These things are important in our lives. I don't think we can have an open relationship if there are entire areas that we can't share." When she looked at him, her eyes were shining. She couldn't be-

lieve they were discussing a relationship. Suddenly, it
seemed that all her dreams were coming true: the syndication opportunity, Dev... And the way he was handling losing the syndication slot elicited a rush of admiration. She doubted she would have done as well if she
had been the one discussing a relationship with the person who had just won her dream.

"I'm not suggesting that we set up conversational ta-
boos. I'm just saying that we need to be aware that the
Devlin Gilpatrick who wants to beat you in the ratings
and who wants to win the culinary contest is not the
same Devlin Gilpatrick who is cooking you dinner tonight and who wants to make love to you."

Her fingers twitched and droplets of wine spilled over
the back of her hand. She held her breath and slowly
expelled it. Somewhere, deep inside, she had known
they would make love tonight. She hadn't let herself
think about it or try to imagine it, just in case she was
mistaken. But she had shaved her legs, and she had
worn her best lingerie. She had spritzed cologne in
places she usually didn't.

"Would it be fair to say the same holds true for you?"
he asked.

"Yes," she whispered, meeting his gaze. And she saw
in his eyes that tonight would end in his bed if that was
what she wanted. And she did. She stared at him and
listened to her heart pound, noticed the tremble in her
fingers. Oh, yes. As uncharacteristic as it was for her to
throw caution to the winds and simply follow her heart,
she knew that was what she wanted. She wanted Dev
with an intensity she hadn't experienced before. That
was what made him so dangerous for her. With him,
circumstances and consequences didn't matter. All that
mattered was the pulse drumming in her ears, the weak-

ness in her stomach when she looked at him, the way the sound of his voice made her feel and the electricity that raced through her body when he touched her. Then, everything else faded to insignificance. Being with him was what mattered, not contests or competitions or ratings.

"The water is boiling over," she said when she could speak.

He tore his gaze from her and moved the pot off the burner with a laugh. "Damn. That's the first time I've done *that* in years!"

The tension between them eased somewhat. Both of them knew how this evening would end. Now they could relax and enjoy the buildup, could talk and tease without doubt or confusion.

Through dinner they watched each other across the table, and Cathy noticed small wonderful things about Dev. She decided she adored the tiny wrinkles at the corners of his eyes, thought it was sexy the way he used his silverware in the European fashion. She enjoyed his memories about growing up in Chicago, made him laugh with her stories of Kansas. They discovered a shared passion for old Humphrey Bogart movies and the early songs of the Beatles. Neither had been to the Caribbean, but both wanted to visit the islands some day and sample conch cakes and Bahamian cuisine.

"Your meal was wonderful," Cathy said, realizing they had talked about everything but cooking. She wouldn't have believed she could enjoy a meal so much without once mentioning the preparation of the main dish or without trying to guess exactly what ingredients had gone into it. She also realized that she had finished every morsel of his excellent cioppino but had no memory of eating a single spoonful. What she would remem-

ber about this dinner were the twin candle flames reflected in Dev's eyes and the way he didn't seem able
to look away from her. She would remember the shiver
of pleasure that ran up her spine when he laughed, and
the heat that raced along her skin when his fingertips
brushed her hand or wrist. Devlin was what she would
remember about tonight.

"Would you like coffee? Brandy?" he inquired in a
husky voice, his gaze on her lips. His eyes lifted to hers.
"Or shall we end this torture?"

Cathy moistened her lips with her tongue and heard
him draw a soft, sharp breath that was almost a groan.
If teasing and game-playing had come naturally to her,
she might have drawn out their time at the table. Instead, what she possessed was a sense of timing. And
she knew that neither of them could bear much more
of the tension that had mounted along with their desire
for each other.

Exactly as she intended, he read her answer in her
eyes. Laying aside his napkin, he stood and wordlessly
drew her to her feet. For a long moment, he held her
in a loose embrace and gazed deeply into her eyes. In
that moment, Cathy understood that this would not be
an impulsive or careless relationship for him, any more
than it could be for her. They were making a commitment to each other. Perhaps it was no more than a
commitment to explore the possibilities that resonated
between them. Possibly it was a commitment for much
more. Whatever she read in his eyes, it was enough that
when he finally kissed her, she gave herself totally, melting into the heat of him and letting the passion they
ignited in each other sweep her away.

Later, she couldn't recall how they got from the dining
room to his bedroom. One minute they were wrapped

in each other's arms, reflected in the dining room windows. The next moment, they were kissing in Dev's master suite. She remembered candles around the bed and romantic music in the background, but didn't remember Dev leaving her for an instant.

Taking their time, drawing out the moment, they undressed each other, pausing to kiss places slowly uncovered. As hands wandered, their lips moved from mouth to chest, from throat to breast. And finally Cathy stood before him in black lace lingerie and he stood next to her in silk boxer shorts. It touched her heart that he too had carefully chosen what he wore tonight.

And then, the time for leisurely exploration had passed. They'd fought to hold emotion and desire in check, but the sight of each other's emerging, naked bodies swept aside all rational deliberation. They came together in a kiss that rocked Cathy to her core. She felt his fingers on her back, fumbling with hooks, and she pushed at the waist of his silk boxers. But all she was really aware of was the thrill of his mouth possessing hers.

When they tumbled onto the bed, locked in a heated embrace, she surrendered herself completely to the urgency trembling through her body. "Dev," she whispered, arching her throat to his hot kisses. "Dev, Dev."

She hadn't doubted that he would be a skilled lover, and he was. His hands and lips coaxed responses from her that she hadn't known herself capable of. Shyly at first, then with growing confidence, she experimented with giving him the same breathless pleasure he gave to her, gratified when she heard his low groans and hoarse voice.

When they finally came together, the moment was cataclysmic. Cathy drew a sharp breath of surprise and joy and opened her eyes to find him looking down at her with an expression that mirrored her own.

"My God," he murmured huskily. His fingers shook slightly when he smoothed a tendril of damp hair off her cheek. "Cathy. Beautiful Cathy."

They made love to each other slowly, then urgently, then slowly again, experimenting with something new and wonderful, convincing themselves that what they were experiencing was not a fragile thing that would shatter, was not a figment of imagination.

Afterward, they lay in each other's arms, waiting for their breath to quiet, for their bodies to cool. Tears of happiness sparkled in Cathy's eyes.

"That was like…like…the first time I ever tasted champagne," she murmured when she could speak. "Surprising, unexpected, and totally wonderful! Wait. It was more like the first truly excellent crème brûlée! Remember your first crème brûlée? Smooth, silky, exciting!"

His arms tightened around her and he rested his chin on top of her tousled curls. "For me it was more like the first time I ate Sacher torte in Vienna. I knew it was going to be different from American chocolate cake, but I had no idea how different it would be." He dropped a kiss on the end of her nose. "Different and wonderful."

"I remind you of Sacher torte? Hmm…" Cathy tilted her head back and grinned up at him. They laughed at themselves, then Dev kissed her, his hands moving beneath the sheets. She gasped. "Yes," she murmured, her voice throaty. "Oh, yes…" Then something furry flicked across her ear and she sat up suddenly, blinking down at Ramses, who had settled himself on the far end of her pillow. Laughing, she shoved a wave of hair out of her eyes. "Before we go too much further, perhaps you'd like to remove our audience?"

"Damn," Dev murmured with an exaggerated frown. "How did you get in here?" After carrying Ramses to the door and closing it on the cat's baleful stare, he returned to the bed. "Now...where were we?"

"There," she whispered with a sigh of pleasure. "Oh, yes...right there."

THE FIRST PEARLY PINKS of dawn had lit the highest mountain peaks when Dev, wrapped in a paisley robe, followed her to his front door. He took her in his arms, kissed her lingeringly, and gazed down at her with sleepy, sated eyes.

"I wish you'd let me drive you home."

"I have my car," she murmured, pressing her head against his shoulder and smiling. "Devlin, thank you for dinner, and... The evening was just...wonderful."

He tilted her face up to him and smiled into her eyes. "You were spectacular."

They stood in the foyer kissing, touching, murmuring goodbyes. Finally Cathy stepped backward with a laugh. "I have to go, really. Romeo will be worried."

Dev grinned. "We can't have that." He kissed her again, his hands possessive on her waist. "We're both going to be frantically busy until after the culinary contest on Saturday. Shall we plan to meet after the awards ceremony?"

Cathy tilted her head and gave him a mischievous look. "If you don't mind waiting while I accept the award...."

He gave her a light pat on the fanny, then opened the door for her and grinned. "Actually, I pictured you in the audience applauding when *I* won the award."

"However it works out, we'll meet afterward." She stepped into the plushly carpeted corridor. "Good luck." She really meant it. Since she had the syndication sewn up, it seemed fair that he should win the Chefs' Culinary Contest. To hell with Annette. Since Annette had already made her decision, it didn't seem to matter much if Cathy took second place in the contest. That settled, she could genuinely wish Dev well and almost hope that he won.

"Good luck to you, too." He hesitated and a frown appeared between his eyes. "I never thought I'd say something like this, but...I don't think I'd mind too much if you beat me. I mean, I want to win, but if I can't win, then I'd like you to." He threw out his hands and looked charmingly apologetic. "I'm not saying this very well, am I?"

Cathy laughed, loving him, wondering if her feelings were revealed in her eyes. "I understand," she said, stepping into the elevator across from his door. "That's what I was trying to say, too."

After the doors closed, she leaned against the elevator wall with a happy, unconscious smile. She hadn't been up all night since college, and she should have been dead tired. Instead, she felt marvelously alive and energized. Love did that to a person, although they hadn't spoken of love. It was too soon to speak of love, she knew that, but it wasn't too soon to feel it and know it was real.

They had sailed through the swamp she had feared the syndication choice would cast them into. Dev was being a graceful loser and she admired him for that. He hadn't actually congratulated her for winning the opportunity, but then maybe he didn't know yet if Annette had actually informed her that the final decision had been made. But in time he would congratulate her, she sensed that. He was that kind of man. Her kind of man.

Now, if they could just get through the culinary contest as easily.

Ten

*He said: Winning may not be everything,
but losing isn't anything.*

DEV BLINKED in disbelief as he stared at his TV screen. Cathy had chosen to structure her entire show around recipes using leftover turkey! And they were damn good recipes, innovative as well as practical, tasty as well as quick to prepare. Dev felt an idiotic grin stretch over his face as he watched Cathy cut wafer-thin slices of cooked turkey breast with as much speed and flair as he'd chopped scallions and cilantro for his cioppino. Damn, but she knew how to put on a good show!

He wasn't sure whether to laugh in appreciation or to feel frustrated that Cathy had chosen to try and win their bet by exaggerating the down-home simplicity of her cooking style. He did know that he was oddly warmed by the knowledge that she was sharing a private, on-air joke with him. Although the joke was really on her, he decided, because however warm and welcoming she made her smile, however often she assured her audience that these were meals that would be easy to duplicate in their own kitchens, her skill made a liar out of her. No viewer watching her shape pastry crust, or deftly arrange turkey-and-walnut salad inside rings of tiny champagne grapes, would doubt for a second that she was an accomplished cook. In some ways, her professional training stood out all the more clearly because she was preparing simple dishes with no exotic ingredients or fancy presentation to compensate for inadequate technique.

Dev rewound the tape and watched it again, refusing to consider why he'd developed this sudden fascination with a thousand-and-one uses for leftover Thanksgiving turkey. He wasn't ready to admit that he'd reached the stage of infatuation where the mere sight of Cathy on his television screen was enough to make him hot and edgy with desire. Yet he couldn't come up with any other explanation for the tension that kept him pacing as he watched her.

When he realized he was holding his breath, waiting for the moment when she would turn and smile into the camera—straight at *him*—Dev gave up the useless struggle to lie about his feelings, at least to himself. God, he wanted her! An ache of loneliness had been growing deep inside him ever since the night they'd made love, and watching her on television provided a bittersweet substitute for her physical presence. He must have been crazy to suggest that they'd be too busy to get together until after the culinary contest tomorrow. He wanted to have her in his bed, and he wanted her now. Hot and passionate, soft and pliant in his arms. Delightfully uninhibited and sweeter than he'd ever anticipated.

Dev groaned at the memories. Shoving his hands through his hair, he tortured himself with a few more visions of Cathy naked in his bed, then realized he was scowling with dislike at the blank wall behind his TV set. Until two nights ago, he'd found the bare, white walls and general lack of clutter one of the most attractive features of his home. Now the whole apartment felt empty because it lacked the essential warmth of Cathy's presence. As for his bedroom and his king-size bed, they loomed as bleak and desolate as the Alaskan wilderness. Ramses had done his best to provide the illusion of company by curling around Dev's feet, or in the crook of his back, but a cat, especially a skinny ex-alley cat, could only fill up so much space on a large bed.

As if summoned by his owner's thoughts, Ramses jumped up on top of the TV, sitting so that his tail dangled straight down the middle of the screen. Dev barked out an impatient command to move. Ramses yawned, then began to wash himself, his tail swishing from side to side.

Muttering slanderous comments on the morals and intelligence of his pet's ancestors, Dev strode across the room and lifted the cat onto the floor. Ramses shot him a look of pained incredulity, and immediately jumped straight back on top of the television.

Dev wasn't willing to accept defeat. He plonked Ramses on the floor again. "You know what your trouble is, fellow? You're spoiled. Keep out of the way—we're just getting to the good part of Cathy's show. She's going to smile right at us."

Ramses jumped back on the TV and licked his paw.

Dev knew when he was beaten. He glared at his cat. "Cathy has a d-o-g," he said, holding Ramses' tail to one side so that he could watch a close-up of Cathy putting turkey pot pie into the oven. "Which proves she's a smart woman. If you're not careful, that's what I'm going to get. A big *dog,* who will bite your annoying tail and chase you into the broom closet."

Ramses, who had heard similar threats on frequent

occasions in the past, showed not the slightest sign of anxiety. He jumped off the TV just as the closing credits for Cathy's show began to roll, and picked his way over the bookshelves toward the CD player, where he began a vigorous bout of scratching. His instinct for finding pieces of electronic equipment on which to shed his fur had recently become unerring.

The phone rang. Dev swatted the cat and simultaneously reached for the phone. "Hello," he said, ignoring the pitiful meows with which Ramses tried to suggest he was a seriously abused animal.

"Hey, Dev, this is Bill. Are you busy right now? Jean's working the late shift tonight, and I could use some company."

"Come on over. I have to double-check my supplies for the contest tomorrow, that's all." Dev frowned. "You sound stressed, Bill. What's up?"

"Nothing much. Something happened tonight…I'll tell you when I see you. I'll be right over, if you're free."

"Sure. Where are you?"

"At KDID. It won't take long. I've got my car back, the roads are clear, and there's not much traffic at this time of night. Give me twenty minutes."

"Okay." Dev forgot he was annoyed with Ramses and scratched behind the cat's ear. "I'll put the beer on ice."

Bill grunted. "Thanks, see you soon."

He arrived less than twenty minutes later. "Jeez, it's cold out there tonight," he said, unwinding himself from a voluminous orange scarf, stamped with the logo of the Denver Broncos. He blew on his fingers. "Gotta get the heater fixed in my car."

Dev grinned. "What you really need to do with that

car is drive it to a demolition yard and have it put out of its misery."

"Bite your tongue, man! Don't you recognize real class when you see it? In another couple of years that baby's gonna be a valuable antique."

"Yeah, right. Collectors are lined up all over the country just screaming for a 1985 Buick." Dev flipped the caps on a couple of bottles of beer and handed one to his friend.

Bill took a hearty swig, but instead of relaxing, he leaned forward in the chair, rolling the neck of the bottle between his hands. "The damnedest thing happened to me tonight," he said.

"At the station?" Dev asked.

"Yeah." He stared broodingly at his beer.

"Gonna tell me about it?"

"Yeah." Bill drew in a deep breath. "I was part of the crew doing the six o'clock news. Paul Lyman called down to the studio right after we went off the air and said he wanted a tape of the broadcast right away. Merilee—you remember her, she's the new anchor? Anyway, Merilee wasn't very happy, because she'd fluffed a couple of cues, and she figured that was why he wanted to check the tape. But since he's the general manager, naturally everybody ran around to make sure he got what he'd asked for. I was through for the day once the news broadcast was over, so I volunteered to drop the cassette off in Paul's office on my way home."

Bill paused to draw a quick breath, then hurried on. "I got up to the executive floor not fifteen minutes after he'd called, but when I knocked on the door to his office, there was no answer. I knocked again. Same thing, no reply. So I turned the handle, discovered the door was unlocked, and decided to go in. I planned to leave the tape in the middle of his desk, where he couldn't avoid seeing it."

"So what happened?" Dev asked.

Bill cleared his throat, looking embarrassed. "I walked in and put the tape in the middle of the desk. I was just about to walk out, when I heard this kind of low, moaning sound. I glanced around, and realized there was another door, not the one I'd come in through, that looked as if it might lead into a separate room, like maybe an inner office. Or maybe an executive bathroom."

Bill actually blushed. "Jeez, Dev, I didn't mean to pry, or anything, but that noise I'd heard was weird. I was afraid that Paul might have taken sick. Damn it, he'd only called down to the studio fifteen minutes earlier! How was I supposed to guess I'd walk into the inner office and find him with a half-naked brunette lying on top of him? And when I say half-naked, I really mean it, man."

Despite Bill's harassed expression, Dev couldn't help laughing. "I hope they didn't see you!"

"I don't think so." Bill sounded glum. "They were pretty intent on what they were doing. But that's not the point—"

Dev clapped his friend on the back. "Come on, Bill, lighten up! There's a humorous side to this you know. It may be inappropriate behavior for the office, but it's kind of nice to know Paul got carried away for once. His wife's been dead for three years, and he's always struck me as very lonely, especially now that both his kids are away in college."

Bill didn't crack a smile. "There's something else you

should know." He tipped his bottle and drained the last of the beer. "I recognized the woman Paul was with."

From his friend's tone of voice, Dev could tell this part of the story wasn't going to be in the least funny. He hoped like hell the woman wouldn't turn out to be married to somebody they knew. The television industry wasn't kind to marriages. "Who was she?" he asked grimly.

"I don't know her name, but I've seen her before." Bill looked up, his expression troubled. "The fact is, Dev, I saw her on Tuesday, right before we started taping your show. She was coming out of your studio. The maintenance crew had already left, and I was just getting ready to finish up in Studio B and move on to your set. Lord knows what she was up to in there."

There had to be fifty million brunettes in America, and it was crazy to assume the woman Bill had seen was Annette Dunning, but Dev realized that he felt chilled through to his marrow. "What did this woman look like?" he asked. "Are you sure it was the same woman you saw in Paul Lyman's office?"

"Yes, I'm sure." Bill finally smiled—a sheepish grin. "I recognized her…um…legs."

"Does that mean you saw her clearly enough to describe her?"

"Yeah. Both times. Tall, skinny, but with a few nice curves in crucial places. Dark hair swept up on top of her head in one of those fancy braids. I'm no good at guessing a woman's age, but I'd have said in her thirties. On Tuesday, she was wearing a black wool suit with a skirt that ended six inches above her knees. I…er…didn't notice her clothes tonight."

Annette fit Bill's description perfectly, but so did lots of other women. Merilee Jessup, the news anchor Bill had mentioned, was a tall, skinny brunette, too. Nevertheless, Dev felt the cold, hard certainty growing in him that the woman lurking around his studio had been Annette. "Did you talk to her on Tuesday?" he asked, wondering how his voice could sound so calm, when his thoughts were swooping like an out-of-control roller coaster. "Did you ask her who'd given her authorization to be on my set?"

"I would have, but right at that moment, Scott Mortimer arrived. And he obviously recognized the woman. The two of them started chatting, and then the news guys were hollering for me in Studio B—" Bill shrugged apologetically. "To be honest, I forgot about her. She looked right at home, as if she and Scott knew each other. You have to realize, Dev, it's only in retrospect that any of this seemed significant. At the time, I didn't know there were going to be problems on your set, and there was no reason for me to pay attention to this woman. If I thought about her at all—other than to notice that she had great legs—I assumed she must be some new hire working up on the sixth floor. One of their market-research people, or something. Even when you and I were discussing the possibility of sabotage on the set, I didn't remember that I'd seen her."

"There was no reason why you should," Dev said.

"Yes, there was. I should have remembered," Bill muttered. "But it makes no sense to suspect her of messing with your equipment, does it? I mean, if she's having an affair with Paul Lyman, whoever she is, she'd have no interest in screwing things up for you, would she?"

Dev went to the fridge and pulled out two more beers, popped the tops, and handed one to Bill. "Look, if you're feeling guilty because you didn't mention seeing this woman, you can quit right now. In the first place, what happened on the set could have been accidental—probably was accidental. In the second place, even if the mishaps were deliberately caused, there's no reason to assume this is the woman who did it. You're right, if she's Paul Lyman's girlfriend, she'd have every reason to want my show to be a success."

Bill appeared relieved. "I guess I allowed my imagination to run away with me, huh? I'm getting good at putting two and two together and coming up with five." He finally leaned back in his chair, nursing his beer on his stomach.

He chuckled. "If you want to hear something wild, I actually spent the drive over here working out some crazy theory that the woman I'd seen was that Annette Dunning babe you abandoned at the altar in Paris. She's in Denver, and I wondered if she'd been trying to get her revenge."

"By fiddling with the faucets?" Dev asked mildly.

"That wasn't the only accident. Anybody who's ever watched your show knows that you never measure oil, you just pour it into the pan with a sweeping flourish." Bill looked grim. "If the cap on the olive oil had failed a second earlier, you'd have dumped a half bottle of oil onto an open gas flame."

Igniting a blaze that might have scarred him? Dev wondered with shock. The possibility hadn't occurred to him before. But there was no point in alarming Bill, not at this stage, and he managed a laugh. "Next time the *National Enquirer* wants to develop a new conspiracy theory for the Kennedy assassination, they should call you."

Bill pulled a face. "Don't bother. I've exhausted my quota for the year."

"But I'm glad you told me this, all the same," Dev said. "I appreciate the information about the woman you saw walking out of the studio, and I'll certainly keep my eyes open from now on. I don't know if those mishaps were accidental or deliberate, but I do know that I'm personally going to triple-check everything from the salt shaker to the fire extinguisher before we start taping next week's show. And if there's anything suspicious, I'll insist that Scott goes straight to security."

They chatted some more while Bill finished his beer. Although he felt guilty about wanting to get rid of his friend, Dev could barely contain his impatience as they analyzed the Broncos' chances of making it through the play-offs, and discussed the old house near Denver University that Jean wanted to buy and restore.

Dev eventually made the excuse—a true one—that he needed to get up early for the culinary contest the following morning, and Bill left, muffled to the ears. Dev scarcely waited to close the front door behind his friend, before he reached for the phone and dialed Scott Mortimer's home phone number.

"Damn!" he muttered, when the answering machine responded. "Scott, this is Devlin. If you're there, could you pick up the phone? It's important."

There was a click on the line, and Scott came on. "This had better be real important, Dev. I have company."

"I need some information," Dev said. "This week, right before we started taping my show, you met some woman in the corridor outside my studio. What was her name?"

"You're calling me at nine o'clock on a Friday night to ask me about some woman I spoke to three days ago in one of the corridors at KDID?" Scott's voice rose in disbelief. "Is this a joke?"

"No, it's not a joke." Dev was torn between wanting answers, and not wanting to make Scott too curious. "Do me a favor, Scott, and just answer the question. Do you remember talking to a tall, dark, good-looking woman? And do you remember her name?"

"She's a business acquaintance of Paul Lyman's," Scott said, after a brief hesitation. "Her name's Annette Dunning. What's all this about, Dev?"

"I'll tell you next week. Nothing important."

"That's not what you said when you asked me to pick up the phone."

"Sorry to have interrupted you when you're entertaining," Dev replied obliquely, and hung up before his producer had a chance to ask any more questions.

Dev collected the empty beer bottles and tossed them into the recycling bin trash. He ought to have been more surprised to learn that Annette had been sneaking around his set. But among the many emotions churning in his gut, surprise seemed the least of them. Nothing Bill had told him tonight contradicted what Annette had told him during their dinner at the Westin. On the contrary, the fact that Annette was having an affair with Paul merely made her story more credible. But somehow, all his old doubts were starting to return, rushing in like a returning tide, filling dark pools in his mind with the flotsam of suspicion.

Annette had always been a skillful liar, Dev reflected, checking his supply list for the following morning. And there was every chance that her lies would have become more clever and more sophisticated in the years since he'd last seen her. At their dinner, when he'd demanded an explanation from her as to why she'd been meeting with Paul Lyman at a time when she was supposed to be in Atlanta, she'd taken a while before replying. She'd seemed irritated by his question, annoyed to have been caught out in a lie. When he'd known her in Paris, Annette had rarely let her irritation show, and Dev had found himself waiting for other subtle signs that the woman he'd once known might have been transformed into someone less calculating, and more sincere.

And he'd seen the signs he searched for, either because they were genuinely there, or because the new Annette Dunning was smarter than the old one, and knew exactly how to lull his suspicions. Instead of giving a glib explanation that he'd never have believed, she'd prevaricated and hesitated before finally confessing that she and Paul had hoped to keep their meetings confidential, except to a few selected KDID executives.

There were valid reasons for their secrecy. According to Annette, KDID and American Universal Syndication were on the brink of negotiating a major deal, but it was imperative to keep the details of the deal under wraps so that the competition couldn't steal a march on them.

The deal she'd talked about was breathtaking in its implications. Paul Lyman had grown up in Singapore, and he'd always maintained close links to the financial community there and in Hong Kong, where his older brother was the head of a major bank. With the growth of satellite TV systems, Paul had become convinced that there was an expanding overseas market for American shows, especially in Southeast Asia. Some months ago, he'd made the decision to form a new company to syndicate American productions in various foreign countries.

Universal Syndication had heard rumors about Paul's plans, and top management had been very interested, since although they were strong in the American and European markets, they'd never been very successful in cracking the tight-knit Asian markets. Annette had explained to Dev, with justifiable pride, that she'd been sent to Denver to be the point person in the negotiations between KDID and AUS. A major meeting was scheduled to take place soon, at which time the money men from Hong Kong and Singapore would be flying in to give their approval of the deal. Annette was authorized to negotiate on behalf of AUS.

"That's a major assignment," Dev had said. "The president of Universal Syndication must have a lot of faith in your abilities."

Annette didn't bother with false modesty. "Yes," she said, her eyes glittering. "But I earned the right to it. I've busted my ass for the president and the other fat cats at AUS."

Dev still had an uncomfortable feeling that Annette was leading him right to the edge of some cliff that only she could see. "With so much on your plate, I'm surprised you've got time to worry about something as insignificant as who's going to be the chef on a new cooking show."

"Oh, Dev, get real. I'm not here in Colorado to decide about who's going to appear in a cooking show, for heaven's sake! That decision doesn't require a senior vice president to fly into Denver and spend a week of valuable time hovering over two rival chefs. We're just using that as an excuse in case any of the competition starts wondering what I'm doing here."

"I see," Dev said. "Does that mean there isn't actually going to be a new syndicated cooking show?"

Annette reached out and patted his hand. "But of course there is, and you're our man, Dev." She gave a patronizing laugh. "Cathy Mallory is a nice enough little thing, but she doesn't compare with you as a chef. And even if she did, I'm afraid she works for the wrong station. Obviously, since Universal Syndication's planning a deal with the owner of KDID, they're going to syndicate your show, not hers."

"That's wonderful news," Dev said, although he didn't feel as happy as he'd expected.

"It's going to work out really well for you, Dev. I know you own a restaurant here, and you're something of a local celebrity. AUS doesn't see any reason why you'd need to go through the dislocation of a move. You can carry on producing your show right here in Denver, at the KDID studios, AUS will work out all the domestic deals for you, and our new joint-venture company with Paul will handle all the overseas markets."

It was almost too good to be true. "How soon is this going to happen?" Dev asked.

Annette ate a shrimp, the first mouthful of food she'd actually swallowed. "Things should be coming together very soon," she said. "We can't get the contracts drawn up until after we have the deal in place between Universal Syndication and KDID, but you can take my word for it, Dev. This deal's going to be big for you. Way bigger than you could possibly have expected."

"And for you, Annette? What's in it for you? It must

be something juicy to have you looking this pleased with yourself."

She wasn't in the least offended by his remark. She lifted her gaze to his, her eyes shining. "I'm going to be president of the new company," she said. "Although it's not official yet, AUS and Paul Lyman have both promised me the job."

Dev had congratulated her, even while his mind was analyzing and assessing what she'd told him. It all sounded very believable, he had decided, much more believable than the original scenario, with two rival chefs in Denver just happening to be the finalists in a nationwide search. Annette's friendly attitude toward him was now explained. She was an ambitious woman who would have been willing to do a deal with the devil if that was what it took to snag the job as president of this new company. Burying the hatchet with a man who'd jilted her would seem like small potatoes if that was what she had to do to keep Paul Lyman on her side. Annette liked to get back at old enemies, but not at the expense of her own future gain.

Finally confident that he knew where Annette was coming from, Dev had walked away from their dinner convinced that his contract with AUS was as good as signed. Not surprisingly, the more he thought about it, the more hollow his triumph had felt. He wanted the chance at syndication, of course, but he'd hoped to win it fair and square because "Dining with Devlin" was a more successful TV show than "Cooking with Cathy." It hadn't sat well to know that he'd won the job because he happened to have been employed by the right TV station at the right time.

Now, in the wake of Bill Sadler's departure, Dev questioned his entire assessment of what had happened at his dinner with Annette. He badly wanted to talk to Cathy, he realized. She knew Annette Dunning. Cathy would understand exactly why he was having all these doubts just because he'd learned that Annette Dunning had been inside his studio a few minutes before a series of accidents occurred.

He'd actually picked up the phone and begun to dial her number before sanity returned and he hung up. Cathy Mallory worked for KBAB, and it would be a serious breach of business ethics if he revealed Paul Lyman's syndication plans to her. And, unfortunately, he couldn't think of any way to explain his nebulous but oppressive doubts about Annette Dunning without mentioning the fact that Universal Syndication and KDID were planning to start a new joint-venture company.

Dev returned to the kitchen and worked methodically through his preparatory notes for the culinary contest. He marked off the final item on his checklist, and shut the doors to the fridge. He'd felt very awkward the other night when the subject of syndication had come up while he was cooking dinner for Cathy, and he'd been relieved that she seemed as anxious to gloss over the details of her interview with Annette as he had been. Belatedly, he wished he'd probed her responses a bit more thoroughly, but he knew this wasn't the time to call and open a difficult subject. Better to leave the whole issue of AUS and syndication decently buried until tomorrow night, when he hoped to have won the contest fair and square.

With Cathy coming in second, he thought, smiling softly. Yeah, he really wanted her to come a close second. He might even be willing to live with a tie. Smiling, Dev got ready for bed.

THERE WERE TEN CHEFS entered in the Chefs' Culinary Contest, and since the proceeds from the event were all destined to benefit the children's wing at the hospital, Denver's media were out in force to publicize the contest. The public wasn't permitted to enter the contest venue at Currigan Hall until after midday, by which time all the chefs had their setup complete. Any minor glitches in equipment and supplies had been taken care of, and the public, for the cost of a five-dollar admission fee, was free to stroll around and watch the ten master chefs at work.

They were also free to explore the other side of the hall, where trainee chefs from all over Colorado were showing off their newly acquired skills and selling tasty samples of their specialties—everything from grilled scallop kebabs to hazelnut biscotti.

The food that the ten master chefs were cooking would not be available for sampling. Their meals had already been auctioned off to the highest bidders, and would be rushed immediately after the judging to ten private homes scattered around Denver, where elegant parties had been arranged to consume the extravagantly opulent dinners.

Dev had competed in many similar contests, although none as prestigious as this one, and he always enjoyed the building sense of excitement as the morning progressed and the first subtle smells of cooking began to percolate through the hall. This was no different from other similar occasions, and he worked swiftly, familiarizing himself with his surroundings, arranging everything so that he could reach for cutlery and ingredients by instinct, rather than by sight.

By chance, Cathy was cooking in the booth next to him, but she was screened from sight and even from most sounds by a temporary, seven-foot-high wall erected between their booths. It would have been easy enough to take a short time-out and have a word with her, but he was afraid that seeing her might break his concentration, and—rather like athletes at the Olympics—at this level of cooking, the difference between winning and losing was often no more than a question of which chef was most on form that particular day.

Assisted by Pete, the sous-chef from his restaurant, Dev worked quickly to assemble the ingredients for the red-wine fish stock that would form the basis of his sauce. He'd brought his own pans, and no chef ever went anywhere without his personal set of knives, but each stove cooked differently, and Dev made sure that he understood the quirks of this one before setting diced yellow onions to sweat in fresh, unsalted butter.

He was tying sprigs of thyme, fresh parsley and bay leaf inside celery stalks to make a bouquet garni when he heard Cathy say his name.

He looked up, unprepared for the surge of sheer happiness that washed over him when he saw her. "Hi," he said. "How's it going?"

"Okay. I was a bit nervous, but I'm dealing with it." She smiled at him, simultaneously shy and provocative. "I must go, but I'll see you later, Dev."

His gaze fastened with deliberation on her lips. "I'm looking forward to it," he said.

"So am I." She laughed softly, a little breathless. "I'll meet you right here, immediately after the awards ceremony. Good luck, Dev."

"Good luck!" he said, but she was already gone.

Surprisingly, seeing Cathy didn't destroy his concentration at all. It was almost as if that brief glimpse of her settled his restlessness so that he found himself cooking with fierce concentration, totally unaware of the crowds gathered in front of his booth, or of the TV cameras filming footage of the contest for the evening news.

It was midafternoon, and he was getting ready to strain his red-wine fish stock through a *chinois,* when his concentration first wavered, then broke. He stretched, and stared out into the exhibition hall, wondering what his subconscious had picked up on to distract him. He didn't have to wonder long. Annette, stunningly elegant in a long-sleeved, low-necked sheath dress, stood directly in front of him, smiling and waving, giving anyone who cared to look an excellent view of her sleek figure.

Dev glanced around quickly, but Paul Lyman didn't seem to be anywhere in sight. Not surprising, since he and Annette needed to keep their relationship secret. He nodded to acknowledge Annette's wave, then turned to pour himself a glass of water. Refusing to speculate on why Annette had chosen to attend the contest, he refocused his attention on the sauce he was preparing.

But when he turned to set down the heavy stockpot, Annette was standing directly on the other side of the counter, in exactly the spot where Cathy had stood a couple of hours earlier. "Hello, Dev." She smiled. "You're looking very professional."

"It's the uniform," he said. "If you'll excuse me, Annette. I can't talk now."

"I quite understand. But I had bad news this morning, Dev, and I felt I simply had to pass it on without delay. The powers that be at AUS have reviewed the tapes of 'Dining with Devlin' again, and they've decided that your style of cooking just isn't what they need for a syndication package. If they're going to sell an American cooking show overseas, it's no good having a program that specializes in Continental cuisine, like yours does." She sent him a smile of ill-concealed malice. "Under the circumstances, I'm sure you'll understand why they've decided to go ahead and award the syndication contract to Cathy Mallory. Her down-home style goes over so well with foreigners. Americana is really hot in Europe these days."

She turned and walked away before Dev could manage to order her to leave. If ever he'd seen a triumphant rear end, Dev thought bitterly, Annette Dunning had it.

Chapter Eleven

She said: Revenge is a dish best served cold.

INSTEAD OF SHAKING her confidence, seeing Dev for a few minutes settled Cathy's nerves. She returned to her booth, smiling and marveling at the changes that had occurred in so short a time. She wanted to win this contest for herself and for KBAB and to help Annette justify her decision to AUS, but if Dev won, it wouldn't devastate her as it would have a few brief weeks ago. In fact, she almost hoped he did win. Winning the contest might remove some of the sting from losing the syndication.

The instant she returned to her own booth and scanned the bowls and ingredients meticulously chosen and arranged on the countertop, thoughts of Dev vanished like steam. Her mind focused intently on removing the skin and fat from the plump duck she had selected for her presentation. By removing the skin and fat, she also removed nearly all the strong gamey odor, always a problem with duck. This task completed, she turned her attention to the dressing, lifting long, rosy stalks of rhubarb to the light for inspection. At her request, the rhubarb had arrived with the broad leaves still attached to the stalks, thereby ensuring the greatest freshness. Pleased, confident that the unusual dressing would win the contest for her, she measured a cup-and-a-half of honey and three tablespoons of cinnamon into a bowl, then prepared to chop enough rhubarb to add six cups.

She had just cut the leaves from the stalks when a purring voice called to her. "Hi, Kansas."

"Annette." Frowning, she looked up, resenting the break in her concentration. Surely Annette realized how devastating it was to interrupt a chef at this crucial point in the all-important preparation phase. "I'm sorry, I can't talk right now." An involuntary glance at the clock informed her that she was not seriously behind schedule, but she would be if she didn't pick up the pace.

"Excuse me for interrupting at such a critical moment," Annette said in a self-satisfied voice. She was wearing that smile. "I know how disastrous breaking your concentration can be right now, but I've received some news that I felt you'd want to hear immediately."

Cathy knew she was being manipulated, knew Annette was forcing her to ask for the "news." And from Annette's expression she understood that Annette was thoroughly enjoying this moment. Heart sinking, she moistened her lips and, hating herself for giving in, she asked the question Annette waited to hear. "What news could be so important that you felt it necessary to tell me right now?"

"Disappointing news. The powers that be at AUS reviewed the tapes of 'Cooking With Cathy,' and they've decided that your simplistic style isn't what they want for a syndication package. They don't believe homespun cooking will sell overseas. I mean, really. Meat loaf in the Orient? Turkey leftovers?" Her smile widened and pleasure glittered in Annette's eyes. "In retrospect, we're all slightly amazed that you made the finals. I assure you, someone's head will roll for such a stupid error. But you don't care about that." She lifted a hand and shook her head as if her words were not carefully calculated to wound. "Given that you have nothing to offer any viewer other than a bored American housewife, I'm sure you'll understand why AUS decided to award the syndication contract to Devlin Gilpatrick. Aside from being a better chef, his flair with international cuisine will sell better in the foreign markets."

The color drained from Cathy's face and throat. Stunned, she stared down at Annette from her slightly elevated position until she realized Annette was drinking in the sight of her shock as if her pain was sweet to observe.

"It was all just a game, wasn't it?" Cathy whispered. She was glad Annette could not see how badly her hands shook around her knife and the stalk of rhubarb. "You planned this from the beginning. You never intended to award the syndication position to me."

"You're a fine one to accuse someone of deceit. Tit for tat, Kansas. Years ago I, too, lost a lucrative opportunity. You may remember the incident since you're the one who turned me in to the college authorities. You wrecked a nice little business, and you cost me my degree. I've been successful despite you, but you caused me a lot of embarrassment and humiliation and I never did get my degree." She shrugged and smiled. "Now you know how losing feels."

White faced and shaking, Cathy swayed on her feet. "Annette, you had your revenge way back then. I had to leave school just as you did."

"But everyone rallied around to help poor little Cathy Mallory. No one came to *my* defense." Annette's lips pulled back from her teeth and her eyes glittered. "I've had to work for everything I've gotten, nothing was ever handed to me!"

"I know you don't believe this, but I wasn't the person who exposed your term-paper scheme. I didn't turn you in to the college authorities."

"You're right. I don't believe you." Her lips curved in malicious enjoyment. "Good luck with the contest. Gee, I hope I haven't affected your concentration." With a laugh, Annette turned and in a moment she was lost within the crowd moving about Currigan Hall.

Dazed, Cathy stared at a point in space. The syndication job was not going to happen. Her dreams and the happy plans of the last few days had been for nothing. Annette had dangled the prize and then had reeled Cathy in like a fish on the line. And Cathy had fallen for it.

That wounded as deeply as losing the opportunity of a lifetime. Even when she *knew* better, she had let Annette play her for a sucker.

Tears of anger glistened in her eyes as she quickly chopped the rhubarb and dumped it in the bowl of cinnamon and sugar. How could she have been so naive? So stupid? Hurrying, aware she was now seriously behind schedule, she finished making the dressing, then stuffed the rhubarb mixture into the duck and placed the duck in a deep roasting pan. She had known Annette was trouble, had known something like this could happen. She had told herself to expect some kind of trick. Even so, she had let Annette convince her that the syndicate job was hers. And when Annette jerked the rug out from under her, it was a total and shocking surprise. How was that possible?

Rushing, distracted, she packed rhubarb dressing around and over the duck. That was the secret to this dish. The rhubarb, cinnamon and sugar cured the meat as it roasted and gave the meat a delicious and different taste. But this was not the moment to bask in the anticipated exclamations of delighted judges. Now was the time to start her pièce de résistance, her special secret sauce.

But she was so upset, so thoroughly distracted, that she burned the first batch of butter she placed on the stove to brown. She ruined the second batch by adding a tablespoon more honey than she wanted. In a contest this prestigious, this competitive, even a wrong nuance was enough to result in a loss. And the mistakes she was making were not of nuance but of substance.

Shoulders slumping, Cathy cast a frantic glance toward the clock. Regardless of how far behind schedule she was, she needed to take a break and settle her thinking. If she could clear her mind of the anger and disappointment she was feeling, perhaps she could regain the level of concentration she had achieved before Annette appeared. The thing to do, she decided, was to clean her work area, then return to the sauce with a focused mind. If only she could stop feeling so foolish and stupid for having believed Annette.

Only vaguely aware that the public had now been allowed near the chefs and an audience stood watching her, she wiped off her cutting board, then crumbled the rhubarb leaves and thrust them into a waste can. Automatically, she washed her hands with strong soap after touching the leaves. Rhubarb leaves contained toxic substances that could cause violent illness, even death, if ingested.

"Oh my God." Worry, then panic, flared in her eyes as she stared down into the sink. Shreds of chopped rhubarb had fallen near the opening to the garbage disposal. But what constricted her chest and opened her eyes in horror were the bits of chopped leaves. Whirling, she spun toward the stove, jerked open the door, and hastily removed the roasting pan. Using a spoon, she poked at the dressing that she had packed around, over, and inside the duck.

At once she spotted bits of chopped leaves. Sick at heart, her throat tight, she stared in disbelief at the flecks of dark green.

When she could move, she sat down hard on a wooden stool, staring in fresh shock at the roasting pan. She would have sworn on all she held holy that such an elementary mistake was simply not possible. Such a stupid error was light-years behind her. A chef of her experience and expertise simply did not, could not, make such a dangerous and unforgivable blunder. It was sheer, and potentially dire, carelessness. There was no excuse for this.

Stunned and shaking, she raised her head and looked at the clock with dulled eyes. She had backup supplies. She could begin again. Except there was not enough time.

Lowering her head, she stared blindly at the white muslin cloth she'd twisted between her hands and fought to swallow a huge lump clogging her throat. This contest had been important to her and to KBAB. And winning today would have helped ease the devastation of losing the syndication opportunity.

Finally, when she felt she could do it without embarrassing herself with tears of anger, frustration and disappointment, she stood and walked to the back wall of the booth and pressed a button that would summon one of the contest officials.

When Paul Lyman appeared at her booth, Cathy

drew a long breath, then said in a trembling voice, "I wish to withdraw my entry from the contest. I'm disqualifying myself." Reaching, she removed her chef's cap and dropped it on the countertop.

What appeared to be genuine concern appeared in Paul Lyman's eyes, but Cathy didn't trust his expression. Perhaps she did him an injustice, but she wouldn't have trusted anyone whom she knew to be associated with Annette Dunning.

"Are you absolutely certain?" Lyman inquired, scanning the roasting pan on the countertop. He glanced toward the saucepans containing her two failed efforts.

"I'm very certain." Her voice surprised her by sounding calmer than she actually was. When she thought how violently ill her dish would have made anyone who ate it, her fingers shook like twigs.

"We'll send someone over to clean up," Paul Lyman said after a minute, looking at her with sympathy. He knew what this contest meant to all the participating chefs.

"No," she said, still speaking with a strange calm. "I'll clean up." She didn't want to risk that someone might sample the toxic dressing. After Paul Lyman departed, she dumped the contents of the roasting pan into a garbage bag and firmly knotted the top. Then, moving like a robot, she poured out the little glass dishes containing the ingredients she would have used for her special secret sauce. When the announcement came over the loudspeaker, she paused and listened with an expressionless face.

"Ladies and gentlemen, we regret to announce that one of our ten master chefs, Miss Cathy Mallory, has withdrawn from this year's Chefs' Culinary Contest."

The people standing before her booth frowned and

murmured to one another and studied her with expressions of speculation and curiosity. Face flaming, Cathy hesitated, then reached for her coat, hat and purse. To hell with the cleanup. She needed to get out of here, needed to be alone.

Annette's carefully timed appearance had produced exactly the result that Annette had clearly hoped it would.

Ducking away from the television cameras and the reporters calling her name, Cathy all but ran out of Currigan Hall.

LATER, SHE COULDN'T remember exactly how she passed the next two hours. She recalled scuffing through fresh snow, remembered seeking someplace warm for a cup of coffee that she didn't taste. But by the time she returned to Currigan Hall to witness the announcement of the winners and the awards ceremony, she had almost come to terms with a very, very bad day.

The syndication opportunity was gone, and she had forfeited the contest. But she still had her cooking show and her catering business. She hoped she still had Dev, hoped he wouldn't get so caught up in the syndication job that their relationship fell by the wayside.

Slipping inside the hall, hoping no one recognized her, she edged through the crowd until she had a clear view of the chefs awaiting the judges' final decision. Her gaze fastened on Dev's stony face, and her heart sank. He wasn't going to win and he knew it. Suddenly she longed to see a flash of his old arrogance and confidence. If she couldn't win the contest, she had wanted him to win and had wanted it badly. She would have bet her treasured collection of antique cooking utensils that he *would* take first prize.

Worried, she watched as Paul Lyman took the podium and leaned into the microphone. "Ladies and gentlemen, we have a champion! This year, the mayor will present the awards. Your honor, will you be kind enough to announce the winner of this year's Chefs' Culinary Contest?"

Applause broke out as Denver's mayor accepted an envelope from the judges then approached the podium. "I've tasted each of the entries and believe me, ladies and gentlemen, this must have been a difficult decision." He smiled for the television cameras, then raised the envelope containing the names of the top three winners.

"And now for the results of the Chefs' Culinary Contest. Third place goes to...Mr. Devlin Gilpatrick, representing KDID Television!" A wave of applause greeted Dev as he stepped forward with a thin smile to accept his award. "Our second place winner is...Mrs. Valerie Radner, representing Denver's own School of Culinary Arts!" The mayor shook her hand then referred to the judge's list. "And the winner of the Chefs' Culinary Contest is...Mr. Dom Salton representing Le Boulevard Restaurant!" Thunderous applause erupted as Dom Salton stepped forward, beaming beneath a tall, blindingly white chef's cap.

Cathy lowered her head. Dev could cook circles around the other chefs. He should have won first place easily. She couldn't imagine why he hadn't. But she had seen that he'd known he wouldn't win. She didn't understand that, either.

She did know that she half wished they hadn't agreed to meet after the photos and the media interviews. His pride would be smarting over losing the contest, and that's how he would see it. Cathy knew him well enough to understand that only first place counted to him. She doubted she would be very good company, either. This had truly been a lousy day.

But when she finally saw him walking toward the booths to meet her, she tried to paste a cheerful smile on her lips. "Congratulations."

"For what?" he asked, thrusting his hands in his pockets and frowning down at her. "I lost."

"Third place isn't a loss," she said lightly. But there was nothing she could say to console him. "Where's your award?"

"My assistant took it with him." Entering his dark booth, he found his topcoat and gloves, then took her arm and they walked through the rapidly clearing hall toward the exit doors. "What happened? I didn't hear the announcement. I didn't know until the dishes were presented that you had withdrawn."

Cathy waited until they were outside, then she drew a deep breath of frosty air. Tilting her head back, she gazed up at the dark sky. "I wish the city lights didn't hide the stars," she said softly. "When I was a kid in Kansas, the sky was spangled with stars. Things were simpler then."

"Cathy?" Frowning, he gently turned her to face him. "What happened?"

She met his eyes. "I did something really stupid, Dev." Not sparing herself, she told him about chopping the rhubarb leaves in with the stalks then packing the toxic dressing around the duck. "There's no excuse," she said quietly, seeing the shock darken his eyes. "That kind of dangerous error is inexcusable, unforgivable."

"And it's not like you," he said, his hands tightening on her shoulders. "You're a professional, not a novice who's careless or easily rattled. You're a fine chef, Cathy."

Sudden tears sprang into her eyes. She was so grateful to hear a compliment right now, and more, to hear the sincerity in his voice. Her confidence had been profoundly shaken by the day's events.

"I have to agree there's no excuse for that kind of error," Dev said slowly, looking into her eyes. "But I'd bet my Corvette that there's a damned good explanation."

"One that I'm not proud of."

A frown appeared between his eyes and the pressure of his hands on her shoulders eased. "If you'd rather not talk about it...."

"Annette came to my booth just as I was preparing to dice the rhubarb." She stared into his eyes, taking courage from his genuine concern. "Dev, I wasn't upfront with you. Annette told me at our initial interview that she'd decided to award the syndication to me. I didn't tell you straight out because I wasn't sure if she'd told you that you weren't going to get it."

His gaze widened, then narrowed, and he stepped away from her, running a hand through his hair. "Annette told you *then* that she'd selected you?" He gazed at the street and swore softly. "That means..."

Cathy interrupted. "I'm happy that AUS decided to award the syndication to you, truly I am. If I can't have it..." She bit her lip and moved up beside him. "But Annette picked a hell of a time to tell me that AUS didn't want me after all, and they'd chosen you."

"Wait a minute. Annette told you during the culinary contest that AUS had selected me?"

"I think it's likely that AUS always wanted you. Annette only strung me along to make it hurt twice as bad when I lost. And I..." Lowering her head, she wandered a few steps away from him. The square in front of Currigan Hall was deserted now except for them. "I let what she said and the nasty way she said it blow my concentration. All I could think about was what a fool I'd been. Consequently, I wasn't paying attention." She ground her teeth together. "And also consequently, I handed Annette another victory. I let her cost me a chance at winning the contest."

Dev surprised her by sitting down on the snowy base of one of the sculptures in the square. He nodded to himself then gazed up at her. "Annette also paid me a visit at a crucial moment." Suddenly, he laughed but there was no amusement in the sound. "I wasn't straightforward with you either, and for the same reason. From the beginning Annette told me that I was her choice for the syndication slot."

Cathy stared. "So you thought...and I thought..." She sighed. "Annette played us both for fools."

"Just like you, I believed I had the syndication job. Then Annette showed up at my booth and announced that the big guns at AUS had decided on you as their choice."

"What?" She blinked at him.

"Frankly, I'm astonished that I won third place. I was so angry, so distracted, that in the end I didn't expect to place at all. I didn't make an error that might have caused the judges to become violently ill, but I sure as hell didn't perform to the standards I set for myself. My errors were just smaller than yours, that's all." Suddenly he grinned and this time his amusement was genuine. "You really and truly mixed rhubarb leaves into your dressing?"

"I did." She sat beside him on the snowy pedestal. "God, Dev. Imagine what could have happened if I hadn't realized in time what I'd done." Lifting a gloved hand, she spread an imaginary headline before them. "Cathy Mallory Poisons Culinary Judges. Can't you just see it?"

Lifting a hand, he created a headline of his own. "Scandal at Culinary Contest. Beautiful Chef Kills Judges."

Smothering a giggle, Cathy waved her glove again. "Death by Duck."

"Mallory's Mallard Madness."

They leaned on each other, laughing. "Demise by Dressing," Cathy said, wiping tears of laughter from her cheeks.

"Culinary Contest Casualties Mount."

They laughed until their eyes were wet and they leaned against each other in limp release. When Cathy started to feel the cold, she took Dev's hand and they stood at the same time.

"She got us," she said quietly. "Again. At least in my case."

"Me, too. My only serious competition in the contest was you. With your entry withdrawn I should have won." He paused. "Cathy, I think it's time you heard the rest of my story," Dev said, gazing into her eyes. "I've tried to be a gentleman, but the time has come to take the gloves off."

She knew immediately what he referred to—that long-ago jilting. "I knew there was more," she said, lifting on tiptoe to brush a kiss across his lips. "A man like you doesn't leave a woman standing at the altar without a good reason."

"Are you ready to hear that reason?" he asked, locking his arms around her waist and looking down at her.

"Oh, yes. And this time I suspect I'm not going to feel even a tiny twinge of sympathy for Annette Dunning."

"SO ANNETTE WAS pregnant," Cathy said, repeating what Dev had just told her. She curved her fingers around a steaming cup of coffee and gazed out the windshield. After stopping at Starbucks to pick up mocha lattes, Dev had driven into the foothills to a spot that overlooked the lights of Denver. She watched the lights for a moment, then shifted on the car seat and looked at his profile in the pale glow from the dash.

"By the time Annette told me about the baby our relationship was all but ended." Dev gazed out at the city spread below them, but Cathy didn't think he saw it. He was gazing into the past. "Learning about Annette's pregnancy changed everything. Suddenly, instead of walking away from each other, we were planning a wedding."

"What happened?" Cathy asked gently when he fell silent. She tried to focus solely on what he was saying, tried not to let herself think about Annette carrying Dev's baby. It was sobering to realize there had been a depth to Dev's relationship with Annette that she hadn't guessed. A baby. Twinges of jealousy and envy stirred within her.

"The night before we were due to be married, some of our friends threw a party for us. Yvonne, a friend of mine who happened to work with Annette, let drop the fact that Annette had just accepted a wonderful new job with a French publishing company, a job that would involve frequent travel between New York and Paris. Annette denied that she had accepted the job and insisted she was merely considering an offer.

"Later that night, I pointed out that we would be making the adjustments all newlyweds do, and in six months she would be having our baby. I was upset that she would even consider a job that would have her flying back and forth across the Atlantic."

"Dev," Cathy said quietly, watching him. "If you don't want to talk about this..." Actually, she wondered if she wanted to hear it. Loving Dev, as she now knew she did, made it painful to visualize Dev and Annette discussing a future together.

"No, I need to tell you, so you'll understand. At first Annette insisted she was only considering the job. Then she started to cry and said she had miscarried our baby. She hadn't told me about the miscarriage because she thought I might not marry her if I knew she was no longer pregnant with our baby. She was right about that. When I learned she was no longer pregnant, my first thought was that we could cancel the wedding. But that wasn't what Annette wanted, and I wasn't enough of a cad to cancel the marriage twelve hours before the ceremony."

"I'm not sure I agree," Cathy said slowly. "Marriage is difficult enough between two people who love each other and want to make that commitment. If you knew that you didn't love her..." She respected Dev's code of honor, but she couldn't stand to think of him planning to marry Annette.

"Of course you're right. But at the time, it was hard to see things clearly. I spent the rest of the night walking around Paris, wondering how in the hell I'd managed to make such a mess of my life. I was about to marry a woman I didn't love and wasn't sure if I even liked. And I'd begun to suspect that Annette was a bald-faced liar, that she would say whatever was necessary to get what she wanted. I started to wonder if she'd been pregnant at all."

Cathy's fingertips rose to her lips and her eyes widened. "Was there anyone who knew the truth?" Even though she knew how the story ended, at least the final result, she hung on his words, caught by the details of his pain.

"I thought Yvonne might. Near dawn I phoned her—got her out of bed—and asked if she was certain that Annette had taken the job with the French publisher or if the job had only been offered. Yvonne said she hadn't wanted to interfere, but she'd been hoping I'd call. And yes, she knew for a fact that Annette had accepted the new job because she had overheard Annette's phone call to the French publisher. While I was trying to think of a way to ask about the pregnancy, Yvonne told me the rest of it. She told me that a mutual friend had accompanied Annette when she had an abortion. Yvonne gave me the name of the friend and that was my next phone call. It was true."

"Oh, Dev. That's so…it's just…I don't know what to say."

"Annette aborted our baby because she wanted that job and a baby would have been inconvenient." He stared steadily through the windshield. Finally he turned to look at Cathy. "I phoned Annette on the morning of our wedding day and I demanded to know the truth. I just couldn't believe anyone could be so ruthlessly ambitious that she would abort a child merely for the sake of convenience."

"What did she say?" Cathy whispered. Though she knew Annette was capable of extraordinarily selfish acts, it shocked her deeply that even Annette would do something this unconscionable.

"She was trapped. She had to admit that she had aborted the baby, but she denied she did it for mere convenience. She'd done it for us, she said." Dev ground his teeth together. "She didn't want us to begin a new marriage with such a large responsibility. She was only thinking of me, she said." He paused. "I told her to call off the wedding. I told her that she disgusted me. I told her I would never marry her. She cried and said I couldn't do that to her. She would be at the chapel and I'd better be there, too." Dev turned on the seat. "That's what happened, Cathy."

"I'm so sorry," Cathy whispered. She took his hand, moved that he was sharing a story so intensely personal. Sitting close to him in the warm interior of the car, she felt the intimacy between them and understood that Dev had deepened their relationship by confiding something so profoundly disturbing and painful.

"Later I heard from friends that Annette did indeed wait for me at the chapel. As far as our friends were aware, I jilted her and she had no idea why. What's sad is that I wonder if she did know why. To her it seemed absolutely reasonable to get pregnant to make a man marry her and then to abort the baby when it was no longer useful to her and had in fact become inconvenient."

They sat in silence for a full minute, holding hands and gazing at the lights spread out below them. "Thank you for telling me," Cathy said softly. "When you first mentioned having jilted Annette, I made some gloating remark and later was ashamed of myself. Actually, I felt a little sorry for her. I don't anymore."

A sigh lifted her chest. "That's one of the awful things about Annette. She absolutely brings out the worst in me. I hated it that I made a remark indicating I was pleased that someone got stood up at the altar. I hate it that I let her rattle me so badly I had to withdraw from the contest. Hate it that she suckered me so easily. And,

Dev, I hate it that she aborted a baby and put you through hell."

Dev's laugh was bitter. "Everything you're feeling, I'm feeling just as strongly."

Cathy pushed a hand through her hair. "I feel so outraged and frustrated! I want to hit back! I'm not proud of this, but I wish I could *do* something! Something that says to her, 'You can't treat people like this. You can't play with people's emotions and hurt them. That's wrong and you have to pay for it.'"

"I know, damn it," Dev said, squeezing her hand. "Annette tramples the people around her and emerges unscathed. Just like she will this time."

In silence, they finished their coffee, then Dev kissed her gently and switched on the car's ignition.

"Wait a minute," Cathy said, frowning, her mind racing. "Dev...Annette told me that AUS intended to award the syndication to you. And she told you that AUS had decided to award the syndication to me." She looked at him. "One or both of those statements is a lie."

He stopped, his hands on the wheel. "She indicated that higher-ups at AUS had made the decision...I see where you're going." A line appeared between his eyebrows. "The question is, who *does* AUS want for the cooking show?" He thought a minute. "Maybe AUS has no idea what Annette is doing."

"Do *we* know what she's doing?"

"Did she tell you anything about the deal she's putting together with AUS and KDID?"

"I don't think so. This is the first I've heard about anything like that." Cathy frowned, trying to recall what Annette had said during their interview. "She mentioned she was working on a business deal, but she didn't reveal any details."

Quickly Dev explained about Annette and Paul Lyman and the syndicate they hoped to form to open Far-East markets to American television shows. "If I understood Annette correctly, Paul can furnish the markets and AUS can furnish the shows."

"Then blowing off the two best candidates for a cooking syndication for AUS comes at a bad time," Cathy said, trying to figure it out. "Wouldn't AUS be trying to solidify their position and nail down the shows they plan to syndicate in the Far East?"

Dev stared at her thoughtfully. "Maybe they don't plan to syndicate the cooking show in the Far East."

"But Annette said something to me about the Orient not being interested in meat loaf recipes," Cathy said. She touched Dev's wrist. "This is going to sound crazy, but could it be possible that AUS doesn't know about Annette's deal with Paul Lyman? And what if AUS is unaware that Annette never intended to award the syndication job to either of us?"

Dev's brow drew tight. "She could go back to AUS and tell them that both of us turned down the syndication offer...she could cover her tracks there. As for her deal with Paul..." He reached for his cell phone and dialed while Cathy watched him. "Paul?" he said a minute later, speaking into the phone. "I know it's late, but something's come up. Cathy Mallory and I would like about an hour of your time."

He listened, then brushed his fingertips across Cathy's cheek. "Yes, Cathy Mallory. Paul, it's important. Thanks, we'll see you in about thirty minutes."

"What do you have in mind?" Cathy asked after he replaced the phone in its cradle and started to back up.

"I've known Paul a long time and I trust him." He smiled when Cathy raised an eyebrow. "If you and I can get taken in by Annette, so can Paul. But when he discovers we know part of the story, maybe he'll tell us what's going on."

"Dev?" Cathy put her hand on his arm. She felt good that at least they were doing something. And they might, just might, figure out Annette's agenda. Annette was up to something more than the petty revenge she'd taken on them. "Dev...I..." She wanted to tell him that she loved him, that she felt closer to him right now than she had ever felt to anyone else. The only thing that stopped her from saying the words was that she didn't want to remember that the first time she told him she loved him followed a discussion about Annette. "I want to tell you that...we're in this together, whatever happens."

He stepped on the brake and studied her for a long moment in the glow of the dashboard lights. "I know," he said softly. "We're a team. And that feels good. Very good."

They smiled at each other. Then Dev took his hands off the wheel and kissed her, deeply and thoroughly.

Cathy murmured his name, shivering with pleasure at the things his hands were doing beneath the edges of her coat. "After we see Paul..."

He laughed, a throaty sound near her ear. "See how much alike we think?"

PAUL LYMAN MET them at the door of his home and led them to his study, a tastefully appointed room done in tones of cream and maroon. The room was as stylish as Paul. Even at this late hour Paul Lyman still wore a silk tie and a dapper three-piece suit.

He sat behind his desk and smiled as Cathy and Dev seated themselves. "I must say, I never expected to see the town's most famous rivals together and looking so cozy with each other." Sympathy warmed the gaze he turned to Cathy. "I'm sorry you withdrew from the contest, Miss Mallory. Your decision must have been difficult."

There was a question behind his comment, but Cathy didn't answer. Instead she glanced at Dev. They had agreed that since he knew Paul, he would speak for them both.

"Paul, I'll get straight to the point. You know that I'm a finalist in the search for a chef to host the syndicated cooking show proposed by Universal Syndication. What you may not know is that Cathy is also a finalist."

"Interesting," Paul said, looking back and forth between them, mild curiosity in his gaze. "But I'm sure you didn't come here merely to inform me that Miss Mallory is also a candidate for the AUS syndication slot."

"Cathy and I were notified that Annette Dunning would make the final decision as to which of us would be awarded the job. Annette's name alarmed us both because we each have an unpleasant history with her." Quickly Dev told Paul about Cathy's experience with Annette in college and then his own involvement with Annette in France. "I left her standing at the altar, Paul," Dev ended quietly.

Paul Lyman touched his tie uncomfortably. "I can't imagine why you've told me these distasteful stories. Frankly, I'd rather not have heard them. I...." He colored slightly. "Perhaps I should mention that I have a personal relationship with Miss Dunning."

"We know," Dev stated flatly.

"We also know that Annette is representing AUS in a deal you're arranging to syndicate American television programs for the Far East," Cathy added quickly. Intuition told her that Paul didn't really believe what they had just revealed about Annette.

Paul stared and then frowned. "How can you possibly know about my personal situation? My relationship with Annette has been discreet. As for any business deals that Annette and I are involved in, to state it bluntly, I fail to see how that is any of your concern." He leveled a scowl at Dev. "Moreover, you've been misinformed. I'll reveal this much—I'm not involved in any business negotiations with AUS."

"Paul," Dev said slowly. "I've known you a long time. We've had a good working relationship at KDID. Therefore, I'm going to assume that you're not lying."

A rush of dark color filled Paul's cheeks. "Of course I'm not lying," he said angrily. "I hope you have a damned good reason for making that statement."

"Annette Dunning told me that she's not in Denver to make a choice between Cathy and me for the syndication job. That is merely AUS's cover story to conceal their negotiations with you, conducted by Annette as their representative." Leaning forward, Dev spun out the details of the deal between AUS and Paul's group exactly as Annette had explained it to him.

When he finished speaking, Paul stared at them with a white face, his fingers gripping the edge of his desk. "My deal with Annette does not involve AUS, and Annette does not represent them in this instance. She is acting as a private individual. What disturbs me is that you've somehow learned of negotiations that I believed were utterly confidential."

"I didn't learn about your deal 'somehow,' Paul. Annette told me about it."

"I find that difficult to believe, since you have so many details incorrect," Paul said sharply. "As Annette is one of the principals, she would certainly know that AUS is not involved. There's no reason whatsoever that she would have claimed AUS is part of our deal."

"Unless she's planning to double-cross you," Cathy snapped, angered by his tone. Then she told him what had happened that caused her to disqualify herself from the culinary contest. "Annette lied to Dev and me. She hurt both of us. And we think it's possible that AUS has no idea what she's done, but you can bet she'll have a story for them to explain it. Just like she'll have a story for them to explain a side deal with you, if that's what she's doing, and just like she'll have a story for you if AUS is involved in your deal, but you don't know it yet."

Paul stood behind his desk, anger narrowing his gaze. "I don't know what you two hoped to accomplish by coming here, but I can tell you it was a mistake. I see no reason to continue this conversation."

Both Dev and Cathy rose to their feet. Cathy noticed that Dev was opening and closing his fists by his sides. "I guess we hoped that you'd be as open with us as we've been with you," he said. "And we wanted to warn you that your deal is not confidential, as you may have believed it was. Think about it, Paul. What if Annette told me the truth and she *is* representing AUS's interests? If that's true, then Cathy's right. You're looking at a double cross."

"It would be wise to end this interview *now*," Paul said, speaking between his teeth.

In silence, Cathy and Dev followed Paul to his front door. Paul said good-night in a terse voice and they nodded, then found themselves standing on a snowy porch looking at each other, the furious sound of the door banging shut still ringing in their ears.

"He didn't believe us," Cathy said quietly, looking into Dev's stormy eyes.

"No. He didn't." Taking her arm, he led her toward his car, parked at the curb. "I'm not willing to give up and let this go, Cathy. Are you?"

She shrugged. "What choice do we have? The sad thing is, I suspect Annette is going to hurt Paul Lyman, just like she's hurt us."

Dev stopped on the sidewalk and faced her with a distracted expression. "And there isn't a damned thing we can do about it."

"Wait a minute." Cathy's mind raced. "Maybe there is something we can do. I've got an idea.... We'd need Bill and Jean's help...."

"What are you thinking?"

"Maybe there is a way we could expose Annette and pay her back for what she's done to us," she said, speaking slowly. Falling into step beside him, she walked toward the car at the curb.

"I'm all in favor of that," Dev said promptly. "What's your idea?"

"I need a few minutes to think about this. I'll tell you about it during the drive home."

The events of the day crowded her mind and overwhelmed her, and suddenly she felt tired and cold. Holding hands, they walked around Dev's car and paused beside the passenger door. Before he opened the door for her, Dev took her in his arms. She hesitated slightly, then relaxed against his body.

"It's been quite a day, hasn't it?" he said, speaking against her hair.

"One of the worst in recent memory."

Dev tilted her face up to his and she felt the vapor from his breath bathing her lips. "Cathy, I want both of us to have the freedom to be honest with each other." He gazed into her eyes. "Are you really in the mood to make love?"

She could answer the way she thought a woman in love ought to answer, or she could answer honestly. Which answer she chose and how he responded would determine the direction their relationship would take.

"Actually, no," she said quietly. "It's been a long and extremely upsetting day." Oddly, she had a feeling that a lot was riding on how she answered his question. "What I'd most like to do right now is go home—alone—and crawl into bed and go to sleep."

Smiling, he kissed her nose. "That's exactly what I'd like to do, too."

Dev opened the car door for her, then walked around to the driver's side. Before Cathy slid inside, she gazed at him over the top of the car. "Dev?" When he stopped and looked at her, she bit her lip and hesitated. "My idea for getting even involves you and Annette. If you agree with what I'm about to propose, it would mean that you and Annette..." She stared at him. "You and Annette almost had a baby together. You came within hours of marrying her. I...are you sure you still don't care for her?" She hated herself for asking, but she couldn't stop the words. Cathy knew Annette was a woman who enthralled men even when they knew she was poison.

Dev studied her across the snowy roof of the car for what seemed like several minutes, but could only have been seconds. Then, his face expressionless, he said tonelessly, "There's nothing between Annette and me."

But his reply didn't answer the question that Cathy had asked.

Trembling with fatigue, thinking about what her idea for revenge would require him to do, Cathy slid into the car.

Oh, Dev, she pleaded silently, looking at him with her heart in her eyes. *There's unfinished business between you and Annette. Be careful, darling. Please, please don't let her seduce you again.*

Twelve

He said: An intelligent man prefers not to believe that he has loved foolishly.

DEV REALIZED THAT his fingers were drumming repeatedly on the table, and he forced himself to stop. Muscles aching, eyes gritty with fatigue, he listened to the phone ring, willing Annette to be in her hotel room and to take the call. Four rings already. Where the hell was she? The hotel still had her registered as a guest, which surely meant that she hadn't yet left town. God, he hoped she was still in Denver! Even more, he hoped that she wasn't spending the night with Paul Lyman.

On the sixth ring, the phone was picked up. "Yes?" Husky with sleep, the voice was unmistakably Annette's. And undeniably sexy.

Dev was so relieved she'd finally answered that he had to swallow hard before his throat loosened up enough for him to answer. "Annette, this is Devlin. I'm glad I managed to reach you." Amazingly enough, once he regained the use of his voice, he managed to sound calm, even a touch blasé, despite the fact that the palms of his hands were slippery with sweat.

"It's two o'clock in the morning, Devlin." All trace of sleep had vanished from Annette's voice, but the sexy throb remained.

"You used to say that was the time when the real fun started," Dev said. He drew in a shallow breath, forcing himself to continue. "Do you remember the nights we spent together that only ended with the dawn? I can see us now, standing on the banks of the Seine, watching the sun rise. I don't believe you've forgotten those early mornings in Paris, Annette. You couldn't have forgotten them."

There was a tiny pause before she replied. "That was years ago, and I've grown up. I realize that you can't work all day and play all night. And some memories just hurt too much—" She broke off, as if she'd said more than she intended. "What's this sudden urge to reminisce really about, Devlin? I have to assume there's a practical reason why you called and disturbed me at this hour of the night."

"There are lots of reasons."

"Start with any one of them and move on."

Hands balling into fists, Dev resisted the overwhelming urge to hang up the phone. Some things had to be done, however unpleasant, and it was vital for him to convince Annette that he was still attracted to her—his whole future depended on it. "I'm sitting here in my apartment, drinking a glass of wine, and wondering when it all went wrong between us. Wondering *how* it all went so terribly wrong."

"You tell me," she said bitterly. "What's your take on those interesting questions, Devlin? Personally, I'd say our relationship unraveled right around the time you left me standing at the altar, holding a bouquet of drooping roses and watching forty guests snigger at my humiliation. Up until that moment, I was naive enough to think that our relationship was going quite well. That you actually *loved* me."

Once again, she sounded genuinely hurt at the painful memory, and Dev's stomach roiled with a mixture of revulsion and regret. Annette was rewriting the past, but he had an uncomfortable suspicion that she truly believed her own heavily revised version of history. "I should never have let our relationship end that way," he said and in this, at least, he could be totally sincere. "I'm sorry, Annette. I wish there was some way to make amends…to make everything come right between us."

"There is," she said crisply. "And I just did it. You wanted the job at Universal Syndication and I took it away from you. You lost out, Dev, and I got even. You didn't just lose out on the syndication opportunity, but in the culinary contest as well. The great celebrity chef, Devlin Gilpatrick, sex symbol to bored housewives, was suitably and publicly humbled. Pity I couldn't get the film of your defeat broadcast on any of the networks, but I can't tell you how good it felt to watch you playing the third-place loser for the benefit of your adoring local TV audience. What's more, before I've finished with Paul Lyman, I have every hope that your rinky-dink little cooking show with KDID will also be a thing of the past. With luck, and a little help from me, your career as a TV chef is about to enter a rapid period of terminal decline. So I'd say everything between us is finally working out just perfectly."

"Annette, can't we talk some more about this? Please?" Dev realized that his fingers were drumming on the tabletop again, and he got up, pacing the den as he talked. Ramses, in a rare moment of solidarity, paced with him. "Let me cook dinner for you tomorrow night, Annette, for old times' sake. We have some wonderful memories to share along with the ones that aren't quite so good."

"Your fixation with our past is becoming boring," Annette said, but she didn't hang up, so he knew she was considering his invitation.

"Remember the first night we made love?" Dev's voice thickened. "I remember that night very well, Annette, and you're still the most skillful and inventive lover I've ever known."

"What about Miss Sugar-and-Spice, all things nice, Cathy Mallory?" Annette asked acidly.

"What about her?" Somehow, Dev managed to keep his voice steady.

"Isn't she the current moppet you have warming your bed?" Annette gave a brief, dismissive laugh. "Not that I imagine she'd be much competition for me. Down-home, fresh-off-the-farm enthusiasm must get a bit wearing to a man of your sophistication. I can just visualize her getting ready for bed and putting on her pink gingham nightie." She laughed again. "That wouldn't exactly be a major turn-on for a man like you."

For a second or two, Dev was incapable of speech. "In the right circumstances, naiveté can be appealing," he said at last.

"Can it? I guess so, although I've never understood why. Are you telling me that you've fallen for Cathy Mallory? You must know that industry gossip suggests the pair of you actively dislike each other, and that seemed entirely believable to me until I saw you together yesterday."

"Where did you see us together?" Dev asked, more sharply than he'd intended.

"At the culinary contest, you know that." Annette sounded taken aback by the edge to his question, and Dev mentally resolved to do a better job of controlling his reactions. The visit he and Cathy had paid to Paul Lyman had been at the forefront of his mind, but there wasn't the slightest reason to suspect that Annette knew about their meeting.

"Cathy's obviously crazy about you," Annette continued. "And you looked positively smitten, Dev. I confess, I'm curious to know what the big attraction is. Why do men fall over themselves for Cathy Mallory? It doesn't seem possible...but am I wrong in assuming that she's boring in bed?"

Boring? Dev shut out the sudden rush of images from the night he and Cathy had made love. "Warm, generous and profoundly satisfying" all sounded like much better words than "boring" to describe the experience. But he couldn't afford to remember Cathy now; too much was at stake to allow himself to be distracted. His career—everything that he'd worked a lifetime to achieve—would be destroyed if he didn't handle Annette just right. He refocused his attention on Annette, shutting out any lingering sentimentality about the sweetness of Cathy's lovemaking.

"What do I see in Cathy Mallory?" he said, trying to sound somewhere between amused and impatient. "Well, I guess I see down-home, fresh-off-the-farm enthusiasm, just like you do. I imagine Cathy will never lose those qualities, even when she's an old woman. When you're with her, even if you're standing slap-bang in the middle of the city, you can always catch a faint whiff of country air. Most men probably find that refreshing."

"How extremely strange of them," Annette said. "Especially since country air rarely comes without a strong accompanying scent of cow manure."

"In the part of Kansas Cathy comes from they grow grain, not animals," Dev said. "But, Annette, let's not waste time talking about Cathy Mallory. She's not important right now, and we are. I called to invite you to have dinner with me tomorrow night." He paused. "I'm planning to make coq au vin and profiteroles."

He heard the hiss of her indrawn breath, and knew she was remembering that he had cooked the same dinner for her the night they first became lovers. But she wasn't won over by the mere fact that he had a good memory.

"Profiteroles are fattening," she said briskly. "Besides, there's no reason for me to come to dinner with you, Devlin. We have nothing to say to each other."

"On the contrary, I believe we have a lot of unfinished business between the two of us."

She laughed. "Not anymore. Yesterday, after five years of waiting, I finally wiped the slate clean."

"Are you sure?" he asked. "Then why are you talking to me right now, Annette?" Ramses had stopped pacing and seemed to be staring at him with distinctly accusing green eyes. Dev turned his back, shutting out the distraction—and the guilt. Unpleasant as he'd expected this conversation to be, it was turning out to be worse than he'd imagined. "Let me prove to you that there's still something between the two of us, Annette."

"Sorry, Dev. When you knew me in Paris, I was still young and stupid enough to think with my hormones. These days, I'm a lot smarter, and you're not rich or powerful enough to be of any use to me. I'm playing in the big league now, and great as you are in the sack, I'm not looking for a stud. So if you want to buy me off, you'll have to find some other method."

Dev swallowed bile. "Have dinner with me tomorrow night and maybe you'll discover that, with my help, you can have great sex, as well as money and power." He barely managed to get out a repetition of his invitation. "Come at six, and we'll have a chance to...talk... before dinner."

She picked up on his hesitation, just as he'd intended. "Dev, don't let's pussyfoot around here. Are you suggesting that we might renew our previous sexual relationship—for a price?"

"It's something that we both want, isn't it? We have the basis for a deal here."

Annette was silent, considering. "And what do you expect in return for your sexual favors, Dev? A promise that I'll put in a good word for you with Paul Lyman? Are you that desperate to keep your foot in the TV door?"

"We'll talk about what I expect tomorrow night." Dev's voice was hoarse with strain, making his words sound husky, almost caressing. "I guarantee you'll like the bargain I'm offering."

Annette covered a moment of electric silence with an audible yawn. "Maybe I will stop by," she said. "But then again, maybe I won't."

She hung up the phone before Dev could speak again.

DEV GRABBED a bare five hours of sleep, then got up and immediately phoned Bill Sanders, who picked up the phone, yawning and protesting. It took Dev less than ten minutes to explain what he and Cathy wanted, but almost an hour to overcome Bill's moral protests and technological objections. Once Bill was persuaded, it took another hour to convince Jean to become an active accomplice to their plans.

With Bill and Jean en route to their respective TV stations to gather equipment, Dev called Cathy. "It's all arranged," he said. "Bill and Jean have agreed to help us."

"Great!" There was a pause. "We're doing the right thing, aren't we, Dev?"

"Yes, we are. We're putting Annette's fate in her own hands. If by any chance we've misjudged her, then we'll be the ones who end up looking foolish. On the other hand, if she's up to the sort of malicious trickery we suspect, then she'll bring herself down."

"You're right." Cathy sounded reassured. "And I guess it's better for Paul Lyman to discover the truth now, rather than months down the road, when his life and his business might both be in ruins."

"Absolutely. Cheer up, honey. This mess is soon going to be over." Dev hung up, wishing there was some less deceitful way to achieve his goals, but knowing there wasn't. He and Cathy had both tried the honorable methods for defending themselves, and those methods clearly weren't working. It was time to play the game Annette had set up, and to play by the sort of merciless rules she herself would follow.

Dev filled his afternoon alternately cooking a dinner he didn't expect to get eaten, and answering frantic phone calls from Bill and Jean. He was putting candles on the table when the Sanderses arrived, lugging heavy cases of equipment.

"We're here," Bill said, unnecessarily. He didn't even comment on the enticing aroma of red wine, chicken and mushrooms beginning to percolate through the apartment—it was a first for Bill not to notice food.

"Glad you could make it," Dev said. "Did you manage to arrange for the roving Minicam? Otherwise I don't see any way to make this work."

"Yeah, we got one, and don't ask how. The van will be here at six-thirty, parked outside this apartment building until seven-fifteen. That's all I could get."

Dev grimaced. "Three-quarters of an hour. Jeez, Bill, that's not much of a window."

"I've called in every favor I'm owed for the last decade, and the next one, too. Have you any idea how much it costs to operate one of those suckers?" Bill's normally cheerful features were pulled into an expression of deep and genuine alarm. "Dev, I sure as hell hope you know what you're doing here."

"I sure as hell hope so, too," Dev said wryly.

Jean and Bill exchanged glances. Then Jean shrugged. "What the heck, let's get to work, lover boy. Where do you want us to set up, Devlin? In the den?"

"Yes, that seems the obvious place."

At five-thirty, Bill and Jean announced that they were ready, with all their equipment fully operational. At five forty-five, Dev showered and changed into black linen pants and a gray cotton sweater. A somber outfit, but then his mood wasn't exactly upbeat. He didn't bother to shave. Annette always preferred the men in her life to look slightly untamed. And, God help him, he wanted her to find him attractive.

At six, Dev started counting down the minutes until Annette might arrive. At six-fifteen, he was pacing the living room, swearing at Ramses. At six-thirty, the phone rang and he damn near jumped out of his skin. It was Cathy, calling from the KDID studios. Paul Lyman had agreed to meet with her in his office, and she was waiting for instructions. Dev told her to call back in ten minutes.

Cathy's voice fell to a whisper. "Is Annette with you?" she asked.

"No." Dev slammed down the phone, tense to the point of exploding. He was on the point of calling Cathy back and apologizing when the intercom buzzed. Hand not quite steady, he depressed the connect button. "Hello."

"It's Annette. Let me in."

Despite nearly snapping Cathy's head off, he hadn't known how uncertain he'd been that Annette would come until he felt relief wash over him in a giant wave. "I've been looking forward to seeing you," he said, giving the thumbs up sign to Bill and Jean. "I'm buzzing you in now."

His friends retreated into the den, issuing last-minute instructions. "Remember, the dining alcove is the best place for you to sit with her from an audio point of view," Jean said. "Don't go too far into the kitchen, and keep her away from the west side of the living room. That's almost entirely out of range."

"And I only have a narrow operating radius for the camera," Bill said. "Try to face her toward the den when you sit down." He frowned worriedly. "Although we don't want her to examine your bookshelves too closely or we're doomed. She'll see the hole I've cut in the drywall."

"I understand the problems," Dev said curtly, resisting the impulse to yell that they'd been over all this a dozen times already. "Close the door. She'll be here any minute."

The doorbell rang within seconds of Bill and Jean hiding themselves. Drawing in a deep breath, Dev prepared to open his front door. He started to smile, then let the smile vanish. No point in trying to be too ingratiating. Annette despised any man she thought she could control.

He stepped back, holding the door wide, and speaking with cool admiration. "Annette, come in. You look—beautiful."

And she did. Wearing a long coat of deep-burgundy wool, she'd turned up the sable collar so that it framed her face and accented both the creamy smoothness of her complexion and the dark, sexy fullness of her lips. She didn't acknowledge Dev's greeting, but stood staring at him in assessing silence before walking into the penthouse, shrugging out of her coat as she passed him. Beneath the coat, she wore a burgundy satin sheath that clung to her body, flaunting the fact that the dress was undoubtedly all she had on except for panty hose and a pair of high-heeled evening shoes.

Dev hung up her coat, taking a minute to get his emotions fully under control. Odd how he could recognize Annette's sexuality, acknowledge its potency, and feel only repulsed. He had already closed the drapes over the windows that looked west, so Annette automatically gravitated to the other set of windows that afforded spectacular views of downtown Denver. If he could move her four or five feet closer to the dining alcove, she'd be comfortably in range of Bill's camera and Jean's microphones.

He crossed to her side, leaning negligently against the broad windowsill. "You're late," he said.

She shrugged. "I wasn't sure if I'd bother to come. In the end, dinner with you seemed more appealing than going to a concert with Paul Lyman."

"I'm glad you chose me. I think you'll find the deal I'm offering is worth your time."

"I doubt it." She tilted her head back, her expression mocking. "You're lucky Paul's so damn boring. I'll be very surprised if you have anything that I want, Devlin."

He let his gaze travel over her face, coming to rest on her mouth. "Liar," he said. "You know exactly what I have, and you want it."

Her lips parted, but that was the only response she allowed herself. "Don't think it's going to be easy to win me over, Devlin. These days, I use sex to control other people. I don't let sex use me. So if you have a proposition for me, let's hear it."

Come on, Cathy, your ten minutes are up. I need to hear from you. "Dinner's the first part of the deal," he said. "I have some interesting wines over here. Why don't you come and choose one? I usually recommend the Beaujolais with coq au vin. It's robust enough to stand up to the sauce, but not too heavy." He strolled over to the small bar, with its built-in wine rack, that marked the division between the dining area and the kitchen. Ideal camera range. For a moment he thought Annette might not follow him and he was sweating by the time he realized she'd moved into almost perfect position.

The phone rang just as she started to inspect his selection of wines and aperitifs. Feigning casualness, Dev lifted the receiver. "Hello."

"Devlin, this is Cathy. I wondered if you were busy tonight."

"Very busy," he said. "I have a guest, Cathy." He saw the sudden intensification of Annette's interest and rolled his eyes, as if irritated at having to deal with the call.

"You said earlier that we might do something together tonight," Cathy said.

"Look, Cathy, I'm way too busy to talk right now."

"What should I do—"

He cut her off quickly. "If you're bored, why don't you watch some TV? I'm sure you can find something entertaining to watch."

"Oh." Cathy sounded breathless. "All right, Dev, I guess that's exactly what I'll do for the next half hour or so. Watch TV."

"Have fun," he said with brutal lack of courtesy, and hung up.

Annette came and stood beside him, holding a bottle of Dubonnet. "For old times' sake," she said, putting the bottle on the counter in front of him. She smiled, looking pleased. "You certainly gave little Miss Sugar-and-Spice the brush-off."

Dev shrugged. "One of Cathy's more endearing characteristics is that she's too sweet-natured to realize when she's being well and truly blown off." He poured two small glasses of aperitif and handed one to Annette. "I'm sure you can see the usefulness of a woman like that."

Annette raised her glass in a mocking salute. "Certainly. Although you have to weigh the advantages against the disadvantages. I know you, Devlin. You're a man who needs a challenge. A woman who's too sweet and submissive could never satisfy you sexually, or any other way."

"You're probably right." Dev put down his glass and moved behind Annette, putting his arms around her waist and leaning down to nuzzle the hollow at the base of her throat. "But you understand me so well because you're just like me. That's what you think, isn't it? That we're two of a kind, ambitious, smart, willing to do almost anything to succeed."

"Maybe." She took his hands and slid them up her body to cover her breasts. She closed her eyes, rubbing herself against him. "Mmm...don't stop. God, Devlin, but you make me feel good! I'm so damn sick of pretending to be turned on by middle-aged Romeos who think slobbering all over me is advanced sexual foreplay."

"So why pretend?" Dev asked, his mouth grazing the bare skin of her shoulders. "Just tell Paul Lyman to get lost."

"For God's sake, Devlin, grow up!" Annette twisted

out of his arms, and reached for her drink. "You think it's easy for a woman to make it in the world of television?"

"No, but you seem to have succeeded admirably. You're a vice president at AUS."

"Yes, because I slept with every damn executive in the place!" Annette breathed hard, her cheeks flushed with resentment. "Besides, I deserve a far more powerful job than vice president of planning. That's one of those titles that sound great, but don't pack any real power. I deserve to be president of my own company. I *would* be president if I were a man."

"Is that why you seduced Paul Lyman?" Dev asked. "So that he'd appoint you as president of this new company he's setting up to syndicate American TV shows in overseas markets?"

"Well, God knows I didn't seduce him because he's such a fantastic lover." Annette tossed back her drink and paced restlessly, moving farther out of camera range with each turn. "No wonder the guy's a widower. I bet his wife died in bed, out of sheer frustration."

Dev grabbed her as she passed, and swung her around, back into his arms. Back into perfect camera range. He looked down at her. "I think it's time for us to talk business, Annette. You want to be president of your own company. I want to be the star of a syndicated cooking show. I think we have the grounds for doing a deal here."

She tossed her head impatiently. "You've lost the chance of syndication, Dev. You and Cathy Mallory are both completely out of the running. I've already told AUS management that neither of you are suitable candidates for syndication—"

"How did you make that lie stick?"

She shrugged. "It was easy. I said that you both

cracked under pressure, and provided evidence to back up the claim."

"What evidence?"

"I faked it. AUS management isn't going to bother to check out my supposed sources."

"That's why you sabotaged the set for my show, isn't it? You expected me to throw a tantrum and you wanted to capture me on tape, losing control."

"You've gotten a *lot* smarter at figuring out, haven't you?" She stood on tiptoe and pressed a kiss onto his lips. "Mmm, you really do have the sexiest mouth, Dev. But I need to keep the big picture in mind here and not get distracted by the sexy package you come wrapped in. I warned you years ago that I'm not a woman who forgives and forgets, and nothing's changed. You're powerless, Dev. I can't see any basis for doing a deal here unless you want to take me to bed and try to persuade me not to get 'Dining with Devlin' canceled."

He resisted the urge to wipe the imprint of her kiss from his mouth. "But I have something that you want, Annette. Something that you want very badly."

She ran her hand down the front of his pants. "True. But unfortunately for you, I don't want it badly enough to forgo the pleasures of revenge."

"I wasn't offering to sell you my body," Dev said coolly. "I was offering to sell you my silence."

"Your silence?" She jerked back, her expression scornful. But when she spoke again, her voice betrayed her uncertainty. "You don't know anything worth paying for."

"Are you sure? You spun me a fine tale about how KDID and AUS are working together to syndicate American television shows in overseas markets. But I don't believe the two companies are working together.

I've known you for a long time, Annette, and that means I know you're up to something."

"Pure speculation on your part."

"No, not pure speculation. As you mentioned yourself just a moment ago, you're not the only one who's gotten older and wiser in the years since we last met. You made a major mistake sending me a tape of Cathy Mallory's show before it had aired. I've been suspicious of you for weeks now—"

"I don't know what you're talking about."

Dev sent her a cool look. "That wasn't a very convincing lie, Annette. No doubt you expected me to keep quiet about receiving that tape of Cathy's show. And then, if I won the culinary contest despite all your efforts to make sure I didn't, you planned to inform the judges that I'd cheated. Same deal for Cathy. Presumably you wanted some backup method to discredit us, just in case either of us managed to jump over all the hurdles you'd put in our way—"

Annette shrugged, no longer bothering to deny that she'd sent the tapes. "When I plan revenge, I like to make sure my schemes are foolproof."

"But your plans aren't foolproof," Dev said softly. "Far from it, in fact. I've done a little detective work, and I've found out that you're playing one company off against the other. AUS thinks you're working for them. KDID thinks you're on their side. You'd be in big trouble if I told Mr. Eugene Montford, President of AUS, that you're helping Mr. Paul Lyman, of Station KDID in Denver. And vice versa. I'm sure both gentlemen would be very shocked to hear about your treachery, especially since I imagine they shared their plans with you in the belief that you were in love with them, and would keep their confidences entirely private."

Annette paled, but she recovered quickly. "There's

no fool like an old fool," she said. "It's not my fault if AUS and KDID are both run by men who can't keep their mouths shut or their pants zippered. Take my advice, Dev, and don't try to blackmail me. Paul Lyman and Eugene Montford are both head-over-heels in love with me. Go to Gene with a story like this and I guarantee he'll have you thrown out of his office. As for Paul, he's even more crazy about me than Gene. Try to carry tales to him, and you'll be the only loser. 'Dining with Devlin' will be canceled so fast your head will spin."

"Surely that would depend on the evidence I could produce to back up my story," Dev said.

Annette frowned, not understanding why he appeared so confident, so much in control. Then horror suffused her face. "Oh my God—you bastard! You're wired! You've been taping this conversation."

He smiled. "Yes, I have."

She gave a howl of mingled fury and despair, swinging her fist at his face in a hard punch, intended to inflict maximum hurt. When he sidestepped, she lunged for him, ripping at his shirt, searching frantically for a mike. "Where is it, you son of a bitch? Don't think I'll let you get away with this! I'll tell Paul you set me up—"

Dev caught her hands and pulled them behind her back, subduing her. "It's too late, Annette," he said gently. "I'm not wired, but some of my friends helped me out and our conversation has been televised, live, straight into Paul Lyman's office. There's nothing for you to destroy, nothing for you to lie about. Paul has already heard and seen everything."

"I don't believe you." But she obviously did. Her cheeks were chalk-white beneath her makeup. Dev could almost feel sorry for her as he watched her mentally recap their conversation, recalling every damning comment.

Bill came out of the den. "I have the uplink established with the KDID studios," he said. "Paul Lyman's waiting to speak to you, Dev."

Annette refused to look at either of the men. "I don't have to stand for this," she said. "I'm leaving."

"No." The command in Dev's voice actually caused her to hesitate. "For once it isn't going to be that easy for you, Annette. You're not going to walk away and leave people wondering if somehow everything that happened might have been their fault. You're going to speak to Paul Lyman, and face up to what you've done."

Annette must have realized that with Bill Sanders on one side and Dev on the other, escape was not an option. In stony silence, she allowed herself to be led into the den.

The television was already turned on, showing a close-up of Paul Lyman seated behind his desk, with Cathy at his side. Paul looked shattered, but his natural dignity stood him in good stead, and when he rose to his feet, there was nothing comic or wretched about his appearance.

He stared into the camera, speaking to Annette without preamble. "How could you deliberately set out to use me like this? To exploit my loneliness after my wife's death strictly to further your own ambitions?"

"That wasn't what I did, Paul. Of course I love you—"

He cut her off with a chopping motion of his hand. "No, don't, Annette. You'll merely embarrass both of us." He shook his head. "You were right about one thing. I was a fool. I wouldn't listen to Devlin and Cathy yesterday, and when Cathy came to me this afternoon and explained what she and Devlin planned to do, I was angry, furious. The only reason I agreed to go along with their plans and actually turn on my TV was because I was so sure they would be proved wrong about you." He laughed harshly. "My God, I still can hardly believe what I heard and saw with my own eyes."

"Don't believe it," Annette said. "They faked it...they coerced me—"

"Everything you said was broadcast live, Annette, so there's no way Devlin and Cathy could have faked anything. Don't let's humiliate each other any more with excuses that can't possibly take us anywhere useful. By the way, I should warn you that I am sending a tape of this broadcast to Eugene Montford at AUS by overnight courier. He deserves to know exactly what's going on."

"No, Paul, please don't do this! You don't understand! I love you—"

Paul Lyman turned his back to the camera. "I've seen enough, Cathy. Cut the link, please."

The television screen in Dev's den went black and silent. Bill broke the quiet by coughing and shuffling his feet. "Jean and I will get this equipment cleaned up, Dev. It'll probably take us thirty or forty minutes."

"That's okay, no rush." Dev was quite glad that he wouldn't be alone with Annette. Now that it was all over, he felt no particular sense of triumph that the tables had been turned so effectively and completely against her. Instead, what he felt was regret, mingled with bone-deep weariness. Annette was a beautiful woman, with a keen intelligence, and a bountiful supply of natural talent. It was truly sad that she had chosen to use her assets to hurt other people.

She thrust past Dev without speaking or acknowledging the existence of Jean and Bill Sanders, and walked defiantly toward the front door. "If you're planning to try and bring criminal charges against me, forget it, Dev. There's not a thing I've done that was illegal and there isn't a jury in the country that would convict me."

Dev disagreed, but he wasn't going to debate the issue with her. He took her coat from the hall closet. "It's AUS and Paul Lyman you have to worry about, Annette, not me. As far as Cathy and I are concerned, you've self-destructed quite adequately. The television industry is a small, closed world and you're going to have a real hard time finding yourself a new job. I figure that's punishment enough. I'm sure Cathy feels the same way."

She slipped into her coat, burrowing deep into the fur collar. "You always were too damn noble for your own good, Devlin. You and Cathy Mallory both."

"Maybe that's one of the reasons I like being with her so much," Dev said quietly.

Her eyebrows rose almost imperceptibly. "You're going to marry her, aren't you?" she said flatly.

He hesitated for a second, but Annette didn't wait for his answer. She opened the door and walked quickly into the corridor.

She didn't look back.

Epilogue

They said: Ain't love grand?

CATHY JUMPED UP at the ring of her front doorbell and raced Romeo to the hallway. Seeing the shadow of a man through the beveled panes of glass, she skidded to a halt, almost tripping over Romeo in the process. *Dev had come.* They were going to be alone for the first time since the night of the culinary contest. She drew in a deep breath, which had no calming effect whatsoever.

"We're being ridiculous," she informed the dog. "Stop throwing yourself against the door, Romeo, and put your tongue back in your mouth! We're both going to be dignified about this, okay?"

Still slightly breathless, she opened the door. Dev stood silhouetted against the bright winter sunshine, his face in shadow, his black hair gleaming. Romeo gave a bark of pleased recognition, then tumbled out of the door into the crisp new snow, buffeting Dev in canine ecstasy. Cathy managed, just barely, to refrain from doing the same.

"Hi," she said, wishing she felt confident enough of Dev's feelings to lean forward and welcome him with a kiss. "Come on in."

"Thanks." Dev stepped into the cozy warmth of Cathy's house, wishing he felt confident enough to take her into his arms and kiss her with all the passion and longing that had been building inside him for the past three days. The smile of welcome she'd given him had damn near melted his bones, but Cathy was so friendly to everyone, it wasn't easy to decide how much of her warmth was directed toward him personally, and how much was just a reflection of her naturally outgoing manner.

She led him into her living room and they sat down on the sofa, Romeo honoring them both equally by sticking his wet nose into Cathy's lap and draping his snow-dampened tail across Dev's feet. Sinking back into the cushions, Dev stretched out his legs toward the fire and felt as if he'd finally come home. It was strange to feel such a deep sense of intimacy with Cathy at the same time as he was afraid to reach across five inches of sofa and touch her hand. Maybe he was inhibited because he wanted so much from this relationship—more than he'd ever wanted from a relationship before. Maybe it was his own feelings that confused him as much as his uncertainty about Cathy's.

"The ratings for last week came out yesterday," he said, still surprised that he didn't care in the slightest that she'd beaten him. In fact, when he'd seen the charts, he'd actually laughed.

"Yes, I saw them," Cathy replied, wondering why she didn't feel more triumphant for having beaten Dev's brilliant program about Mediterranean cuisine—with a show built around leftover turkey, no less!

"'Cooking with Cathy' beat 'Dining with Devlin' so you won our bet." Dev reached inside his jacket and extracted a small, flat package, about the size of a paperback novel. "I owe you ten bucks, but I fudged a little and brought you a gift instead."

Cathy took the package, but she didn't open it. "I didn't really win," she said. "I bet that I'd beat you by three points in the ratings, and I didn't. There wasn't even a whole percentage point between us. It was just over half a point.''

"Yeah, I know." Dev hid a smile. "Your win was barely significant, statistically speaking. In fact, to all intents and purposes, our two shows came out neck-in-neck in the ratings."

She sat up straighter, and her eyes flashed. "Well, I wouldn't say that. We're talking about five thousand more homes in the metropolitan viewing area tuning in to my show…"

Delighted that she'd risen to the bait, he cut her off in midstatistic and leaned forward, kissing her firmly on the mouth. She kissed him back with great enthusiasm for a couple of minutes. Then to his deep regret, she wriggled out of his arms and faced him with a stern glare. "Oh, no, you don't, Devlin Gilpatrick. You're not going to seduce me into forgetting that I beat you!"

He grinned, unrepentant. "I can sure as hell try." His smile fading, he took her hands and wrapped them around the gift he'd brought. "Open it," he said.

Cathy wasn't sure what she expected to find when she opened Dev's package, but she suspected it would be something much more important and valuable to her than a ten-dollar bill. She tore off the wrapping paper and discovered a battered black-leather box. She unlatched the dented silver clasp, pushed open the lid, and found herself looking at a set of six antique coffee spoons, nestled on a bed of velvet that had no doubt once been a rich midnight blue, but was now frayed and turning gray with age.

A lump lodged in her throat as she stared at the spoons. Over the past few weeks, Dev had proved unexpectedly perceptive and thoughtful in many ways, but even so, she was caught off guard by the fact that he'd been so observant. She lifted her gaze to his. "Dev, I'm overwhelmed. You noticed my collection of antique cutlery, and you saw that I didn't have any coffee spoons. Thank you, these are truly beautiful.''

"I'm glad you like them."

"I love them. Where did you find them? And still in the original box, too."

"I didn't buy them," Dev said. "They've been in my family for almost a hundred years. My great-grandmother worked as a maid on the Earl of Londonderry's estate in Galway. The other servants gave her those spoons as a wedding gift when she came to America to marry my great-grandfather."

Cathy discovered that she had tears in her eyes and an ache throbbed somewhere in the region of her heart. She dashed her tears away with the back of her hand, disconcerted by her emotional reaction to his gift. "I can't possibly accept something as precious as these spoons in settlement of a bet I didn't even win," she said, closing the box and holding it out to him. "Dev, these belong in your family, to be used on special occasions, and then passed on to your daughter when she gets married...."

"Yes, that's what I think, too." He'd known that Cathy would understand right away how important the coffee spoons were, but he hadn't expected his stomach to turn somersaults at the prospect of telling her why he wanted to give them to her. He'd spent a good part of the past three days planning exactly how he was going to hand over the spoons and then propose to Cathy. All in all, he'd been rather proud of the eloquent speech he'd prepared, listing all the reasons why they were well suited, explaining in cogent detail exactly how they would mesh their careers and their lives. Unfortunately, he couldn't remember one word of his eloquent speech.

"Oh, hell," he said, reaching out and pulling her into his arms. "This isn't the way I planned to say this, but I love you, Cathy, and I can't bear the thought of having to live without you. Could we...would you marry me?''

His words dispelled the ache in her heart, which suddenly swelled with a great rush of joy. "You love me? I love you, too, Dev, so very much. Oh, yes, I'll marry you!''

The gap between them that had seemed so difficult to close when he first arrived now vanished without a moment's thought. Dev opened his arms and Cathy slipped into them as if they'd been rehearsing the move for years. He kissed her with passion and tenderness and a deep sense of wonderment. He traced his hands over her body, shaping her firm breasts, her tiny waist, the flat plane of her stomach. He imagined his child growing inside her and was shaken by the sudden intensity of his longing to watch her grow big with his baby. In the past, whenever he'd contemplated marriage, it had always felt as if he'd be sacrificing his freedom. But now, far from narrowing his choices, marriage to Cathy seemed to open up a dazzling new world of possibilities.

She had never realized that love could feel so comfortable and so exciting at one and the same time, Cathy thought. Her hands were shaking as she took off Dev's sweater, and her body tingled wherever he touched her. And yet, somewhere beneath their sexual passion, she was aware of a trust and a tenderness toward him that she'd never experienced with another man. Desire mounted far more quickly than she'd anticipated and Cathy recognized, to her chagrin, that they weren't going to make it as far as her bedroom before their lovemaking reached its climax.

Surrendering to the inevitable, she stopped worrying about what the neighbors would think if they knew she was making love on her living room couch in the middle of the afternoon. Sometimes a woman just had to stop thinking like a small-town girl from Kansas, she decided. She locked her mouth on Dev's, and slid down among the cushions of the sofa, her skin turning slick and her body growing taut with anticipation when he stood up to strip off his remaining clothes. Heavens, he was gorgeous! Devlin Gilpatrick was everything she'd ever wanted in a man: the friend who supported her, the colleague who challenged her and the lover who fulfilled her.

"I love you, Dev," she murmured.

"I love you, too." His mouth burned a line of fire down her throat and across her breasts. She heard herself give a low groan when his tongue circled her nipple, sending streamers of pleasure rippling outward.

The husky murmurs of Cathy's pleasure were the most arousing sounds Dev had ever heard. She was everything he wanted in a woman: intelligent, generous, talented. And beautiful. God, she was beautiful! Looking down at this woman who had come to mean so much to him in such a short time, Dev was seized by a powerful need to possess her. Now. Immediately. He held her hands pinned above her head and watched the flicker of delight cross her face as he entered her, plunging deep. He felt a primitive, bone-deep sensation of male triumph when, within seconds, she convulsed in a shattering climax.

His triumph didn't last very long. Cathy tugged her hands free of his grasp, and linked them at the nape of his neck, pulling his head down and kissing him fiercely. Then she arched her hips upward and rocked. That was all it took to send him over the top. Dev's world exploded, gloriously.

A COUPLE OF HOURS later, showered and dressed, Dev sat on a bar stool in the kitchen and refrained, with difficulty, from telling Cathy how to make grilled-cheese sandwiches. She seemed blithely unaware of how noble he was being, since she chatted away about nothing in particular, spreading Dijon mustard over the bread, and not even noticing when he winced.

But when she pulled up the stool next to his and put a golden-brown sandwich in front of him, he saw she was laughing. "What's so damned funny?" he growled.

"You are. Look, Dev, it seems to me we have two choices here. We can order out everything we eat, or we can try to accept the fact that the world isn't going to come to an end if one of us uses Cheddar cheese in a sandwich where the other one would have used Swiss."

"Jarlsberg," Dev said, letting out the breath he'd been holding for what seemed like forever. "Jarlsberg makes the best grilled-cheese sandwiches."

Cathy considered murdering him, caught sight of the antique coffee spoons sitting on her counter, and decided to kiss him instead. Which she did to their considerable mutual satisfaction.

"I had a phone call from Eugene Montford yesterday," she said when she was finally sitting down again. "He mentioned that he'd already spoken to you."

"Yes." Dev bit into his sandwich, and shot her a surprised glance. "Hey, you know what? These are pretty good."

Cathy smiled sweetly. "You'd almost think the person who cooked them knows what she's doing, right?"

Dev grinned. "I'll check that out over the next few years and get back to you." He took her hand and laced his fingers through hers. "I'm sure Gene told you the same thing he told me about Annette."

"She's been fired," Cathy said.

"Yes. And from the way Gene was talking during the call, she's lucky she didn't get charged with criminal conspiracy to defraud."

"It was the same when he spoke with me," Cathy

agreed. "He told me he's making sure that she'll never work in the television industry again." She sighed. "What a mess Annette managed to make of everything, Dev. Paul Lyman seemed devastated by the extent of her betrayal. I just wish we hadn't been forced to shatter his illusions so brutally."

Dev squeezed her hand. "Much better that we shattered them now than that Annette shattered them later. And you know Paul's knee-deep in negotiations to establish his new company right now, so that should give him something to think about besides Annette and all the despicable ways she lied to him."

"I'll never understand what drives her," Cathy said. "She's smart, attractive, and well educated. She could succeed on her merits, so why does she have this compulsion to deceive people and try to trick her way to the top?"

"Obviously Annette has some pretty deeply rooted insecurities beneath all the surface glitter. But maybe this experience will be a wake-up call for her. Perhaps she'll finally realize that you can't get through life without a few friends to help you along the way." Dev captured her wrist as she started to take his empty plate away. "Leave the dishes for a moment, Cathy. I need to talk to you about AUS. I'm sure Gene's suggested the same deal to you that he has to me."

Cathy nodded and looked at Dev, realizing that she had no idea what he was thinking. She sat down again, admitting to herself that the only area in which she still didn't feel entirely sure about Dev's reactions was in relation to their profession. "Exactly what did Gene suggest to you?" she asked.

"He proposed producing a trial package of six shows featuring you, and six shows featuring me, making a dozen shows in all. He'll try to sell the pair of us as a single deal, with the stations that buy the package alternately airing your show and mine.''

Dev's voice gave no clues as to what he thought of Gene's proposal. Cathy took a sip of cranberry juice. ''What did you think of the idea?''

''That it sucks.'' Dev shrugged. ''TV stations want to have the same programs scheduled each week in the same time slot, otherwise the audience can't find the shows. From our point of view, neither of us can build a name and a national reputation when we're only getting half an hour of airtime every other week.''

''I agree,'' Cathy said. ''That's why I suggested to Gene that we should scrap 'Cooking with Cathy' and 'Dining with Devlin' as separate shows. In their place, I proposed that the two of us should come up with a new concept and a new show. I suggested that we should call it 'In the Kitchen with Cathy and Devlin.'''

Devlin laughed, and Cathy stared at him, offended. ''It's not that crazy an idea,'' she said.

''That's not why I was laughing,'' Dev said. He got up and spun her around on her bar stool, clasping his arms around her waist and holding her tight against his chest. ''I laughed because I also suggested to Gene that we should come up with a single show, starring both of us. Only I called it 'In the Kitchen with Devlin and Cathy.'''

Cathy tilted her head back and pretended to consider. ''I can be bought,'' she said finally, smiling. ''In return for a large diamond-engagement ring, a guarantee of mind-blowing sex after we tape each show, and a lifetime supply of white-chocolate mousse, I'll agree to let your name appear first in all the credits.''

Dev slowly lowered his mouth to hers. ''Honey, you've got yourself a deal.''